Deceit

Deceit is first published in English the United Kingdom in 2022 by Corylus Books Ltd, and was originally published in Icelandic as *Launsátur* in 2021 by Mál og Menning.

Published by arrangement with Mál og Menning, Iceland.

This book has been translated with financial support from:

ICELANDIC LITERATURE CENTER

Corylus Books Ltd

corylusbooks.com

ISBN: 978-1-9163797-9-4

JUN 2023

Deceit

Jónína Leósdóttir

Translated by Sylvía Bates and Quentin Bates

Published by Corylus Books Ltd

JÓNÍNA LEÓSDÓTTIR

Thursday 02.04.2020

There are forty Covid-19 patients currently at the National Hospital and one in hospital in Akureyri.

Precautions have been tightened in Ísafjörður, Hnífsdalur and Bolungarvík.

More than a million people worldwide have been diagnosed with coronavirus and approximately fifty-three thousand people have lost their lives, including around a thousand Americans and close to a thousand people in Spain over the last twenty-four hours.

1

"OK to drop by? There's something I need to run past you." Soffía sounded breathless and rushed. "It's really urgent."

"Can't we talk this over on the phone? I'm supposed to be in self-isolation."

Adam left out the fact that he was also deep in a crime drama showing on Netflix.

"Self-imposed isolation," she corrected. Soffía had never managed to break the habit of correcting his Icelandic, even though by now his command of the language was almost flawless and virtually free of his English accent. "And, no. This is too sensitive for the phone. I'm at the station, I'll be with you in a quarter of an hour and coffee would be great."

Adam ended the call without a word. Soffía hadn't called to ask if she could come, but to announce that she was coming. There were good reasons why his parents referred to their former daughter-in-law as the Bulldozer. This elaborately courteous middle-class English couple had never taken to the confident, straight-talking woman who had captivated their only son.

Coffee? Soffía knew perfectly well that he was a hardcore tea addict who never touched coffee. But she also knew that Adam kept a stockpile of decent coffee and chocolate, in case their daughter should drop by. The girl was even more hooked on coffee and chocolate than her mother, whose habit was serious enough.

Adam kicked off his sandals and pulled on socks and a pair

of tracksuit bottoms over his boxers. He wasn't inclined to let Soffía find him with bare legs and feet, even though she knew all of his failings and secrets. Next, he boiled water, and as Soffía burst in with her coat flapping, two steaming mugs were waiting in the living room, one containing black coffee on the dining table and another of tea on the coffee table.

"Two metres," he told her, backing away from her as he took a seat on the sofa.

Soffía's hair had been recently cut, far too short in Adam's opinion, and dark streaks had been added to her fair hair. He felt sorry for her, unable to grow her hair down to her shoulders, let alone longer. Her hair was so thin that it caused her endless trouble. All the same, she hardly needed to crop it that close to the scalp. His own hair was a floppy brown mop that refused to be tamed, and which he habitually wore in a bun at the back of his head.

"Lovely!" Soffía dropped into a chair, slipped her coat from her shoulders and shook her arms out of it so that it became a heap on the seat behind her. Then she hunched over the mug and eagerly breathed the coffee aroma deeply.

He didn't have to wait long for her to get to the point. She had no time for small talk about the weather or superficial enquiries about anyone else's wellbeing.

"I'm thinking, y'see, about doing people harm," she said, as if it were the most natural thing in the world. "Not someone in particular, just anyone."

"You're what?" Adam stared at her. He was used to Soffía's unpredictable outbursts, but she had never been malevolent, not even in connection with her role as a detective on the city force that brought her into close contact with scumbags of every description, both criminals and colleagues.

"Not me personally! This is something I want you to look into with me. As a psychologist."

"But you said..."

He didn't get to finish his sentence.

"This is absolutely confidential, Adam. Massively sensitive.

2

But I managed to get permission to share this with you, on the basis that you might be able to help us on this one. The suits sat up and took notice when I mentioned your name, as you really made a difference in that domestic abuse case last year. And one of us at the department is Covid positive, and because of him we have ten others isolating. This is panic stations."

"And do I get paid?"

Although a great many people were struggling with anxiety and depression due to the pandemic, the practice Adam ran with a couple of colleagues had seen a serious drop in bookings as soon as the virus had arrived in Iceland. So Adam's earnings had fallen dramatically.

"If we can get something useful out of you." She glared a challenge at him.

"OK. What's going on?"

He interpreted this as meaning that he would be able to invoice the police, as he had on two previous occasions when he had been able to provide the force with support for its investigations.

"Crimes against innocent people. Assault, in fact."

He digested this for a moment.

"Terror?" he asked.

"Well..." Soffía frowned and sipped hot coffee. "Terror? Sure, you could look at it like that."

"Are you going to explain, or is this some kind of new version of *Twenty Questions*?"

"Yes, y'see ... It concerns a little shop in the Grjótathorp district. A sort of hippie-style wholefoods place. It's a popular smoothie bar as well, and they do some revolting shots with loads of ginger."

Adam couldn't stop himself smiling. Soffía had described it with a scowl on her face, and it was obvious this was the kind of place she would never enter other than to investigate a crime.

"They do hot food to take out. Vegan, of course. Bean stew, brown rice and green stuff. All very healthy." Soffía sighed as if healthy food was something unimaginably bad. "The problem is that foreign bodies have been found inserted in the fresh fruit."

"What kind of foreign bodies?"

"Needles."

"Hypodermic?" He took a sharp breath. "Could they be carrying an infection? Have they been analysed?"

"Sewing needles. They've been cut down and just the sharp tips used. That's probably so it's easier to push them into the fruit. Or just to make them smaller. That way there's more chance of them being swallowed. I don't know if there was anything on them. They're being analysed."

"Hell. Who does that kind of thing?" Adam was stunned.

"You're the psychologist."

Soffía glared, as if he were a suspect under interrogation.

"So is this directed at any particular customers? What fruit was this? Could anyone have picked them up?"

"A banana, an apple, an orange. All in the same basket on the counter. More than likely all contaminated at the same time. Who would take a chance going there repeatedly? But the fruit was sold over a two-day period."

"And was anyone hurt?" Adam felt a twinge of guilt for not having asked this question earlier.

"Could have been worse. Nobody swallowed a needle. The man who ate the banana got a nasty cut to his tongue. But nothing life-threatening. Another person got a needle stuck in a gum eating an apple. It seems it was incredibly painful and they needed a dentist dressed up in full PPE to remove it. But the woman who bought the orange wasn't badly hurt. She pricked her finger when she was peeling it."

"Hopefully there's no toxin associated with the needles." Adam wondered if anyone could be crazy enough to try to use this vile method to infect people with Covid-19. He wasn't even sure if this was possible, and decided not to say anything.

"These people were put on antibiotics." Soffía didn't seem overly concerned. "Just to be certain. They haven't developed any symptoms. Not yet."

"You're sure the needles were introduced into the fruit in the shop? Could it have happened at the wholesaler, either abroad or here in Iceland? Or when the goods were being delivered?"

"Not abroad. The fruit comes from different sources. But all from the same local distributor."

Adam sipped his tea. If Soffía was expecting any concrete information from him concerning a possible culprit, then she was going to be disappointed. He had far too little to work on.

"Has there been a search for more needles?" he asked. "And when was this fruit sold? Could there still be fruit out there that people have bought but haven't yet eaten?"

Soffía sat upright.

"I suggested we use a metal detector." She was clearly pleased at her own initiative and paused, as if expecting a word of praise. "We went over everything in the wholesaler's store, including the vegetables. Nothing there. But the woman in the wholefoods shop sliced up fruit that hadn't been sold and she found two needles in some avocados."

"And all this fruit was in the shop at the same time?"

Soffía nodded.

"All in the same delivery on Monday, and sold on Monday and Tuesday. We were notified yesterday."

"What day is it today? Every day seems the same when you're isolating."

"Thursday."

"I'm surprised there's been nothing in the news. Or that there's been no social media hysteria. I haven't seen anything like that."

"You're on social media?" Soffía stared at him in astonishment. "You said that was hopeless for a psychologist."

During the misery of Covid, Adam had found his way onto Facebook, Twitter and Instagram, admittedly with an anonymous avatar and not under his own name. But that was none of Soffía's business. She wouldn't be able to track him down.

"Is there CCTV in the shop?"

"Look, Adam. None of this cop stuff. That's our job. And you can be thankful for that. I had to drag descriptions of her customers on Monday and Tuesday out of her. That was a struggle. So you can just focus on the psychological side of things. Who does this sort of thing and why?" She hesitated for a moment. "There's no security camera there. It's a tiny shop."

"I know this shop well and I've often been in there." Soffía's comment about cop stuff had irritated him. "But I need to have all the relevant information so I can build up as clear a picture as possible, such as how much of a risk the perpetrator might have taken."

"We don't have a lot to work on. The owner says she doesn't know personally the customers who were injured. So she says. They don't know each other, or so they say. Two women and one man. That's all I know." Soffía felt for her coat behind her and thrust her arms into the sleeves. "Can you give us an initial report quickly? Within an hour?"

"Give me a couple of hours. I'll have to read up on this and it's not textbook stuff. But tell me something... How does such a tiny shop manage to stay open through this pandemic? And how do they cope with the two-metre rule?"

Soffía was on her feet.

"Maximum of three customers at a time. One can be at the counter which is also the smoothie bar. The other two can be elsewhere in the shop as long as there's space between them. It's all set out on the sign outside."

Adam still felt this was scant information to work with and tried to fish for some more details.

"What do these customers have in common?" he asked. "Apart from eating fruit and doing their shopping in the same place, I mean? Do they work or live near the city centre, maybe in the same place?"

"We haven't found anything that connects them."

Soffía stood at the door with her right hand resting on the handle.

"Any similar incidents connected to other shops, any vandalism?"

"Nope."

"What about the owner? Any disputes with other shopkeepers, or a landlord, or a jealous husband, or...? You get my drift?"

Soffía shrugged and put in her mouth a piece of chocolate from a packet that crackled in her coat pocket.

"She's a vegan-yoga type. She was married to a Danish guy and can't divorce him. The man disappeared. He might be dead, or not. Now she lives with a woman." Soffía opened the door and gave Adam a wave. "That'll have to do. Call me as soon as you have something. We need to know what sort of nutcase does this kind of thing."

She banged the door behind her with full force before he was able to ask her to close it gently. The couple upstairs had a new baby, and sound carried easily between flats.

"Who and why. Not asking for much, are you?" Adam muttered to himself as he squirted disinfectant onto a cloth and wiped down the door handle, the table and everything else Soffía had touched.

When he had meticulously washed his hands in soap and hot water, he picked up his laptop from the dining table and typed 'food tampering' into a search engine. General information from news sources around the world would be a good start. He half-remembered having seen reports of foreign bodies in foodstuffs, but couldn't remember any details.

2

Adam didn't have the time at his disposal to search through articles in professional journals or scholarly essays, but he found several articles from different countries that mentioned foreign bodies inserted into foodstuffs, including some that specifically mentioned needles. On the other hand, little was known about the mental states of the perpetrators as it hadn't been easy to track down the culprits. With more time in hand to immerse himself in the subject, he could undoubtedly have dug out more, but Soffía had given him a tight deadline.

The best known example concerning needles was from Queensland in Australia. A man had been admitted to hospital suffering from acute stomach pains after eating strawberries. Needles began to be found in strawberries across the country practically as soon as the incident had become public knowledge, and subsequently in apples, bananas and mangoes.

In such a large country, it was considered impossible for a single perpetrator to be behind every instance. Adam wondered if Soffía was aware that once it was known that needles had been found in the wholefoods shop, there would be a strong likelihood that others would start to do the same, not just the original perpetrator. He shuddered at the thought. Covid had given the police enough to cope with already, without adding a spate of needles in foodstuffs.

The Australian police had caught a youngster hiding needles in a punnet of strawberries, and a woman in her sixties who had inserted a needle into a banana. Both incidents appeared to be unconnected to the original one in Queensland, and the question of who had started off this frightening trend remained unanswered. Adam decided to look more closely at that later.

He saw reports of very similar incidents in the USA, Italy, Japan and elsewhere, but more research would have to wait. He had already used up forty-five minutes of the two hours Soffía had allowed him, and he was determined to pay a visit to the wholefoods shop before delivering an initial report. Maybe speaking to the owner would give him some clues, even though the detectives had failed to get much out of the woman. He often shopped there, and they were on speaking terms.

Adam picked up a packet of wipes and a bottle of disinfectant, took his down anorak from its hanger and pulled on a fleece-lined woollen hat. He knew he would still be cold making his way downtown from Kaplaskjólsvegur. Icelandic winter temperatures suited him as badly as customary indoor temperatures in Iceland suited him well.

It was a huge contrast to the Essex market town where he had grown up, where the summers had been long and pleasantly warm, while winter had meant dressing to keep out the cold indoors, with a dewdrop on his nose and cold fingers and toes. Although his parents had been relatively well-off university lecturers, they were careful with heating the old house they lived in, and the central heating came on according to the calendar rather than the temperature. If Adam complained, he was told to put on another jumper, or to take a hot water bottle with him to bed.

"I'm not made for this country," he had moaned through his childhood. "Why couldn't I have been born in Spain or Italy?"

His father had laboured the point during his speech at their wedding. There had to be a roaring flame behind their love, considering the warmth-loving Adam was prepared to follow a girl all the way to the Arctic Circle. But after seventeen years, when the marriage came apart, his parents were surprised by his decision to remain in Iceland.

Adam pulled his hat further down over his forehead and ears, trying to focus on the police case while he walked along Hofsvallagata and past Landakot. What could he tell Soffía and her colleagues if chatting to the shop's owner left him none the wiser? He pondered the possibilities, despite the scarce information he had to hand.

One theory was that this was a dangerous practical joke perpetrated by an idiot. Now that schools and sports clubs were running at a minimum activity level, boredom and a lack of other diversions could prompt youngsters to get up to all kinds of things.

On the other hand, this could be down to an adult who could not protest a lack of understanding of the seriousness of all this. Anyone with common sense should understand how heinous an act it was to sneak something sharp into food. What on earth could make someone do this? To answer that question it would be necessary to establish who the intended target of the crime might be, and this was the difficult part.

Adam wondered if it was just pure coincidence that the wholefoods shop in the Rock Village district had become the scene of the crime. Of course, that was a possibility. If that wasn't the case, then the perpetrator had to be aiming these actions at the shop's proprietor, whether there were business or personal reasons behind all this.

The further Adam walked and the more he thought it over, the less likely he found it that the perpetrator could have had any other victim in mind than the shop's owner – assuming that the location hadn't simply been chosen at random.

It would be impossible for the perpetrator to know who might eat the fruit. Even if he or she had some supernatural way of guessing who might buy this produce, there was still no certainty that they would consume it themselves. So the target had to be the woman who ran the shop. She would be the key to this.

There was something else of which Adam was certain. If this

wasn't a childish prank, then the perpetrator had to be either devoid of the slightest empathy, or else in a dire mental state when the deed had been done. Anyone with a conscience or able to think logically for themselves would hardly choose to endanger the lives of complete strangers, however much enmity they might bear towards the shop's owners. All the same, he couldn't speculate further without more information.

As he approached the building in the Rock Village, the shop looked closed. This was confirmed by a note on the door, along with the message that anyone with an urgent errand could ring the doorbell for the upstairs flat. The owner presumably lived above the shop, a similar arrangement to what Adam had seen of small businesses in Britain. His childhood best friend had been a pub landlord's son, and back then Adam had envied his friend his access to illicit crisps and fizzy pop. Later on, their interest had focused more on beer.

Adam went up the set of steps covered in a layer of trodden snow and pressed the doorbell under a gilded nameplate engraved with two names; Arngunnur and Katrín. A few seconds later a tall woman in a colourful, billowing dress stood in the doorway, looking down at him over a pair of pink-framed reading glasses perched on the end of her nose. She was hardly much older than fifty, but the shoulder-length fair hair pinned up at the back of her head was starting to turn grey and her complexion told him that she had either drunk or smoked for most of her life, or both.

Old sins can rarely be escaped, Adam thought, recognising the shop's owner.

"Hello." She gave him a cheerful smile. "Can I help you? Are you looking for tea or herbs?"

Adam quickly stepped down two steps.

"Actually, I need a word with you, but it would be great if I could do some shopping while I'm here."

"No problem. I'll open up for you."

She shut the door without another word and Adam made his way down the snow-covered steps.

He had no urgent need of any herbs and his parents kept him supplied with shipments of tea from England, but it would do no harm to stock up on turmeric, rice and beans. The woman undoubtedly needed the business now that fewer people were about in the city centre and many of them now had their groceries delivered.

Adam saw the shop's owner make her way through the tiny, poorly-lit shop and was surprised that she was not more watchful. Even though she knew him by sight, he could still be the one who had hidden the needles. It was more than likely that whoever had been behind this was a regular customer, familiar with the layout of the place. Otherwise this person would hardly have been able to do what he or she had done with the fruit basket on the counter.

"Come on in." The woman opened the door wide and extended her hand. "I'm Arngunnur Andersen. I don't think we've spoken before, but I recognise your face. Do you work around here?"

He hid his hand behind his back and nodded politely.

"My name's Adam Newman."

"Oops. Sorry," she apologised. "When will people be able to shake hands again?"

"I don't work downtown. But I often shop here. You have the freshest herbs and the best rice."

She paid no attention to his compliment.

"Newman? I didn't realise you're a foreigner. You don't have an accent. You said you needed to speak to me?"

"Could we sit down?" He gestured towards two wooden stools that stood behind the counter. 'I'm a psychologist. The police approached me about the needles that were found in the fruit.'

'So that's it.' Arngunnur looked at him with interest, turned and made her way past the brimming shelves to the little workspace behind the counter.

Adam hurried behind and looked her up and down. She was taller than he was, probably around one metre eighty, but carried her height well in a gaudy dress woven from some African cloth and bright yellow rope-soled sandals. He recalled that these were what were referred to as espadrilles. Clusters of bangles jangled on her wrists, from chunky wooden bracelets to finely worked metal rings, and around Arngunnur's neck hung what looked like a rosary.

Could it be possible that the damage had been done by some deeply religious customer who had been shocked at the sight of a rosary worn as an accessory?

"Excuse me, but do you recall anyone ever having mentioned what you have around your neck?"

With gloved hands he moved aside one of the stools to maintain maximum distance between them before sitting down.

Arngunnur's hand went to the string of beads hung with a cross, as if afraid that he would rip it from her.

"Mentioned this? No. Why do you ask? Do you think that someone set out to hurt innocent people because of the way I dress?"

"Some people are intolerant of unusual uses of religious imagery. Madonna and Lady Gaga have both been criticised for that kind of thing."

"That's quite a comparison!" Arngunnur tilted her head back as she laughed out loud. But her laughter was short-lived and she assured him that nobody had said a single word about the rosary.

"Of course I can't read people's minds. It may well be that someone disapproved without saying anything. But, really, do the police think this might have something to do with religion? I mean, a random attack on a Reykjavík wholefoods shop's customers? Come on."

"I can't speak for the police," Adam said, quick to put things straight. "But considering they came to me, they can hardly have many strong leads."

"Am I interrupting?" a voice behind him said. Adam started, and twisted on his stool through ninety degrees.

In the doorway leading into the building stood a bony woman with short grey hair and a prominent tattoo where her neck met her chest, a red rose entwined around a purple shield. She wore loose white trousers and a low-cut striped shirt, stroking a long-haired cat that purred in her arms.

"This is my partner, Katrín." Arngunnur pointed first at the woman in the doorway and then at him. "And this is Adam. He's a profiler with the police."

"No, not exactly," he said, hastily correcting her. "I'm not a specialist. Just a normal psychologist. But I'm fascinated by why people behave the way they do, especially criminals. My ex-wife is a detective, and sometimes she asks me to look at cases they are working on."

"Can Púrra and I listen in, or is this confidential?" Katrín asked, looking at Adam, but Arngunnur didn't give him a chance to reply.

"Katrín looks after the books and some of the purchasing. So this is her business as well. And the cat is very discreet."

"I was brought up in my grandparents' shop," Katrín said, laughed and came closer.

Adam put up a warning hand.

"Two metres," he said, more sharply than he had intended.

"Of course. Sorry." She stopped short and leaned against shelves of spice jars, still stroking the cat. "Don't let us interrupt. We'll be as quiet as mice."

"The police seem to be very interested in the man I'm supposed to be married to," Arngunnur said with a questioning note in her voice as she looked at Adam enquiringly.

"He's not easy to track down?"

"Well, he's no nine-to-five type," Arngunnur said with an airy gesture. "We met in Christiania."

"When were you last in touch, and where was he living then?"

"Look, these needles are nothing to do with Morten. I gave up on him in Copenhagen back in the last century. At that time he was living in a squat, puffing weed and dreaming of moving to Jamaica. I'm sure he's long dead."

"But he could be still living and not feeling particularly charitable towards you?"

"He was so stoned that he didn't even notice I had gone. I heard that through mutual friends."

Katrín giggled quietly. She must have heard the tale many times before.

"Last year I went to Denmark and reported him formally as a missing person," she continued. "If he doesn't pop up within the next five years, then I'm automatically registered as a widow. Unless the Danish bureaucrats grant me a divorce before then, which could happen."

Adam felt that she had a cold attitude towards a man for whom she must at one time have had strong feelings.

"Is a divorce important for emotional or financial reasons?"

"Simply being practical." Arngunnur shrugged. "I have a bunch of grasping half-siblings and I don't want Katrín to have any problems in that direction when I pop my clogs."

"I keep telling her that I could end up going first," Katrín said, sniggering as if it were a joke. She came across as a light-hearted personality. "After all, we're the same age."

"But you're in better condition," Arngunnur said, as if she were referring to a used car.

"But you still use the Danish surname?" Adam asked.

"Ach, yes. I've been Andersen for so long now that it would cause all kinds of headaches if I were to change it." The flippant expression faded from her face and she became serious. "Do you think that these needles are some kind of an attack on me personally? Could I have some enemy who might try again, with something aimed directly against me, or both me and Katrín?"

"Or Púrra," Katrín broke in, hugging the cat. "I loathe people who are cruel to animals."

Adam couldn't avoid giving a reply, but did what he could to soften his words.

"Yes, assuming that we're not dealing with crazy kids. There's a strong possibility that the person concerned is considerably unbalanced and wanted to do you harm, Arngunnur. Or it could be some unprincipled person who has a business advantage to protect. My opinion is that the danger is still very real."

3

Adam gave CID an informal report during an online meeting when he got home. The police team, which consisted of Soffía and a pair of youngsters, didn't try to hide their disappointment. Repeated sighs told him clearly that they had expected something meatier, although nobody was more aware than they were of how little they had to work on.

"Do we need to take precautions?" Soffía took the lead as she seemed to be in charge of the investigation. "Concerning Arngunnur, I mean."

"She could certainly be in danger." Adam was aware that this was the last thing the overworked police wanted to hear. "If the perpetrator had expected some other reaction, such as dramatic media coverage, the shop being closed or even news of Arngunnur having been injured ... well, there's a likelihood that he or she may have been disappointed and could choose to escalate things."

"50-50 chance, or higher?"

"There isn't enough information to be able to make an estimate. I'll look at all this more closely this evening and I'll email you if I come across anything that could be of use. But don't expect too much."

"Can't you get stuck into this right away?"

"I have a meeting with colleagues at the clinic. We're trying to get a temporary reduction in the rent. The practice on Ármúli is pretty much empty these days."

"Don't you offer consultations online?"

Soffía clearly saw this as no problem. Adam wasn't inclined to explain to her that many people found it difficult to discuss sensitive subjects via a computer. Even if they trusted themselves to try this, there was no guarantee that they would have the necessary privacy at home, with a spouse and children in the next room.

Before ending the conversation, he asked Soffía if she had heard anything of their daughter Margrét, who fluttered like a butterfly between departments at the University of Iceland, as well as from one boy to the next, none of whom her parents ever got to know. Adam had expected her to appear for dinner, until she had cancelled without explanation. But Soffía said that she hadn't heard from Margrét for a week.

This wasn't something they were going to worry about. The girl was in her twenties and had quickly become independent and kept herself busy. At the moment she was living in a semi-commune in Skerjafjörður, spending weekends and evenings working in various coffee houses, until the pandemic had shut them all down. She would be in touch when it suited her.

With Margrét unlikely to show up for dinner, it was time for Jenný to make an appearance once the phone meeting with the colleagues at the clinic was over and he was almost finished preparing a meal. This time cannelloni with ricotta and spinach was in the oven and everything needed for a salad was laid out on the worktop.

Jenný was able to see things from a fresh point of view and Adam appreciated her perspective on the challenges he grappled with. Right now he couldn't keep his mind off the needles in the fruit. Should he maybe have mentioned to Soffía that copycat incidents could pop up if details were to leak out? In one of the scholarly articles online he had read that in such foodstuffs-related incidents, there was one common factor: emulation. Before long, someone would start to copy the initial perpetrator.

"A psychologist can only work with the facts available. If

Soffía wants to predict the future, she should have gone to a fortune teller."

Jený crossed her bare legs and admired the bright red lacquer on her toenails, looking satisfied with herself. She wore a brown leather skirt with a white blouse and light-coloured sandals, so that the nail polish was shown to full effect.

"The most likely explanation is that this was a stupid prank and that nothing more will happen, even if it's reported somewhere else. People are only thinking of Covid-19 now. It's not certain that a case like this is likely to have the same kind of effect as it would with no pandemic." Jený wrapped a lock of her long hair around her index finger, as she did when she was thinking through a problem. "But of course you could send the police a link to some articles about copycats. Then Aunt Soffía can't fuss and complain to you if something happens."

Jený smiled. She liked to compare Adam's ex-wife to the witch in the children's play *Kardimommubær,* although he always spoke politely of her. But she and Soffía were not friends, so Jený felt she could call her whatever she liked.

"It's a shame we can't tell if it's directly aimed at this Arngunnur or not," she added. "That would actually be better. Not for the shopkeeper, of course. These acts of barbarity that can affect anyone are just horrible. Like gunmen who mow down anyone in their path."

She stood up from the couch, adjusted her skirt and went to the fridge.

"One pink gin before dinner. I'm not on the wagon!"

She reached instinctively for the bottle of pink Beefeater from behind the recycling bin before choosing a small yellow can of tonic and half a lime from the vegetable drawer in the fridge.

She chose a tall glass, half-filled it with ice, splashed in gin, then filled it with tonic. Finally, she cut a thin slice of lime and held it up to the light.

"Just to be sure," she muttered and let the slice drop into the glass. "No needle."

The ice cubes in Jenný's drink clinked when she sat down and placed the glass on the coffee table. She turned up the volume of the television, which these days was almost always on and tuned to BBC News with the sound off so that Adam could follow the news ticker at the bottom of the screen for pandemic news.

"Do you think this needle business is related to coronavirus?" Jenný stared, distracted by a BBC news story showing images taken at an overcrowded morgue in Italy. "Maybe all this terrible news has affected some already vulnerable person so much, now they feel compelled to hurt others? Someone who otherwise wouldn't hurt a fly, except that the world has turned upside down?"

Adam's phone rang the moment Jenný finished speaking. *Margrét*, the screen announced.

"Hi, Magga love."

"Can I change my mind about dinner?" When Adam didn't reply straight away, Magga added, "I don't need anything hot, just a sandwich or something."

"Of course you can come, there's a cannelloni in the oven. I have a bit of work to do first and need about half an hour to finish it. But you're welcome any time after then."

"Do you have a cold? You sound like you do. Have you been washing your hands and using hand sanitiser?"

"I'm fine, love. I'll see you in a moment. Bye for now."

Jenný sighed disappointedly and downed most of the pink drink in one. She knew what to do. With Margrét on her way, Jenný would have to make herself scarce.

When his daughter rang the doorbell, Adam had just finished writing Soffía a very short email in which he asked her to read the two attachments. He could have sent her academic journal articles, but instead decided to send the media stories, as Soffía always wanted information in what she referred to as plain language.

He was immediately much relieved. He had now pointed out to the police that copycat incidents had occurred in similar instances abroad. No doubt people in Reykjavík would quickly spread the word if anyone had been hurt by needles in fresh produce, as this was such a small community. Now the police would be prepared for copycats, although it would be very difficult for them to prevent any further incidents.

"Hi, my love." He happily greeted Margrét. "No hugs for the moment. Clean hands first, then you can eat at the table and I can eat on the sofa."

Adam put on latex gloves to prepare the salad while Margrét washed her hands in the bathroom. When she returned, she sniffed the air.

"Doesn't it smell wonderful?" He dipped the wooden spoon into the hot dish. "It's so much better when you make the sauce from scratch with cherry tomatoes."

Margrét looked at her father quizzically.

"Have you started drinking again? I smell booze."

JÓNÍNA LEÓSDÓTTIR

Friday, 03.04.2020

A new security app from the Directorate of Health, which is managed by the Civil Protection and Emergency Management's infection control team, is released for public use.

The first temporary hospital for coronavirus patients has opened in Britain.

4

The next morning Adam was woken by his phone. Soffía didn't give him a chance to say good morning, she got straight to the point.

"It's on the internet," she snorted. "First the woman with the needle in her gum. She posted on Facebook. Then the media picked it up. And then the banana man joined in."

"Hell!"

"Arngunnur is still bloody lucky. Nobody said where they bought the fruit."

"Doesn't that seem strange?" Adam hadn't seen any mention of such discretion during his research yesterday. Perhaps this meant that the 'victims' were really responsible, and now felt guilty?

"I talked to her. These are regular customers. They don't want to cause her trouble. But everyone's under suspicion, shops and wholesalers alike. Those businesses are under the cosh."

"So early?" Adam didn't quite believe her, aware that Soffía was prone to exaggeration.

"It's nine-thirty!" Her indignation was obvious. No doubt she herself had started her day at the gym hours earlier.

"Oh. So, why are you calling me?"

He turned off his alarm, which was set for ten o'clock. The man whose wife was a compulsive shoplifter had already cancelled his noon appointment. The couple had started working from home and all the shops she had visited regularly were closed. The enabling husband was now no longer in a state of constant tension, and seemed to have stuck his head in the sand for the moment. Adam was now more concerned with the clients who had volatile relationships with spouses or children, and who were now locked up with them for most of the day. The situation for those families had to be close to boiling point.

"This stuff that you sent me yesterday." Soffía sucked her teeth and left it at that.

"Are you calling about the copycat?"

"Yeah. Do I need to worry about that?" It was obvious that Soffía wanted him to say no.

"Yes, but not as much as you would under normal circumstances, I think. But still." Adam could not give an answer that went against his own judgement.

"Don't talk in riddles."

"They're not riddles. Just common sense, Soffía."

She waited for him to explain further so he continued:

"What do primary school kids and secondary school students do when they don't have to go to school? They sleep half the day away and then spend the rest of it online. Do you remember Magga during the teacher's strike? If kids were spending time outside, like they did before, then it's more likely that some moron would think it really clever to copy this needle business after they saw it online."

"Are copycats always kids?"

"Actually, no."

Soffía sighed.

"Would you ask shopkeepers to be on their guard?" she asked after a moment's thought.

"That could work both ways. If managers make a big deal out of this with their staff, then some disgruntled employee could put needles into produce. Or just pretend to find needles."

"It could happen anyway. Now that this is in the media."

"True." Adam was irritated with himself. He wasn't

thinking clearly, woken so abruptly and before his first cup of tea of the day.

"And the police will get the blame. For not warning business owners."

Now it was Adam's turn to sigh.

"Why are you wasting time talking to me, then? You've already decided what you're going to do."

Soffía pretended not to hear him.

"The original perpetrator could also continue," she said.

"Exactly so."

It occurred to Adam that Soffía had really called him so he could add a day's consulting to the invoice he would send to the police. Soffía knew that purchasing his property had been tough, even though it was a small basement flat, which he referred to as the ground floor, in an old apartment building. Adam could have bought a bigger place further out in the suburbs, but location was more important than square metres. He wanted to be within walking distance of downtown.

After the divorce Soffía had bought herself a place in Grafarholt, a district Adam considered uninhabitable. It wasn't that she was better off than he was, but rather that she had a regular salary that meant she could get a bigger loan. She was also less afraid of debt than Adam, who preferred financial security. He repaid his mortgage as fast as possible and went everywhere by bus or on foot.

"Listen, Magga changed her mind again and came for dinner last night," Adam said, when he realised that he could not come up with any clever ideas about the needle man, as he had privately started referring to the perpetrator. "I thought she was very careless, no gloves or sanitiser."

Soffía burst out laughing.

"My darling Adam! She's so young. Kids think they're immortal. Don't you remember what that was like?"

No, he didn't remember. He had never taken risks, although he had sometimes acted careless so as not to stand out from the crowd when he was younger. But it had always gone against the grain.

"She isn't going steady now and I have concerns about that. I asked her to put off boys stuff until the infection numbers go down, but she just laughed."

"But have you talked to her?" She emphasised the three words dramatically.

This hit Adam like lightning from a blue sky. He froze for a moment before taking a deep breath and answering smartly, "We talked for two hours yesterday."

He hoped that this news would show Soffía how she had no grounds to question him. This was none of her business.

"You have to talk to her, man."

Adam took offence.

"Don't you have research to do? And business owners to warn? I'll keep looking and see if I can find anything else as soon as I've had some tea and checked my email. I'll let you know."

There was a snort from Soffía as she hung up without a goodbye. She still thought she could boss him around despite the many years they had been divorced.

Maybe he should have moved back to England after the divorce, he thought to himself. There would have been advantages to that. But Margrét had been a teenager at the time and Adam hadn't been able to bear the thought of living so far from his only daughter. Now she needed him much less, but it was too late to change his mind and leave. He had never worked as a psychologist in England, only here in Iceland, and he had neglected most of the friendships of his younger years.

After he had drunk two cups of tea, written one appointment into the diary, and read the online comments on needles in fruit, he began again to search for academic articles on malicious interference with foodstuffs.

Some people would call this kind of crime terrorism. This made some sense because the perpetrator did not care who got hurt. Adam found no evidence that the attacks had a religious or political motivation. Actually, it was a guess as only a few cases had been fully concluded, not least because of the copycat effect. The motivations of the original perpetrator were almost secondary to the chaos created by copycats.

It was midday by the time Adam finally stood up from his computer, stiff and with his back aching. He would have to go for a walk to relax. But first he was going to listen to the radio news.

This was something of an old-fashioned attitude, a deep-rooted respect for the BBC from his childhood – but if the news reported the attacks, in a dramatic tone, then Adam would know that the problem was much more serious than if the coverage remained limited to the internet. However, he completely missed the lunchtime news report.

At 12:15 there was a call from the clinic, Sáló. It was the office manager, Guðrún Inga, always called Gunninga, on the line. She was easily stressed, and now sounded breathless.

"Can you take on another patient?" she asked, having given her name and said good morning all in one breath.

Adam suppressed a groan. She had been reminded more than once not to refer to Sáló's clients as patients. And the question itself was silly. Gunninga knew as well as the psychologists she worked for how dramatic the reduction in appointments had been.

Of course he could take on another client. He had grimaced at the sight of his online bank balance last night, when he had transferred a small amount over to Margrét. His emergency fund was still intact, but if things didn't improve he would have to dip into the savings that gave him such a sense of security. That would be hard to do.

When the pandemic was over, he planned on seriously considering working for the National Hospital or another practice where he could rely on a fixed salary, even if it meant a lower overall income. The freedom of being self-employed was an expensive commodity during a recession. This was the second time Adam had encountered this in his career, first during the Financial Crash, and now with Covid-19.

"Yes, of course I can take on clients, Gunninga. I could take on another dozen. Do they want to meet in the office or have an online consultation?"

"At the office and straight away, absolutely right now if possible. I told him I sanitised all the door handles and other surfaces frequently during the day and that all patients are provided with latex gloves and face masks if they need them."

Now he let slip a sigh.

"Did you use the forbidden word?"

"Ah, I don't remember. No, but, I'm sure I said *cli-ents*." Gunninga said the word slowly and clearly, as if talking to someone reading her lips.

"OK. I can be in the clinic in an hour."

"He'll definitely be there, it seems very urgent."

"Do you know what the problem is?"

"Not exactly. It was a man, about middle-aged or older. He said it was his daughter who needed help, but she won't be coming with him."

5

An hour later Adam sat three metres from a sweating, suited, shaven-headed man who introduced himself simply as Björn. It was Gunninga's job to deal with names and ID numbers of their clients, so Adam was happy with just a first name. It had taken many years for him to adjust to the informality in Icelanders but he had come around to it, and now when he visited Britain he found being addressed by title and surname uncomfortable.

Next to Björn there was a small table where Gunninga had arranged hand sanitiser and a box of masks, which Adam politely invited him to use. The man was satisfied with just using the hand sanitiser, but Adam put on a mask, even though the chief epidemiologist had emphasised that masks gave a false sense of security.

The new client was clearly preoccupied with something other than Covid-19 and it weighed heavily on his heart. The words poured out as soon as he had cleaned his hands.

"I'm looking to you for the sake of my daughter, my only child, who is utterly miserable, just utterly. Poor girl has just been diagnosed with a terrible illness which I have never even heard of until now, the apple of my eye, a terrible blow." Björn wiped the tears from the corners of his eyes. "I wish I could take this burden myself instead of her. I've lived a good life for almost fifty years, it would be all right if I got this, an old guy like me's no loss. But such a young person! The future just snatched away from her, a girl in the bloom of youth."

"What...?" Adam had no chance to ask what this illness was. The shattered father wasn't ready for a discussion until he had told his story.

"But as if this wasn't enough, then... yes, she won't focus on her health and doesn't want to accept the little help that she can get. She won't listen to anyone, not me, not to her friends. My darling girl is so deeply angry, even more with her mother who is dead and can't do anything at all. She is angry at everything and everyone. And thinks only about finding the person she thinks of as *the culprit*."

"Did someone infect her?"

Adam doubted that the man had heard the question. He didn't respond to it. The only thing Adam could think of when the man had mentioned a culprit was that it was HIV. But it was very dramatic to claim that the girl had lost her whole future to it, nowadays it was possible to control HIV with drugs and lead a normal life.

"The culprit," repeated Björn and gestured in despair. "She calls him that, her natural father. The man from whom she inherited this illness. I'm not, you understand... her mother was pregnant when we met. She didn't even know herself at the time, it came as a surprise to us both, and she considered going... to deal with it... you know? But it was never something I thought about, never, I have always considered Rebekka Rósa my daughter, completely, unconditionally."

Björn looked quickly down and drops of sweat rained down into his lap from his shiny head.

"But she didn't know this until now. We were so clueless, her mother and me. Delusional, I should probably say. We didn't think it a problem, because we always thought of her as my daughter, both of us. We didn't think about how she might have a very different opinion on the matter from us. That was short-sighted, utterly unforgivable, because now the mystery won't be solved."

Adam looked quizzically at the man. He didn't know to what mystery the man was referring.

"Because Fanney is dead."

The tone indicated that this was something that Adam should already know. But he didn't know any Fanney, living or otherwise. Perhaps the man had told Gunninga the whole story and thought she had briefed Adam on the matter.

"It's been a year," Björn carried on, before Adam could get another word in. "And now this has happened and there's nobody who can tell the girl who her biological father is. Only the two of us knew that I wasn't her biological father, I would have taken this to the grave if it hadn't been for this illness. I had to tell Rebekka because of the diagnosis. She wouldn't let up. The doctor got her riled up, telling her that this was an inherited condition and not something that just appears out of nowhere. But this illness isn't in my family or Fanney's, at least, not to my knowledge."

Finally Björn paused, took a tissue from the box and wiped his shaved head and face.

"Your wife... Fanney... didn't she tell you who the father was?"

"I asked her not to, I didn't want to know. This man didn't matter to me. I only knew that he didn't treat her well."

"I understand."

"She told me straightaway, when we met, that she had just broken up with someone. No details, just that she had thought that it was serious until he went off abroad. Without even saying goodbye, as far as I remember."

"Do you know which country he went to?"

"Nooo." The word died on Björn's lips. "Maybe the Netherlands. But I don't remember whether Fanney ever told me, or perhaps she didn't know. We never talked about that boy, he didn't matter."

Not until now, thought Adam. Now the nameless biological father suddenly mattered. Secrets could pop up out of nowhere when least expected. This was why Soffía was always going on about how he ought to 'talk to' Margrét.

Adam pushed from his mind the conversation he ought to

have with his daughter and asked the man whether Fanney had had other children beside Rebekka.

"No. It didn't happen." The tension relieved, Björn sagged into the chair like deflated balloon. "The problem was with me and there wasn't anything I could do about it. We could of course have found another way... Ach, I don't remember what it's called, using a sperm donor. But Fanney wouldn't have it."

"Could you tell me about this illness that your daughter was diagnosed with?"

Björn cleared his throat.

"You have to really just look it up and read about it, about this illness, I mean. It's so complicated to try and explain. I'm only now learning about this, I can't really describe it properly. It's called Huntington, or Huntington's disease, have you heard of it?"

Adam knew nothing more than that Huntington's disease was a rare inherited condition that was invariably fatal. He'd never had a patient with it, nor had he any experience of it within his family. But with this information he could understand Björn's distress and why he wanted his daughter to talk to a psychologist. The girl had been dealt the most crushing blow possible, just as she should have had her whole life ahead of her.

"Don't the doctors know all the families here in Iceland that this condition runs in?" he asked. "This is such a small community."

"Yes, yes, they do, the doctors. They know that."

"I assume that your wife had no relatives in this group, since this diagnosis came as a surprise. And that she died from another cause."

"Exactly. Fanney had cancer." Björn stared ahead, as if hypnotised.

"But can't the biological father be identified this way? Surely he has to be related to the other Icelanders who have, or have had Huntington's?"

Adam could not remember if someone could pass on the

condition to their children without suffering from it themselves. He thought that it was unlikely. The biological father could well be dead.

"That's the peculiar thing..." Björn remained in his half-trance. "The neurologist, who knows the families, has ruled it out."

That was one theory, thought Adam. Had adultery, which had never been acknowledged, been taken into account?

"There are, thankfully, not many people," Björn continued flatly. "They're all descended from one long-dead couple, if I understand it correctly. And nobody in this group is a fit. Their ages rule them out, and we can be a hundred per cent sure of that."

"Even if the father had been much older than Fanney?" Adam said, deciding not to mention adultery.

The question startled Björn, who scowled as if Adam had suggested something unpleasant about Fanney.

"They were about the same age, I'm sure of that. He was at most only a few years older."

"Could the biological father have been a foreigner?" Adam did not know why he had taken on the task of interrogating Björn about his sick daughter's paternity. This was not a typical conversation between a psychologist and a client, even if the man in front of him was not looking for advice for his own sake.

"Fanney would have said if he was a foreigner, and she never did. And after she died, I found two or three letters from him that she had kept. They aren't very long but they're in perfectly ordinary Icelandic."

"You have letters?" Adam couldn't understand why the man hadn't mentioned this before. "Aren't they signed?"

Björn shook his head.

"Just an initial, a single S, and they were posted from Borgarnes. There's no other information in them, nothing that can be traced."

"And Fanney definitely wasn't a carrier herself? Could her paternity have been wrongly attributed, is that possible?"

The man muttered something which Adam took to be a no. Björn had sunk into the chair and his eyelids were drooping. No doubt Björn had hoped a conversation with a psychologist would be a lifeline he could snatch at for help. He was realising that a psychologist couldn't just snap his fingers and make the problems disappear. Despair had taken hold and he slumped in the chair, overcome with grief.

Adam had always been able to remain at a distance from his clients' problems. People had a right to understanding, support, and suggestions for realistic measures. Adding his own pity or concern for them would do nothing for his clients.

But now, facing Björn, Adam felt a deep sympathy and was overwhelmed by an impotence and a sadness that he knew would follow him home to Kaplaskjólsvegur and into the night. It was bad enough that Björn had lost a beloved wife, but also his only daughter and the apple of his eye was now facing a bitter end that he had no way of averting. Their relationship had become strained at this delicate point in their lives, instead of being strengthened, due to the girl's anger at the secrecy around her paternity.

"Do I understand it correctly, Björn, that you want your daughter to come and talk to me?"

Björn straightened up in the chair and stared in confusion at Adam, as if he had just woken up in some strange place and needed a moment to orient himself.

"What? Yes, yes, the girl, she needs help. Lots of help. She's in a blind rage. The neurologist offered to make an appointment with a psychiatrist. But she just stormed out. I thought perhaps that she might prefer to meet a psychologist. It seems more gentle."

"I understand."

"But she doesn't want to... She says some guy downtown can't change anything. Because there is no one who has a cure for her, you see? She just wants a cure. Nothing else. So I was thinking ... yes, that you could give me some ideas on how to get her to come to you."

Adam was filled with anxiety at the thought of explaining to Björn that psychologists find it hard to help people who don't come to them of their own free will.

"A young woman receiving such a diagnosis must experience severe trauma, of course, great emotional turmoil," he began. "It starts a grieving process, all kinds of difficult emotions. Where do you think she is in this process, Björn? Do you think she is still in the grip of this rage?"

The man grasped a tissue and twisted it as he muttered something indistinct.

"All she can think about is to find... find..." Björn fought for breath. "To find... her dad."

"This is a common desire with people who find out about their biological parents." Adam tried to sound reassuring. "It doesn't mean that they are abandoning the parents who brought them up. It just means they are trying to find out more about their origins, trying to find a ... connection."

Björn looked wide-eyed at Adam and spoke in a voice that trembled.

"No, you don't understand. Rebekka has no desire to give this man a hug, quite the opposite. She says she's going to kill him."

JÓNÍNA LEÓSDÓTTIR

6

After Björn left, Adam sat in the office for a long time, staring straight into space and trying to summon the energy to get up and hurry home. He was startled by an unexpected knock and the door opened without him having invited the person in.

"You wife's coming over," Gunninga announced, loud and clear from the doorway.

"Who do you mean? My ex?"

"The police officer, yes. Do you have another wife? She says that it's vital that she get hold of you, but your phone's switched off. Please talk to her so she'll leave me in peace. I've dropped two stitches because of the phone ringing all the time."

Adam decided not to point out to Gunninga that she was paid to deal with enquiries and messages, and was the only person at the company who had remained on a full salary during the pandemic. But he didn't want to go into that right now. He just thanked her with the courtesy instilled in him as a child, and gestured for her to close the door. Since he was supposed to be the police adviser in this strange needle case, he would probably have to call Soffía.

"I have to be able to reach you as soon as something comes up!" There was no greeting and Soffía didn't just yell at him, she hissed like an animal in attack mode. "More needles have been found!"

The news surprised him. Deep down, he had thought that

the incident at the health store downtown would be a one-off, simply because of the state of society. The focus was all on Covid-19, and Reykjavík was like some kind of ghost town due to the authorities' request that people stay at home as much as possible.

"How can someone sneak needles into something when everything is pretty much shut down?"

"They could have been there for some time. They were in toilet paper."

"But there is no toilet paper to be had anywhere. Or ... if there is any, it's rationed."

Adam felt his daze slough off, as if he had knocked back a pick-me-up. This strange needle case had once again ignited his curiosity.

"It wasn't in a shop. It was in one of those quaint cafés."

"Quaint cafés?"

"Ach, you know. Sourdough bread with hummus and mashed avocado. Loud coffee machine, overpriced bottled beer."

"Aren't all restaurants and cafés closed?"

"Not quite. The owners are siblings. Sesselja and Dóri. They own three places. Just keeping one open. In a big old warehouse. So there's room for a small number of people with a two-metre distance. And sanitiser and gloves, of course."

"Are there really any customers?" These days, Adam would not care to eat something prepared by someone else, people who might rarely wash their hands and sneeze into their palms.

"It's always full. Then they do food to take away. It's allowed. But regular customers get a bottle of beer as well. Free, of course. It goes without saying that this is a grey area. Very grey."

"Icelanders are unbelievable!"

Adam had recently received a shipment from a supermarket and wiped down every single item with alcohol before arranging his purchases in the cupboard. The delivery guy had been wearing gloves, but that was no guarantee of hygiene. Adam had seen a cashier in a shop rub his nose with a gloved hand and then continue to scan products for an old woman. And were bars now giving away beer to keep customers?

"But what about these needles in the toilet paper? Anyone hurt?" He had almost forgotten the main point.

"Yes. Dóri, one of the owners. The places are named after him. Dóri Bar One, Two and Three. But most people call them Bar One, Bar Two and Bar Three."

Adam swallowed at the thought of a man, a visit to the toilet and needles.

"Calm down. He's not a drop-wiper like you. The needle didn't even scratch his arse. It just hurt his finger. And his sister Sesselja kissed it better."

Soffía had always made fun of the fact that Adam, unlike most men, avoided the urinals, preferring to shut himself in a cubicle to pee. This wasn't just because he couldn't pee standing in a row of fat-backed men, willies in hands, but because he preferred to be able to 'dry the drop' as his father had taught him. This was to ensure that no yellow spot would appear in the white pants he was always made to wear as a child. Adam had never got over the habit, even though he had worn dark boxer shorts for years. He found this a form of hygiene that was self-evident.

He decided to let the sarcasm pass.

"If they're so busy, how long could that roll have been there?" he asked.

"The rolls are in a basket on the floor. A big heap. And not used in any particular order."

"Could the needle have been there for several weeks?" Adam wondered what the implications could be if the perpetrator had been active for some time. Then the needles in the fruit could even be the last of many that had been planted.

"Not many weeks. Possibly just a few days. And this wasn't a single needle. Two broken needles in one roll, two in another."

"Hopefully there's no need to unroll all the toilet paper in the place to look for needles. There was no paper in the shop I ordered from the other day." Adam found it uncomfortable to see pictures of empty shelves in supermarkets, especially when the shortage was about basics such as cleaning products and bread.

Soffía made no comment, but asked straight out if he could come with her.

"Where?"

"Bar Three. To speak to the owners."

"Haven't you talked to them?"

"Yes, sort of. On Zoom. Not face to face. I'll be outside in ten minutes."

"No, I ..."

But Soffía ended the call, cutting off his protests. When Adam was a boy and had seen characters in movies behave so rudely, he had thought it unbelievable that someone would actually hang up like that.

It was impossible to keep a two-metre distance in a car, but these days Adam carried sanitiser, face masks and latex gloves in his coat pocket. He had also managed to get used to not touching his face. All of this gave him a sense of security, even though the chief epidemiologist considered masks to be of little use except in hospitals. Adam found this dubious. It was like saying that vitamin pills worked better in the north of the country than in the Westman Islands or something like that. Either masks worked or they didn't.

Gunninga sat with a crossword puzzle at the desk at reception, apparently giving her knitting needles a rest for now. It occurred to Adam to ask if she knew anything about the siblings who ran Dóri's Bar. The woman was a walking gossip magazine. But she was really at her best with gossip about people of middle age and above. The siblings could be outside her field of specialist knowledge.

"Dóri and Sessí? Of course I know who they are! They advertise everywhere, you can hardly open a magazine or turn on the TV without seeing something about them. They have three coffee shops, very popular with young people."

Adam saw in Gunninga's expression that she found it bizarre that the existence of such prominent people could have passed him by. No doubt she attributed this to him being a foreigner, something she thought explained most of what she considered to be the peculiarities in his behaviour.

"So they're wealthy?" The idea came to Adam that the needles might be a form of blackmail.

"You never can tell if there's real money behind something like this." Gunninga scratched her head with a pencil. "You remember the house of cards that collapsed in 2008, even whole banks. But they're highly visible, those two. Dóri owns a detached house that he has completely renovated inside. There's just one big open-plan space inside, even the bathtub is in the middle of the bedroom floor. You couldn't offer me something like that."

"Does the sister live there too?"

"No, of course not! She lives in a penthouse apartment in a new neighbourhood. She also has a summer house that's like a luxury townhouse."

Adam heard a car horn outside and there was no opportunity to ask Gunninga any more questions. He hooked a mask over his ears and ran out.

The moment he was in the passenger seat, Soffía put her foot down. He barely had time to pull the car door shut.

"Can this be a copycat already?" she asked, leaving the parking lot so fast that the unmarked police car slid on the icy street.

"I think it's too early to say." He fumbled to fasten his seatbelt. "Not until we know how long each toilet roll had been in the basket."

"But this is so different. Fruit and toilet paper. Doesn't that tell you something?"

Adam felt Soffía's words betrayed a desperation.

"Unfortunately," he said. "The information we have is far too limited."

Soffía hammered the steering wheel like a drum, but without touching the horn.

"There's loads of pressure," she explained as the drum solo came to an end. "We're so massively understaffed that we don't have time for this. People messing around with needles! And the bar owners absolutely don't want this to get out."

"Someone messing around, Soffía? Needles hidden in unexpected places can be extremely dangerous. This could be just the start of it. Just imagine if someone had swallowed a piece of fruit with a needle in it. That could mean major internal injuries for a child, and could even be fatal."

"But we're in a worldwide pandemic, Adam. Civil protection measures cranked right up to red alert! A bunch of cops in isolation! What the hell am I supposed to do?"

"Don't tell me you're on this case on your own?"

"It's not even seen as a case."

"Really? Do the police think it's OK for someone to get people to swallow sharp needles, or stab themselves?"

"Not me." Soffía let go of the steering wheel for a moment to reach for a bag of liquorice that rattled on the dashboard. "That's why I asked for you. But we have to be quick. This needs sorting out today."

She grabbed a handful of the sweets without the courtesy of offering him any. Adam avoided everything that contained liquorice because of its effects on blood pressure. But Soffía never let that stop her and usually had liquorice of some kind close at hand.

Adam wasn't sure know whether to laugh or cry, whether because of the laughable time limit, or Soffía's liquorice addiction. In the end, he did neither. He also stopped short of asking Soffía what an ordinary citizen could do if he knew a girl was looking for a man with the intention of killing him. She would have told Adam that he wasn't in a position to judge whether or not a man's life was genuinely in danger, or whether this could be attributed simply to the girl's emotional state.

What complicated the matter even further was that nobody knew who the man was. Even if the police were alerted, there was nothing they would be able to do.

7

"I have to make a little confession." The man, who had introduced himself as Steindór Hansson, made a poor job of appearing modest and regretful, coming across instead as artificial. "What I told the boys over Zoom this morning wasn't one hundred per cent correct."

Steindór, known as Dóri, leaned back in a broad-backed black desk chair in the spacious office behind the kitchen at Bar Three. He crossed his long legs and dangled one foot, wearing light brown suede shoes from an exclusive brand. Apart from the shoes, he was mostly dressed in black: skinny black jeans and a light black wool sweater with the collar of a dark grey shirt visible at the neckline. He was fidgety, fiddling with the objects on his desk like a nervous child.

"We didn't find the needles this morning but a week ago last Friday," Sesselja explained after her brother had hesitated for an uncomfortably long time.

"First only one, completely by accident," Steindór broke in again. "When it pricked me."

"And then we didn't dare not check if there might be more."

Adam wondered if the siblings were twins. Sesselja was almost the same height as her brother and they were both lanky, with high, prominent cheekbones and unusually light grey eyes.

The hair made them even more similar – the same dark colour, cut a little below the ears and freshly blow-dried. Steindór had a centre parting, but Sesselja's hair was cut in a fringe. Adam suspected, however, that such impeccable hair wasn't natural but 'created' by a master hairdresser and maintained with expensive potions in chic bottles.

"We didn't want to let any customers get caught up in this."

"It was actually luck that it was Dóri who stabbed himself."

Her brother nodded, raising an index finger with a plaster on it, a pained look on his face as if to illustrate just how unpleasant the experience had been.

"Business is tough enough as it is, without needing to scare people away," he said.

"You still have a plaster?" Soffía looked questioningly at the finger Dóri had waved.

"Ach, yes. It got infected."

"He had a high temperature and we were terrified that he'd caught Covid."

"The swelling's going down," said Dóri proudly, moving his fingers to emphasise the point "I've finished the course of antibiotics."

Adam wondered if the infection could be traced to something on the needle, or even Covid? But Soffía had asked him to get involved in the conversation as little as possible. In addition, speculation about a viral infection could trigger even more of a panic.

"We found another broken needle in the roll that Dóri injured himself on and two more in another toilet roll in the same basket. But that was all. Now we've removed the baskets and we only have one roll in each toilet."

"Of course it's extra work for the staff," Steindór added. "They need to keep an eye on things so it doesn't run out."

"There are four toilets in front." Sesselja pointed to the kitchen door, through which Adam and Soffía had been hustled when they arrived at the café. "And then one here for the staff. We check the toilet rolls frequently every day."

Sesselja seemed especially keen to demonstrate there was no longer any danger. But Adam instinctively wondered if this toilet paper checking would be done with gloved or sanitised hands.

"Can we definitely trust you to not go to the media with this?" Dóri shifted in his chair. "It's hard enough running the business with only one place open."

"We close every day at seven," his sister pointed out. "This is to avoid any trouble with the number of customers and to maintain the two-metre distance and all that. People are more likely to follow the rules when they have kids with them and so on."

"But they prefer to drink coffee than beer," Dóri continued. "I don't remember the last time we sold a cocktail. This situation is going to take us down. So the last thing we need is some kind of panic over needles."

Dóri was a picture of self-pity.

"But we still felt we had to tell you about this. Or I did." Sesselja looked apologetically at her brother. "When we heard broken needles had also been found in fruit."

"Do we really have to worry about these jokers putting needles in the food?"

Dóri's question was directed at Soffía, but Sesselja replied first.

"I have already told you that's not possible, Dóri. All the food is in the kitchen and our staff are absolutely brilliant. They are not connected to this and take great care with everything."

"It was absolutely right of you to get in touch. But you must be aware that this is a criminal case. People could be at risk. We can't keep quiet about it." Soffía spoke gravely, when she finally got a word in. "And needles could be found in food. Maybe not on customers' plates. More likely in ingredients in the kitchen. So the staff should be cautious."

Dóri sighed and shot his sister what looked like an accusing glance.

"This is just someone fooling around. We could easily have handled this without calling the police."

"Someone fooling around?" Soffía snarled. "Then whoever this is has a strange sense of humour. One woman got a needle stuck deep into her gum. And a man got a needle in his tongue. This is no joke."

The crestfallen siblings looked at each other, and became even more sheepish when Soffía asked them to hand over the needles. These turned out to have been thrown out.

"How were we supposed to think that there was some kind of serial case going on and that this was evidence?" Dóri had turned from defensive to remonstrative.

Soffía snorted as she made for the door.

"OK, then. Let's take a look at the bathrooms."

"But there are guests out there!" Sesselja looked at Soffía with entreating eyes, realised that this could not be avoided, and made to escort them to the restaurant.

Dóri followed at their heels and Adam came hurrying behind them into what turned out to be a wide, dimly lit corridor with four doors.

"Jesus, I hope nobody thinks you're from the Health Inspectorate," whispered Sesselja, opening the disabled toilet. "The needles were in here."

Soffía pulled her phone from her pocket and started recording video. When they got back into the police car after the toilet inspection, Adam ripped off his gloves and sprayed himself with sanitiser.

"Was there any investigation into whether the fruit needles were contaminated with anything?" he asked. "I'm wondering if the infection in Steindór's finger was from something like that."

"Those people were prescribed antibiotics. To be on the safe side."

"But nobody checked the needles?" Adam felt that this was a departure from Soffía's usual high standards.

"I already told you they are. Do you know what it's like at the station? This needle thing isn't a priority at all. It's all about Covid. But I'll push for that later."

"It may be too late now. Of course, I'm not a pharmacist, but a possible poison could have disappeared in a few days."

"Chemist, not pharmacist." Soffía put her foot down. "What about the timeline? Does this change anything? And why a disabled bathroom? What's the psychologist's take on this?"

Adam smirked. Although the situation looked bleak, he subtly enjoyed seeing Soffía so bothered about the slow pace of the investigation. She wasn't a woman who liked to admit to mistakes.

"The psychologist is concerned there are more needles hiding somewhere around the city," he said.

"Why?"

"Because this clearly wasn't a copycat. Not unless the perpetrator travels in time. Therefore both attacks, if we use that word, must be the work of the same individual. And this person appears to be in no hurry. The toilet rolls with the needles could have been buried under fresh ones used to refill the basket, and wouldn't be revealed until whenever."

"What about disabled people? Are they in particular danger?" Soffía glanced quickly at him.

"Then you might just as well ask whether the perpetrator is angry with people who eat fruit or have to use toilets."

"You're the psychologist."

"The most high-profile cases around the world weren't about perpetrators harming consumers, that's to say, the original perpetrators. They reckoned they had grudges against the manufacturers of the products, if I remember correctly. They wanted to damage sales and thus cause them financial loss. Copycats have nothing in mind but to amuse themselves and cause trouble for others, just like other vandals."

"Fruit and toilet paper rolls. Any connections there?"

Her phone rang before Adam could answer. The phone seemed to be connected to the car's speakers so the ringtone echoed around them before the call itself was put through.

"Soffía."

"Yes, hello. Steindór here. Dóri. You were here with us just now."

"Hello, Steindór. Did you find the needles?"

"No, they went into the waste, as we told you. No, it's something else, a personal matter, that I wanted to mention to you. I just didn't want to say anything earlier in case my sister heard, as it would stress her out."

"What's this about?"

"Well, it's pretty hard to explain but ... I feel ... well, like the last few days or maybe a couple of weeks ... that someone has been ... actually watching me."

Dóri ended his fragmented sentence with a deep sigh.

"How so?"

"It's really just a feeling. I don't have any direct evidence. Someone has just been sitting outside in a dark car, both at my house and here at work, for a long time."

"Do you have security cameras outside?"

"Yes. I've just looked through the recordings but ... they're not clear enough. Whoever was there, if I'm not imagining this, kept his distance. I tried to take pictures out of the window but they weren't clear. And one time, as soon as I started taking pictures, the car drove away."

"Did you get the registration?"

"No."

"What about the make or model?"

"It was too dim to see. But the car's dark, as I said, black or navy blue. A family car. Then I've seen other mysterious cars, so maybe this person doesn't always use the same car."

Now it was Soffía's turn to sigh.

"Look, this is very vague. And you know what the current situation is. The police are fully stretched right now."

"I understand." The man's disappointment was audible. "I just wanted to mention it to someone. To the police, I mean. Because I'm really not happy about this. It's very uncomfortable when some spooky person is shadowing you."

"Spooky in what way? Can you describe this?"

"No, I'm sorry. It's just a manner of speaking. I mean, there's something shady about all this."

Soffía quickly ended the conversation with Dóri. She was the uncrowned Icelandic champion at ending unproductive conversations. All the same, Adam noticed that she did not hang up without saying goodbye. It was as well she did not use her usual method on people in distress who turned to the police, even though she thought it was acceptable to use this on a man she had once been married to and with whom she had a child.

"Poor baby!" Soffía growled. "Pissed off that Sesselja called the police. Ha! But he still needed to talk to us himself."

JÓNÍNA LEÓSDÓTTIR

8

Adam was relieved to be able to shut the front door behind him and leave the virus-infected world outside. He had always been home-loving and the expression that an *Englishman's home is his castle* suited him perfectly, even here in this small basement apartment. He felt it was important to have a safe refuge and welcoming surroundings.

His attitude toward the home had been one of many that differed from Soffía's, and was the root of endless disagreements during their marriage. She did not care in the least what dishes she ate from, whether the cutlery was part of a set, or whether she wiped her mouth with a napkin or a piece of kitchen towel. Adam, on the other hand, used all of his senses to eat and enjoy his food. He was unable to separate the messages received from his taste buds from those that came from his other senses. The appearance and aroma of the food could elevate it to a higher level. The same went for tableware, placemats, a single rose in a vase, and so much else that contributed to a beautiful overall picture.

Soffía never understood how it could disturb his sense of beauty or his appetite if she dumped a milk carton, bread in a bag or a packet of ham straight onto the table. He himself always took pains to arrange food tastefully on a plate, and he poured milk into a jug, even if it took a little longer.

"It all ends up in my stomach, mashed up together," was a phrase Soffía often uttered when confronted.

"We all end up in the grave too," Adam had replied. "Might

we not as well top ourselves right away?"

"All psychologists are crazy."

Now he was free from this kind of squabbling. This was one of the reasons for his feeling of wellbeing here on Kaplaskjólsvegur, as there were never any dishes in the sink, the bed was made every morning and everything else was exactly as he liked it. This was where he could shut the world out.

This was also where Jenný flourished. Here she lacquered her toenails, shaved her legs, tried out different hairstyles and clothes she had ordered online, tripped around in high heels and sipped pink gin from a frosted glass.

In fact, Adam had never been happier than after he moved here. The only thing that was missing since the spread of coronavirus around the world were short trips abroad. He was starting to feel claustrophobic. Jenný needed to be out among people, but not in Iceland. So in recent weeks a considerable internal tension had built up, which became even harder to bear due to the uncertainty over how long this situation could last.

Adam heated some tea for himself. A mug of hot tea made everything better. Then he turned on the computer and opened a search engine, far from confident of finding anything useful on academic websites. He typed in 'needles, toilet paper, vandalism' in English, and immediately regretted it. The images that accompanied the search results were revolting.

Many of them showed messy, clogged toilets where drug addicts had used needles. There were also bloody toilet rolls that addicts had used to clean syringes, and the sticking-plaster-covered hand of a man who had jabbed his finger on a used syringe that had been left in a paper dispenser in a public toilet. But no matter how hard Adam tried, there was nothing relevant to be found. He did not find a single example of sewing needles in toilet paper.

Since the internet showed him nothing new, Adam decided to check whether his grey cells and old-fashioned thinking might be a better option. He put on a Chopin piano concerto and lay down on the sofa to think as the notes filled the apartment. A person with a master's degree in psychology, over twenty years of work experience and a semi-completed doctoral dissertation ought to be able to build up an idea of how a person would be likely to commit consumer attacks. That was assuming the perpetrator was not a complete idiot who had no idea of the potential harm to innocent people inherent in hiding needles in consumer goods.

In fact, stupidity was the only thing that Adam considered it almost safe to write off. An impulsive child prankster might have been able push needles into fruit, in the same way that children, for example, had been known to figure out how to loosen the wheels on their schoolmates' bicycles, often with terrible consequences. But needles had been inserted into the toilet rolls before the fruit incident. He decided that a child would be less likely than an adult to push broken needles inside a toilet roll in a bar in the eastern part of the city and then follow up with tampering with fruit in a small shop downtown.

Adam jumped when the phone rang and when he looked out the window it was obvious that some time had passed since he lay down on the sofa. He must have fallen asleep.

"I just heard from a vet. A dog was injured. Just now. Very seriously." Soffía was breathless. "It ate some sausages with needles in them."

"At Bar Three?" Adam looked at the clock and saw it was half-past six.

"I'll send you a car."

"I'm not getting in a car with anyone but you, since I have done that once today. If you have the virus, you've probably infected me anyway."

"Jesus, how stressed can you get? Have you talked to a psychologist?" Soffía guffawed.

"It's great that you can laugh about a life-threatening illness that's affecting the whole world and may kill millions of people."

Soffía stifled her laughter.

"But it's out of my way. I'm at home. This is in the Holt district."

"This what? The vet?"

"The gallery."

"What gallery?" It got on Adam's nerves when Soffía acted as if he could read her mind.

"Well, where the dog was injured."

Adam desperately wanted to quit all consulting and, for a change, hang up on her. If Soffía wanted his help, he shouldn't have to drag every morsel of information out of her by force.

"What was a dog doing in a gallery?" he asked, from between clenched teeth.

"It was an exhibition opening."

"Who opens an exhibition in the middle of a pandemic when everyone has been asked to stay at home? And who would even think of attending? Especially with a dog?"

"I will be right with you. Make sure you're ready."

Adam sat confused on the couch with the phone at his ear and his head reeling. Soffía was no longer on the line. That was just standard practice.

The police would be getting a hefty invoice for his expert assistance. This would include double time for an evening call-out, and even a double weekend rate for a Friday night. But deep down, he was curious about this latest turn of events in the needle case, even though the thought of an injured animal was disturbing. There had been a pale Labrador at home when Adam was a boy, and the whole family had been devastated when the dog had been diagnosed with cancer and died shortly afterwards.

If Soffía had given him more detailed information, he could have considered the development of the case while he munched a banana and waited for her. The keywords 'dog, sausage, gallery, exhibition opening' weren't enough to form a theory.

When Adam got into the car, he finally got more to work on. Soffía did not know what breed the dog was, only that it was small. That didn't tell him much. But she thought that the needles had been in small, bacon-wrapped cocktail sausages that were part of the canapés for the two-legged guests at the opening. The perpetrator had presumably intended to injure a human being, not an animal.

"What kind of show is this, who's the artist?" Adam asked, hardly expecting an answer to this question. Soffía had little interest in art and probably hadn't considered the artist's name or work to be an important factor when she had been notified.

"Tapestries by a Greek woman, I understand. She didn't come to Iceland for this. But the gallery owner kept to the distance rules. Two people let in at a time. Wine and nibbles outside. Fire in an old charcoal grill. An accordion player. All perfect. Until the dog got a sausage. Or sausages. He swallowed two needles. Or something. They're stuck inside him. Do dogs have an oesophagus?"

"It's not known whether the dog ate one sausage or two? What does the person who gave him the food have to say?"

"Nobody's admitting to it. Guilty conscience dot com."

"Could the dog have got the sausages himself?"

"Not a chance, the owner says. He owns the dog. The gallery owner."

"Then he must be at the vet's place. Shouldn't we go there rather than to the gallery?" Adam found this obvious. "Surely it's the owner of the place we need to talk to, the one who presumably ordered or even prepared the nibbles himself."

"Leave me to it, please. First the scene, then the vet."

"You didn't tell me it could take all night. I could have something else on."

"You? Going out? Now?" Soffía chuckled. "D'you know any other jokes?"

"Well, or expecting guests for dinner." At times, it infuriated Adam that she knew him so well. "You didn't say that we would be running around from place to place."

"Guests for dinner?" Now she howled with laughter. "Yesterday you treated me like I was a leper. I've no doubt you sanitised the chair and the coffee mug after I left. Yes, and the doorknob. Don't try to deny it. I could have been about to burst and you wouldn't have let me use the toilet."

Adam decided to let her uncharitable remarks pass without comment.

"You dragged me to a café today and now you expect me to go both to a gallery and to a vet's clinic. Do you think that Víðir or the Covid committee of three would approve?"

Soffía turned down a side street, which Adam did not remember having passed before, and stopped the car in front of a gallery he had never heard of. In the window hung a tapestry that showed colourful houses and mountains in the distance. A poster with a photograph of a dark-haired woman and a short text had been pasted on the window, no doubt information about the Greek artist.

On the pavement stood a battered charcoal grill in which scorched pieces of wood floated in water. The fun seemed to have ended abruptly after the dog got into the bacon sausages.

9

The small gallery was illuminated but nobody was to be seen in the exhibition space. Soffía rapped hard on the window and a young girl in a wheelchair appeared in a doorway leading off from the room. When the girl had let them in, she pulled a tissue out of the sleeve of her jumper and turned around.

"My name's Sunna. Aren't you from the police? Emil asked me to wait for you."

The girl was sniffling and her eyes were red. Adam hoped it meant she was crying rather than suffering a viral infection. To be on the safe side he kept as far away from the girl as the space allowed, but unfortunately this was one of the smallest galleries he had ever visited.

"Do you have news about the dog?"

Adam mentally awarded Soffía points for starting by asking about the dog. It showed a warmth that she sometimes lacked in human communication.

"Mango? The vet put him to sleep."

"Really? It was that serious?" Soffía seemed shocked.

"No, wait, not like that." Sunna caught her breath. "He's being kept heavily sedated because he was so badly hurt and was trying to bark even though he couldn't. Emil said they were waiting for a woman who assists the vet with the operation."

"Is it possible to extract the needles?"

"The vet doesn't know. Or yes, sure. But the injuries are

internal, so even if the needles are removed, he might still not make it."

"Did this happen in here?"

"No, outside. Most of them were there. Poor Mango was suddenly so agitated and started whining, we didn't know what was going on."

"Do you work here?" Soffía looked around her.

"Sometimes. If I'm not at school and Emil needs to see a doctor or something. But sometimes he just puts a sign on the door."

"Does he often go to the doctor? With the dog maybe?"

"No, himself. You see, he's not well."

"Something serious?"

Adam sent Soffía a meaningful look as a sign that she had crossed the line. The poor girl was upset about an injured animal she loved and now she was being grilled about the gallery owner's health. If his medical history was relevant, which was highly unlikely, Soffía should ask the man himself, instead of expecting the girl to reveal things that were her employer's personal business.

But Soffía did not look at him and Sunna didn't seem to realise that she could decline to answer.

"He has cancer."

Adam ostentatiously cleared his throat and took a step closer to Soffía, who finally looked quickly in his direction. Although neither of them spoke, he willed her not to ask what kind of cancer Emil had. She had certainly meant to ask about it, but turned her attention elsewhere.

"Tell me about the sausages," she said. "Were they bought in? Are there any leftovers?"

"Wait a minute."

Sunna rolled into a side room off the exhibition space and quickly returned with a deep white bowl, the bottom of which was covered with a layer of grilled cocktail sausages wrapped in bacon. She carefully handed Soffía the bowl, as if both the container and its contents were poisonous.

"These are the leftovers. Sorry, but I don't know where Emil got them. Maybe you want to get the rest too? There are marshmallows that people could warm up on the fire, really cosy. And then there are red and white wine boxes. And of course also toothpicks for the sausages and long skewers for the marshmallows."

Soffía shook her head.

"No, that's fine," she said. "Did anyone else find a needle?"

"Nope."

"Did anyone check the leftover sausages?" Soffía lifted the bowl up to her face and looked critically at the sausages.

"We didn't know what had happened to Mango, so it didn't occur to anyone. Emil only told me about all this when he called from the vet's surgery and he had been examined. Mango, that is. And by then everyone had gone."

"Do you have a bag for this?" Soffía handed the girl back the bowl. "Just the sausages."

Sunna went back into the back room, which was presumably the owner's office, and came back with the sausages in a thin plastic bag.

"Sorry, I only found plastic ones."

When the girl held out the bag, Soffía indicated that she should give it to Adam. Although he didn't appreciate this, he tried not to show it and kept the bag slightly away from his body, as if the bacon could transfer grease directly to him.

He noticed that Sunna stared in amazement at the latex gloves he was wearing and Soffía's eyebrows were raised for the same reason to the roots of her hair. But Adam was unfazed. Under the circumstances, it was each individual's responsibility to take their own health precautions.

"Do you have a guest list?" Soffía looked around the hall. "Or a guestbook?"

Sunna looked guilty.

"I accidentally spilled red wine over the guestbook, so Emil put it on the radiator to dry. So nobody could write in it. But he has an email list and he advertises everything on Facebook."

"I understand." Soffía was unimpressed.

"Do you think any of the guests ... could have ... intentionally put needles in the sausages and then ... then given them to Mango?" The girl's lip quivered.

"That's the question. Who planted the needles? When? And why?"

Soffía posed the questions to herself rather than hoping for answers. Then she walked around the small exhibition space for a minute or two, lost in her thoughts, as if she were alone in the world.

"We have to talk to Emil," she said abruptly and looked at Adam. She thanked Sunna for her assistance and for the information. Then marched out of the gallery.

Inside the car, Adam handed Soffía the plastic bag with the greasy sausages.

"I'm not your pack horse," he grumbled through clenched teeth.

He was even less pleased when she burst out laughing and threw the bag on the floor in the back of the car, before greedily tearing open a bag of sweets and offering him some. He shook his head, even though he was hungry. Since these were sweets from Soffía's own pockets, it was certainly something containing liquorice. Why didn't she have dangerous hypertension? Adam had a blood pressure monitor that he used regularly and he immediately suspended using salt if it went over 130.

He was really looking forward to going home, cooking something heavy on the carbs with a pile of grated cheese, and then relaxing. Although the work for CID was welcome, it brought with it an awkward proximity to his ex-wife. It was simply a question of whether it was worth the money.

Now, however, Adam was forced to go with Soffía to the vet. He couldn't walk away in the middle of the enquiry, which would be highly unprofessional. But on the way to the clinic, he did not utter a word, other than to answer the questions that Soffía asked him.

"Who gave the dog a sausage?"

She sounded commanding, as if she thought he could come up with a name, address and ID number, but he didn't let that put him off.

"I find it a little strange that the person who did it didn't own up," he said. "That's to say, if the person in question had nothing to do with the needles. The silence is suspicious."

"Could he just be ashamed?"

"That is a possibility. Few people want to hurt animals. Or other people, for that matter. Perhaps this person finds the whole thing so unpleasant that he can't bring himself to accept having been responsible, even if his intentions were nothing more than to spoil the dog with a treat."

"But ... was it definitely in the sausage?"

"Isn't that what was reported to the police?"

Soffía nodded.

"Maybe the dog then vomited a sausage, or a sausage was found when the vet examined him." Adam shrugged his shoulders. "The vet wouldn't mention sausages without reason."

"Toilet rolls, fruit, sausages. Is that definitely the right order?"

"It seems to be. Unless the cocktail sausages were cooked a while ago and then frozen. I'm going to check." He picked up his phone and googled. "It's possible to freeze bacon-wrapped sausages and then thaw them when you want to use them. But when the food was prepared might not matter, maybe the needles were stuck in the sausages at the party itself. Someone might have fished one out with a toothpick and stuck a needle into another sausage at the same time."

"Damn, it's complicated!" Soffía groaned. "Everyone down at the station thinks I'm messing about. Just some cosy little case. While they're dealing with Covid."

The veterinary clinic was on the ground floor of a commercial building, behind a discreet exterior. Adam worried that they would not be allowed in. The office was closed, so the vet and the assistant were probably in the middle of the operation. But a thin man in a dark overcoat, who was smoking outside the building, provided the solution.

"You're from the police?" the smoker asked uncertainly, and took such a long pull on the cigarette that his cheeks formed deep cavities.

When Soffía had nodded and introduced herself, without mentioning who Adam was, the man in the coat stretched out his hand before immediately pulling it back.

"My name's Emil. I'm the one who called you. I own the gallery. And Mango."

"Is he...?" Soffía jerked her head in the clinic's direction.

"They're trying to ... to save him."

Emil dropped his cigarette, which he had smoked right down to the filter, and crushed it underfoot. It seemed to Adam that he was about to burst into tears.

"Can we go inside?" Soffía asked, pointing to the entrance.

Emil pulled a key out of his coat pocket and waved it to indicate that the locked door was not a problem. But when Soffía stepped up to the door, he hesitated.

"If you don't mind, I could do with another. That was my first smoke in two or three hours." He pointed with his toe at the crushed filter on the ground. "First I was busy with the opening... and then... I've just been here."

He had already lit up again.

"I'll just take a few puffs," he promised, smoking with the same intensity as before.

"Then we'll just start right here." Soffía pulled out a small notebook and pen. "Were the needles definitely in the sausages? And who prepared them?"

Emil exhaled a great column of smoke.

"Yes, Mango threw up bacon and also bits of sausage. But you probably already know, it seems nobody is inclined to own up to giving him anything. That's just nuts. The bowl was on a tall table, so it wouldn't have been possible for Mango to get to it by himself. The only thing that I can think of is that

someone accidentally dropped food and didn't realise Mango
would get it."

"And who prepared the sausages?"

"I'm no chef, so I got them from Bar Three. They always
prepare something for me when I have an event."

Soffía looked at Adam and then back at Emil. Now there was
a connection between two of the elements in this strange case.

Adam hoped that this meant that the mystery of the needles
was now on the way to being solved. Inwardly, he was also
thankful that it was too late in the evening for a visit to Bar
Three.

10

Soffía wanted to talk directly to the owners of Bar Three after the visit to the vet, but then Adam put his foot down and said that enough was enough. She could go to the owners' home or anywhere she saw fit. He, on the other hand, was completely done with playing detective for the day.

When Soffía saw how close to the edge Adam was, she gave up and drove him back to Kaplaskjólsvegur in the western part of the city. But on the way, she continued to bombard him with questions.

"Did you see how ill Emil looks? It has to be serious."

"Soffía. Really."

Adam found her words distasteful. All the same he knew exactly what she meant. Emil had been not just been slim, but emaciated. It was clear to see when he took off his coat inside the clinic, the man's shoulder blades protruded and his limbs were like straws. There was considerable swelling to his face and a yellowish hue to his skin. Adam's grandfather, who had died of cancer, had had a very similar appearance in the last few weeks of his life.

"The yellow skin colour. Smoking or cancer? What do you think? Liver cancer, maybe?"

"Would you mind, Soffía? Show the man a little respect. Isn't it enough that he's seriously ill, but could be about to lose his dog as well?"

She hastily changed the subject.

"Did you understand the vet?"

"I thought she was talking in circles," Adam said with a sigh. "She was so gloomy when she came into the waiting room I thought she was going to tell us that the dog had died during the operation. Then it turned into let's hope for the best, wait and see. Poor Emil was completely confused. Didn't you find it touching when he asked to stay with the animal overnight?"

"I'd have asked for that too."

"Really?" Adam was startled. When Margrét was small, it had always been his job to take care of the little girl if she was unwell.

"Yes, rather than pay for a nurse. That's going to cost something. It's a night shift."

Soffía was someone who knew the value of money. But before Adam had time to be offended, she fired the next question.

"Are all the needles linked to Bar Three?" she asked, with no let-up in her demands of her psychology adviser.

"Obviously in two cases out of three," he replied after brief reflection. "Or what do you think? You went to these fruit importers, were any of them connected to Dóri and Sesselja? Maybe they run a wholesale business, or own a share in some such company, to get cheaper supplies for their establishments."

"I talked to the CEO. And had him go over the stock. The metal detector, remember. But I didn't check ownership." When Adam did not respond, Soffía continued. "It was the first case. Some kids finding an outlet for bad behaviour. That was the most likely option by far. It didn't occur to anyone that there could be more."

In other words, she had only grudgingly looked into the fruit case. This was what Adam had suspected.

"If these siblings are involved in importing fruit, then it's likely the connection is there, in their company," he said. "Although not necessarily with them."

"Hold on, what are you saying? That this could all revolve around Dóri and Sesselja?"

"Well, that strawberry case in Australia seems to have started as revenge directed at the producer. But then, naturally, the whole thing got out of control." Adam thought for a moment as he put together his conclusion. "So, yes, the perpetrator could be someone that the siblings have fired or mistreated in business. Something like that."

"Not a sacked employee. Then he would no longer be there."

"That's true. This would have to be someone with access to the food and the toilet without attracting attention. But the needles could have been inserted into the sausages afterwards, by someone who knew there would be a connection with Bar Three. The same goes for the fruit, however that theory depends on the wholesaler, and we don't know if there's a link there."

"Maybe he had help?" Soffía glanced questioningly at Adam.

"Of course," he said, although he wasn't fully convinced. "If the person with a grudge is a former employee, he could have arranged for someone else to plant the needles in the toilet so he wouldn't need to be seen there. That's a possibility. But for the sausages, the person has to work there, doesn't he? They must have been cooked in the kitchen."

They were both silent for a moment.

"If these attacks are aimed at companies, as they were in Australia, then Bar Three seems to be the most likely company that the perpetrator would want to discredit," Adam said, thinking aloud. "Unless he bears a grudge against people in general, and dogs. That would be very sad."

"This thing with the dog was pure chance," said Soffía firmly. "It can't be anything else."

Adam agreed. The leftover sausages from the party also needed to be examined. Maybe it was just luck that there had been no more needles to cause harm at the exhibition opening.

"I think, unfortunately, that this is going to be a big thing, at least on social media." Despite the temptation, he resisted finding fault with the online world. "There hasn't been anything negative about Bar Three simply because it was Dóri himself who was injured, and not some customer who would immediately have posted pictures and made a fuss. So the perpetrator was out of luck. And this thing with the dog happened this evening, so the news hasn't come through yet."

"But Sunna didn't know where the cocktail sausages came from, let alone the guests. How could needles in sausages at a tiny gallery discredit Bar Three?"

Adam understood that Soffía thought that this was far-fetched, but he wasn't prepared to let go of his theory.

"I know that the sausage case doesn't come across like an obvious attack on Bar Three, considering what we now know," he explained. "But something else must surely come to light, something that explains this, some connection. Let me come with you to talk to the siblings tomorrow. Just not too early."

"You're getting excited about this." Soffía was delighted, as if she had uncovered a secret. "Go on, admit it."

"Let's say I want to get to the bottom of it. This is like solving a crossword."

Adam sometimes wrestled with English online crosswords, especially the challenging cryptic variety. Unfortunately, he had never been able to interest Soffía or Margrét in this. Part of the fun of these riddles was consulting other crossword addicts, just as his parents habitually did at home in Essex. In his childhood home, it had been a tradition to discuss the day's Guardian crossword over dinner.

His father and mother were so obsessed that they had their favourite crossword compilers, and the paper always published the author's pseudonym with each puzzle. Adam missed these little everyday conundrums. Why hadn't he thought of discussing the crossword in video calls with his parents? They hardly talked about anything but depressing statistics these days, about how many had been infected and the situation in hospitals in the UK and Iceland.

DECEIT

When he finally returned to Kaplaskjólsvegur and felt sure he would not be disturbed any more this evening, it was time for Jenný to make an appearance. Adam rarely had as much need of her as he did right now – and Jenný really needed a pink gin with plenty of ice. He mixed a drink as soon as he had thrown away his latex gloves and washed his hands long and thoroughly with plenty of soap.

The crystal glass awaited Jenný, frosted and tempting, when she appeared a little later in the living room in a royal blue glitter dress and with a matching Alice band.

"Wonderful!" she whispered, taking hold of the engraved glass. She had been waiting for this all evening, if not all day.

SATURDAY 04.04.2020

Approximately 1,400 individuals in Iceland are confirmed to be infected with Covid and roughly 6,300 people are in isolation.

Forty-four patients with Covid-19 are at the National Hospital, eleven of them in intensive care and eight of them are on ventilators. The youngest is thirty-seven years old.

Four people have died of the virus in Iceland.

11

Finding no fresh news about needles online the next morning, Adam decided to read up on the illness that Björn's daughter had been diagnosed with. The further he read, the deeper his sympathy grew for the young woman and her father. The blows that people received through life could rarely be as devastating as this, and Björn's concern was entirely understandable.

Huntington's disease is a progressive degenerative disease that affects thought, emotion and movement, he read in one source. Its onset is seen in changes in behaviour and personality, depression, increased irritability and anxiety. In the early stages there are often difficulties in recalling memories, in brain function and judgment. As the illness progresses, memory problems become increasingly severe.

Adam felt crushed. This illness was even more terrible than he had recalled.

It was no surprise that Rebekka was preoccupied with her paternity as it seemed clear that the condition was not in her maternal line. Although the threat of murder was certainly an exaggerated reaction, this young woman had been confronted with a terrible illness linking her with sinister bonds to a complete stranger. Many folk had obsessed over other people for lesser reasons.

Adam knew that Rebekka needed psychological help and wondered if there was a way to approach her. Maybe Björn could appeal to her closest friends, get them to sit down with her and talk to her about their concerns. Tactics of this kind often worked well when people needed treatment.

Adam was unused to making the initial approach to a client, but this case was unlike most others. He was reminded of the depth of the anguish Björn felt for his daughter. He would contact the man later today, if only to see how he was doing. Even though it was the girl who was sick, Björn was Adam's client. It would be inhumane not to bend the rules for someone undergoing such a crisis who appeared to have limited family to call on.

But first he had to visit the siblings at Bar Three with Soffía. She had asked Dóri and Sesselja to meet them at the café shortly after its eleven o'clock opening.

As they walked through the door, Adam was once again astonished that people would risk going to a café to eat and drink in the middle of a pandemic. A young couple had even brought a baby, which slept in a pram outside. Adam was completely baffled. Would they go outside and fetch the baby if it were to wake up and start crying? Would it be allowed to put its fingers on the table, drink something from a glass and play with the teaspoons?

Nothing but the need for an income and oxygen could get him to set foot past the threshold of his home on Kaplaskjólsvegur. Except, of course, if Margrét were to desperately need him for something; but absolutely nothing else. These young people were hardly at work as they lingered over coffee, sourdough bagels with salmon, and their phones.

"Can people just chatter in here with a latte as if there's no pandemic going on?" he said softly to Soffía, without leaning too close to her. "Wouldn't Víðir have something to say about this?"

"God, you can be so English!"

Soffía never hesitated to make fun of English people, despite the fact that her only daughter was half-English and she herself had spent some years at university in England. She felt that the English obeyed rules too willingly and without question, that they were too quick to form an orderly queue, and that they were constantly apologising. Even though Adam had acquired Icelandic citizenship, she always regarded him as English. This wasn't flattery.

Sesselja appeared suddenly, as if she had sprung up from the floor. Adam looked up and saw two security cameras; no doubt the owners had seen them on a computer screen.

"If you don't mind, Dóri is inside," she said, politely but coldly, and placing a hand on Adam's back, as he was walking behind Soffía. She clearly wanted to get this over with.

Dóri slumped rather than sat in the office chair, his legs diagonally across the table, playing with a thick elastic band. He put Adam in mind of The Pink Panther.

Making no attempt to stand up, he just nodded and indicated a yellow-brown leather sofa by the window. The siblings' patience for the police investigation seemed to be fading.

"More needles have been found," Soffía said bluntly, as soon as they had sat down. "They were in food from here. And this time there was harm done."

If her intention had been to shock them, then it worked very well. Dóri lost control of the elastic band so it shot up into the air and then dropped to the floor.

Sesselja gasped.

"This has to be some kind of misunderstanding, nothing has happened here," she blurted out. "The staff would have let us know."

"It happened at an event in town. The food was bought in."

"No, that's not possible," Sesselja continued to object." We don't have ..."

"Were the needles in bacon-wrapped sausages?" Dóri interrupted, glancing from Soffía to Adam and back.

"They were."

"*Oh, my God.*"

Dóri hauled his legs sluggishly from the desk and his suede shoes thumped to the floor.

"*Emil!* Emil wanted sausages for some opening." He held his head in his hands, elbows on the desk. "Now I understand. I have a bunch of missed calls from him and messages that I haven't opened yet."

Sesselja glared at the man hunched over the desk.

"Have you been feeling sorry for Emil again?"

Dóri muttered something else into the desk. Adam heard some mention of cancer and imminent death.

"Shit, man! Are you ever going to stop indulging him?" It was clear from Sesselja's tone that this was something she wouldn't have agreed to if Dóri had asked her.

"Who prepared the sausages?" Soffía directed the question to Dóri.

"His name's Tóti." Dóri straightened up again. "That's to say, he's called Tóti. What's his name again, Sessí? Thórarinn?"

"No, Thórsteinn, I think. I can look it up in the accounts."

"But he's been with us since we opened, he'd never..." Dóri let the sentence fade away.

The anxiety was clear in Sesselja's expression.

"Who got hurt? Didn't you say someone get hurt, what did you say again?" She looked at Soffía in horror.

"It was the owner's dog. Emil's dog, that is. He swallowed two needles. And had major surgery."

"Were no *people* injured?"

"By pure luck. Another needle was found. In a leftover sausage."

This was new information for Adam. So there had been three dangerous sausages in the bowl and by some miracle one had been left untouched.

"Have you heard how the dog's doing?" he asked Soffía, even though she had asked him to keep quiet.

"It's touch and go."

Adam wondered if this was true, or if Soffía was deploying scare tactics.

"Is this Tóti at work?" Soffía directed the question to

Sesselja, who seemed more likely to be thinking clearly right now.

"Now?" They looked into each other's eyes, and the siblings shook their heads in unison.

"It's his weekend with his children," Sesselja explained. "But I can ask him to come in."

"Yes, please. Absolutely. To the station."

"Do you mind if I ...?" Sesselja pointed to her phone and then to the door of the café to indicate that she preferred to make the call from the other room. She didn't wait for an answer, but hurried out of the office when nobody said anything.

"Do you think that the needles in the toilet rolls and in the cocktail sausages have something to do with those found in fruit from the health food shop the other day?"

Dóri looked questioningly at Adam. "I saw something about it online."

Soffía hurried to answer so Adam wouldn't speak on their behalf.

"We can't rule it out. But don't mention it to anyone."

"No, of course I won't. This isn't something I want to advertise, this is absolutely terrible for us. First Covid-19 and now this needle business!"

They waited in silence for Sesselja to return, but eventually Dóri seemed to find the silence uncomfortable.

"I am a hundred per cent certain Tóti has nothing to do with this," he said. "I mean, a skint weekend dad? Why would he do something that causes more trouble for his own workplace? We've already had to lay off people and cut shifts. I don't see how this shit is going to end?"

"Is there anything that comes to mind? Anyone who might bear a grudge? An employee, current or former? Or a business rival?"

Adam waited with interest for Dóri's answer. Soffía was finally getting to the heart of the matter. The siblings should be able to point to an individual who wouldn't shed any tears

73

if their business were to fail. There might even be a few people who could fit the bill.

"No... I don't remember anyone, not anyone who'd do something like that." Dóri scratched his head so that his hair stood on end. "I mean, not all the animals in the forest are friends, not in business, and that goes without saying. But this... someone has to be off their head..."

Dóri looked up, his eyes wide and his face a picture of horror.

"But... don't you think...? Do you think that this might be connected to what I mentioned yesterday, this person spying on me, day and night? Isn't it likely that it's the same person?"

"We don't have a lot to go on there."

Adam felt that Soffía was unnecessarily gruff, as it was clear that this so-called spying was preying on the man's mind.

"It's because he's too clever." Dóri looked entreatingly at Soffía. "He always stays far enough away that I don't see the licence plate or his face and ... it's not always the same car."

"I need more than that." Soffía wasn't giving way. "But I'll bear this in mind. Right now we focus on the needles. And the spotlight is on Bar Three."

"What about Arngunnur's health food place? Isn't the focus on her too?"

"You know Arngunnur?" Soffía asked in return.

"Know her?" Dóri threw up his hands, as if disappointed with the police. "She's my sister! Emil told me what happened to her."

"*What?*" Adam and Soffía chorused.

Dóri was taken aback by the force of the reaction that came from the couch.

"Well, half-sister, actually," he explained, as though he wanted to backtrack. "Just like Emil. Same father. But she and Emil don't have the same mother."

"What, Emil as well?"

Soffía was so startled by this additional information that

she shot to her feet, planted her palms on the desk and leaned forward until her and Dóri's noses almost touched. If either of them had the virus, there would be no question of an infection.

"Are you telling me this now? Why the hell didn't you say so before?"

"Didn't say what?" Sesselja had returned without anyone noticing.

"Well, just about Arngunnur and Emil," Dóri muttered to his chest. "Sorry."

Adam wondered why the man was apologising – for not having mentioned the family ties earlier, or for having mentioned them at all?

12

"Well, now..." Soffía sighed as she sat behind the wheel. "Now I want to hear your thoughts."

Adam had silently watched her take initial statements from the siblings, who had been summoned to make a formal statement at the police station in an hour. Arngunnur and Emil would also be called down to the station, and the whole business of the needles in the fruit and the cocktail sausages would be examined again in the light of this fresh information.

Dóri and Sesselja had denied any connection to importing fruit, but the information about this family connection had completely changed the situation. These were attacks on companies owned by individuals, all linked by family ties. This was certainly more than coincidental discoveries of needles across the city.

"This must be something personal," was Adam's first cautious assessment. "I don't remember coming across anything comparable, neither in any academic journal nor in the news. The initial attacks, in the cases I read about, were aimed at companies, followed by idiotic copycats who were just fooling around."

"These are still actions against companies. Not the siblings themselves. Dóri's finger was a coincidence."

"Yes, but is it worse to get a little prick from a needle or for people to boycott a place that's your livelihood?" Adam asked and immediately saw that this was a flawed theory. "But needles ended up injuring living creatures, both those who ate fruit and then the poor dog. It wasn't right for me to say 'a little prick'. It could have been much worse than a scratched tongue and a needle caught in someone's gums. And we don't even know if the dog will survive."

"So...? These are attacks on particular people? And their livelihoods? Not something accidental or plain stupid? Is that the conclusion?"

"Well..." Adam thought a little longer. "It can hardly be anything else. It may be silly to call it a family affair, but that's the feeling I get."

Soffía seemed unconvinced.

"But they aren't close. There's no communication with Arngunnur. And Emil's also kept at a distance. Sesselja was not overjoyed when she knew that he had been provided with those sausages."

"The attacks may have the same roots as the lack of communication," Adam suggested. "Of course I don't know what it could be, it's just an idea. If I were you, I would want to know why they have such a distant relationship."

"I tried that. You heard what he said. 'We're just half siblings. Not brought up together.' No doubt they'll stick to that explanation."

"All the same, it's personal," Adam repeated. "It has to be."

"So you think it's right to warn the other brother? The one who runs a hotel?"

There was hope in the question that Adam would say no, even though Soffía herself knew she would have to. She was a perceptive investigator, and Adam often admired her professionalism. He decided to tell her that, if the opportunity were to arise.

"Absolutely," he replied. "Although there are probably no guests at the hotel right now, someone could try to play a trick on the man."

At that moment, Adam felt sorry for Soffía. He had no responsibility for this, and could just sit back and air theories without worrying about the consequences. She had to deal with the practicalities of the investigation and to be fully and ultimately accountable for everything she did – or did not do – to her superiors.

This issue would probably end up under the media spotlight with all the accompanying criticism and vicious online comments. What if someone were to be seriously injured, someone on two legs? Then things would really kick off.

"But the sister in the old people's home? The one they said was off her head? Should I warn her?"

"These are called nursing homes in the twenty-first century, Soffía. *Heedfulness in the proximity of the soul.*"

Hell, he shouldn't have been critical. But now it was too late and she'd take it badly.

"You are so totally Icelandic. Quoting the nation's poet."

There was no warmth in her voice.

Adam sighed. Either Soffía thought he was too English or too Icelandic. He'd never be able to get it right. But he decided to let this issue slide. They were beginning to sound exactly like what they were: a middle-aged divorced couple.

"There must be some arrangements for the sister in the nursing home," he said. "Although it may not be possible to talk directly, as it seems she has dementia."

"Which complicates things."

"Exactly," he agreed. "Warnings about needles and risks can make a person feel stressed, even if they don't fully understand what it all means. In any case, a sick woman isn't likely to be alert. It wouldn't do any good, and would just be counter-productive."

Soffía did not respond, chewing instead on a sweet from a newly opened bag, and glared at Adam, as if she wanted him to hand her a magic wand.

"Consult the people who take care of the woman." Adam felt his shortcomings keenly, as he had no obvious solution to offer. "The staff will know best if there's any point in warning her. But you have to ask that everything – literally everything

– that woman consumes is checked. Every bite, every sip."

"That will make them happy."

"You can't worry about that, Soffía. It needs to be done."

"Agreed."

Soffía drove fast westwards along Miklabraut. After dropping Adam at home she decided she would go straight to the police station. There she would demand more manpower. Now that the case had developed in a whole new direction, she could no longer manage the investigation practically single-handed, even with the support of Adam's informal involvement.

"Of course you are very important," she added, to his surprise.

She continued to question him on aspects of the case along the way, as her need for support from a psychologist hadn't diminished with Dóri's unexpected revelations of the family connections.

"Hell, that's a complicated family."

Adam realised that this was a question rather than a statement.

"Yes, it's not easy to figure out who was who, who is whose son or daughter, and the full or half-siblings." He pulled a folded sheet out of his pocket and smoothed it out. "I noted down the names, like you did, but I don't know if I quite got it all."

"They all have the same father," she said, as if Adam were a slow student.

"Yes, this Hans. Wow! They're all Hansson or Hansdóttir. It's like an extended joke."

"And not funny."

Adam disagreed.

"And Hans seems to have been something of a philanderer."

"Don't beat about the bush. He was a philanderer."

"OK." He peered at the list. "He had children with four women: Arngunnur with one, Dóri, Sesselja and Bergsveinn the hotel owner with another, Hafdís in the nursing home with the third and Emil with the fourth."

Adam waved the scrap of paper.

"I don't envy you keeping all this in your head. One man, four women and six children."

"And five of the children run companies. All except the invalid. Four people have been in trouble with this needle business."

"Maybe needles represent something special in this family?" Adam suggested. "Possibly something related to sewing?"

Suddenly Soffía started giggling.

"Or congenital pins and needles?" she suggested and they screeched with laughter, not that either of them felt that laughter was appropriate. They were like kids on a sugar high.

Soffía was the first to pull herself together.

"What do you advise me to do? What do I need to ask them later?"

Adam had an answer ready.

"I'd try to find out how they get along, whether there have been any disputes over inheritances. Yes, and definitely check their finances. Family disputes frequently revolve around money."

"Several needles. Covid in full swing. And I should request a financial investigation? Forget it."

"I know of a man who hasn't spoken to his siblings for many years because he didn't get to inherit a basket that his parents had used for weekend picnics. Just a very ordinary basket with a lid. People can turn into bitter enemies because of the most ridiculous things when it comes to inheritance."

"Enemies." Soffía repeated the word thoughtfully.

"Of course, this is just a guess."

"So ...?" Soffía left the question in the air.

"Look, I've never faced anything or heard of anything like this ... a stranger attacking different members of the same family. I'd like to consult a colleague in the UK before I go further into this. He was a long-time consultant at Scotland Yard."

Soffía nodded.

"Rich people often step on each other's toes," she said. "Much always wants more."

"Why are you asking me? You are very capable of this yourself."

Adam tried to sound encouraging.

He omitted to mention that Hans's grown children did not appear to be particularly wealthy. There could hardly be much profit from Arngunnur's health foods business, Emil ran a tiny gallery and Hafdís probably did not live in luxury, confined to a nursing home. Only Dóri and Sesselja lived well, but that could be a house of cards. And Adam had never heard of the hotel that this Bergsveinn owned. It could hardly be that big or profitable a business.

"Use your intuition, Soffía," Adam continued. "And it's OK to be demanding. Except maybe with Emil, he naturally got the worst of it with the dog. If the dog's dead, for instance, I'd be inclined to leave him completely out of any questioning today, just to show a little sympathy."

Soffía turned so quickly into the parking lot that the car slid. They ended up a few centimetres from a jeep with a blue disabled parking placard in the window. This left Adam with his heart racing and he could hardly open the door quickly enough.

"I'll send you an email if I can think of anything or if I can reach my colleague Brian. Don't you keep your phone on your desk during interrogations?"

"Yes. OK, fine. I'll call after the statements have been taken. I'll really need some advice then."

It was a pleasant feeling for Adam when he realised that Soffía clearly needed him and that she took notice of his opinions. Both of these had been sorely lacking in the last years of their marriage.

13

Adam felt a little guilty when he had settled comfortably on the sofa with a stack of academic books, a computer, and a mug of hot tea. The TV screen on the wall opposite showed the BBC announcer, with the volume on low, while the latest news of the pandemic flashed on the red *Breaking News* banner.

He had not felt this content for many days, even two, three weeks, and the reason was that other people were struggling. It was shameful but true. Innocent people and a defenceless animal had been injured by these needles, the dog perhaps life-threateningly. Businesses were also threatened. Last but not least, every hope for the future of a young woman had been dashed, and she had channelled her frustration over this tragedy into dreams of revenge on some unknown person. And here sat Adam – in perfect health, with everything he could desire, immersed in his psychological activities and as cheerful as could be.

He had never before felt so palpably how directly his self-respect was linked to his work. Although he certainly had bouts of idleness, like anyone else, this was mainly to recharge his batteries. He was in his element when seated opposite a client, or immersed in thinking over what could improve their quality of life. That was when the adrenaline flowed at the speed of light through his veins and time flashed by.

Adam had known this before, but he sensed even better now how gloomy and forlorn he had been since the state of emergency was declared and people had been asked to stay at home as much as possible. It had been an oppressive and tense time that, unfortunately, had not yet come to an end.

The former Scotland Yard consultant had not responded to repeated calls or text messages. This left Adam in limbo until the information from the statements was to come from the police and he decided to call Björn, the father of the girl with the Huntington's diagnosis.

He was not used to bothering Gunninga at weekends, but now he called her without the slightest remorse. It wasn't as if she had been rushed off her feet at work recently.

"Adam! Is something wrong?" Gunninga had obviously seen his name on the screen and been startled.

"No, no, nothing like that. I just need a phone number for the new client who came to me yesterday, this Björn. I can't look him up, I don't know his full name."

"Do you think he's going to do himself in?"

"*Gunninga!*"

"OK. I know I shouldn't ask."

"It's not just that. This is a form of words we don't use. But this isn't about a risk of suicide, I just need a word with him. Do you remember the last name or do you have to go down to the office and look it up?"

"No, darling, I have it all in my head. Just wait a moment."

Gunninga was no epitome of humility. When she returned to the phone a moment later, she read out a number that Adam hurriedly jotted down.

"So you did remember the phone number?"

"No, not exactly. But I remembered he lived next door to the mother of my friend's ex-daughter-in-law. Well, or where she used to live, I mean. She died last year, bless her, and the eldest granddaughter bought the apartment. They were so pleased it stayed in the family."

Adam felt his head swim. All these connections between people in Iceland were a jungle that he would never manage to find his way through, no matter how long he were to live here. But he took care not to ask what was remaining in which family. If Gunninga realised that he had lost the thread, she would explain everything to him at even greater length. He had what he needed.

"Thank you for that, Gunninga. And sorry for the inconvenience. See you after the weekend."

Although she had not included Björn's last name in the flood of information, Adam could probably find it online now that he had the phone number.

But he did not call right away. First he wanted to inform himself better of what Björn and his daughter were up against.

He looked up references in two books and read through some online educational materials, including a website for and about people who had been diagnosed with Juvenile Huntington's Disease, as the illness was called when it affected young people. It was heavy reading. Children who inherited the disease could be diagnosed at primary school age, but in other cases this spilled over into adolescence or up to the age of twenty. The young people seemed to have slightly different symptoms to adults, and their life expectancy was also shorter. If people became ill in adulthood, they could live for decades after diagnosis, but children and adolescents were expected to survive for an average of only about ten years.

Rebekka, Björn's daughter, must certainly have read descriptions similar to those that Adam had found. It was no surprise that the girl was angry and upset. Adam also found it understandable that she wanted to know who her biological father was. The illness created a strong bond between them, though it could not be considered a good or happy link.

He could also sympathise with Björn's anguish, as he had no doubt absorbed every available piece of information about Huntington's in the hope of finding some spark of optimism. But so far no medicine or other treatment seemed to be able to slow the progress of the illness. Patients could only be helped in managing the symptoms. Björn had known this when he came to Adam's office, as he had been a picture of helplessness, clutching at straws.

Adam suspected that the unfortunate man had been deeply disappointed by the time he spent at Sáló. Perhaps he would not care for the psychologist's further involvement in the case. He had seen that Adam could not produce any silver bullet that could alter the fate of father and daughter. Yet Adam felt he had to make at least one attempt to reach the man. So he quickly entered the number Gunninga had given him before he lost his nerve.

Björn answered instantly, curt and obviously stressed. This alone told Adam that Rebekka was still wandering, alone and engulfed with rage, in search of the mysterious father with the initial S.

Adam doubted that the girl would try to do anything to the man, in the unlikely event of his being identified. She was probably more likely to take her own life. It clearly worried her adoptive father, even though he had not said it out loud at Sáló. This thought had just hung in the air.

When Adam had introduced himself, he asked if it might be a bad moment, suggesting that he could call back later. But Björn said there was no need for that.

"It's fine, I'm just home alone," he said, seeming in spite of everything to be glad to hear from Adam.

"Have you mentioned to Rebekka the idea of coming and chatting with me?"

"I've not made contact with her since I saw you, no contact." Björn sighed heavily. "But I've talked to her best friend. They live together, the girls. And she promised to mention this to Rebekka."

"Good to hear."

Björn coughed awkwardly.

"Forgive me, Adam, but if she'd prefer to talk to a woman or someone else then of course that's up to her. Rebekka must have that choice."

"Of course," Adam responded. "The main thing is that she gets support. Hopefully she'll get help as soon as possible. When did the friend expect to..."

"Now that's the problem. She said that Rebekka rarely comes home. She appears late at night, sometimes not even that. She is so torn, alone with these terrible thoughts. Well, or with some man."

"Man?"

"I gathered that from her friend, yes. She has one of those ... apps and ... yes, meets all kinds of men. I'm worried about this, deeply worried. And not just because of corona, you see." Björn was about to burst into tears. "It's so easy to take advantage of a girl ... in this situation."

"Björn, you mentioned her anger and other reactions to the diagnosis. But what are the symptoms she mainly struggles with?"

"I'm sorry, wait a moment." Björn was heard blowing his nose, but then he came back to the phone. "Look, these symptoms have been developing for quite some time, probably two or three years. It's easier to see it in hindsight."

Björn fell silent and seemed disinclined to continue, so Adam tried to get him back on track.

"Have these been mainly physical symptoms?"

"Not mainly, no. After her mum died, I attributed it to grief, we both did. Rebekka's movements became so heavy. Yes, and clumsy. Stiffness, you understand, always dropping things and struggling to cope with steps. It was very strange. Here at home she had always run up and down the stairs with no trouble."

"And has that stiffness got worse?"

"Yes, it has."

"What about symptoms other than physical?"

"I also attributed those to Fanney's death, I felt it was so obvious why the girl was depressed. I was sad myself, anxious for the future, anxious for everything. We felt exactly the same. That's why it took so long for me to realise."

"How about her studies?" Adam asked after a short silence on the line. "You said she's at university now, so she's graduated from college."

"She graduated, yes, but she wasn't the high-flyer she had been. Far from it."

"Did she struggle to concentrate?"

"Absolutely." Björn sighed. "She tried, the poor girl, to focus on her books. She was determined to finish college. Her mother made her promise that immediately after she was diagnosed. The cancer was incurable, that was obvious from the start. So Fanney knew what was going on and the last thing she wanted was for it to affect Rebekka's studies. The girl also wanted to keep this promise. She wanted to, but often she just sat and stared into space."

"Do you know how her studies are going now?"

"Obviously this has all become distance learning now, because of the pandemic. I can't imagine that she's making any progress. She sees everything as meaningless. 'Why, Dad? Why?' It's the same story with everything I mention."

Adam wanted to ask Björn if Rebekka used drugs, but thought better of it. He realised that a person in this state of mind would look for ways to numb the pain. Considering she was having one-night stands during this chaotic time, it was to be expected that she would certainly drink alcohol, smoke dope, and perhaps take sedatives. It would only increase Björn's discomfort to talk about it now that it was uncertain whether Adam would be more involved.

The conversation with Björn gradually faded away. Adam, however, managed to encourage him to take care of himself, even though he knew that it would hardly be easy for him to follow such advice under these circumstances. He also suggested that Björn consult a family doctor about antidepressants, despite being generally opposed to the use of psychotropic drugs. This desperate father needed all the help available.

After the call, Adam turned up the volume on the television and switched to the daily briefing from the Icelandic public health team, Víðir, Thórólfur and Alma.

Some time later, he realised that he had not absorbed

anything of what the trio had said at the briefing, nor what the reporters had asked.

His mind was still on Björn, who he hoped would make contact with his daughter as soon as possible. Maybe there was a reason to fear that Rebekka would commit some atrocity if she were to find her natural father. It was even possible the young woman could convince herself that this would be a positive act – by killing the man, she could prevent him from having more children who would suffer a similar fate.

14

"Can I come by?" Soffía sounded exhausted.

"Don't you have a *team* on this with you?" Adam regretted his sharp reply. He hadn't intended to sound so curt.

Soffía groaned so loudly that it sounded as if a storm were raging around her.

"Three more in isolation," she said when she calmed down. "And you're still the psychological consultant. We're relying on you."

This warmed Adam's heart. He didn't miss the plural 'we'. Had Soffía said 'we' because she did not want to admit that she – singular – was relying on him?

"OK. Come on by, I'll make coffee."

In fact, he was happy. He was most content when he was busy and had challenges to deal with. The role of consultant in this strange needle case was a welcome addition to the few clients who continued to seek psychological help despite Covid-19.

While he waited for Soffía, it occurred to him that it would be a good move to write a journal article during this slump in his usual work. A fresh scholarly article would reflect well on him if he were to apply for a permanent government position. He could also make himself more relevant by sending material to Icelandic online media, such as supplying helpful articles about what people could do to make their own lives and those of people around them easier during quarantine. He could get involved in the debate about the increased risk of domestic violence in these circumstances.

If he was more outspoken, perhaps some broadcaster would ask him for an opinion on the psychological effects of social isolation, or advice for office workers, teachers, and others who now had to work from home. This should be a good time for psychologists. He just needed to turn the defence into an attack.

Some kind of public recognition by the police of his work in resolving the consumer product attacks would also be helpful. That would certainly attract attention. But first, of course, they had to resolve the issue.

When Soffía arrived, Adam slightly upped the ante by asking her to wash her hands. Meanwhile, he sanitised the door handle on both sides. He would have preferred to give her a mask, but that would have triggered a storm. This would have to be enough.

He handed her a large porcelain mug filled with strong coffee, and again she was directed to take a seat at the dinner table. There was a basket with cinnamon rolls, which Soffía immediately looked at longingly, but she was unhappy with the seating arrangement.

"We sat side by side in the car," she said irritably.

Adam did not respond to this, as this was something he wasn't prepared to argue about. He simply felt the need to continue to obey the emergency regulations, even though he had been forced to make exceptions. And this was his home, his territory.

He sat himself on the sofa with his mug of tea, with a pad and a ballpoint pen to hand and surrounded by books and website printouts. Neon-coloured post-it notes stuck out from the books and piles of paper, according to a system that Adam had contrived for himself. The bright pink ones were for the most important things he had found when searching psychology textbooks and academic articles, and yellow was for moderately interesting things. Green labels were for material he considered unlikely to have a use for, but had marked just in case.

"Well, did anything new come out of the formal interviews?" he asked.

"Nothing that explains the needles."

Soffía dispatched a cinnamon roll with two quick bites.

"Nobody angry about not getting a basket from the estate?" Adam teased.

"Emil's mother was put out. She was living with the old man when he died."

"Wait, was the estate divided even though Hans had a wife? I thought that the surviving spouse could live in an undivided estate in Iceland."

"It was an unmarried cohabitation. In that case she needs the consent of her stepchildren, which she didn't get."

"So it got turbulent?"

"Yeah. But this was complicated. The estate in this case was a real estate. A fully operating farm. And Emil's mother had no interest in farming."

"She could probably have hired someone to run the farm?"

"No doubt. But she seems to have got over it all. Currently lives in Tenerife. Happily and with another man. And properly married. Once bitten, if you get what I mean."

"Good for the old lady."

"She's only fifty-five. Just over twenty years younger than the old man was. And had Emil at eighteen. Do you think that's right and proper?" Soffía bit another roll in half, didn't wait for an answer and continued with her mouth full. "I called her and she cried with joy. Do you believe this? Because Emil got to enjoy his inheritance. Before he got sick, she said. Such a strange person."

Adam scratched his head.

"How can she be so young? I thought Emil was forty-something."

"He's thirty-seven."

"Really? He's obviously seriously ill, and that can fool you." Adam changed his tone and now sounded a little accusatory. "I guess you were inquisitive about what kind of cancer he has."

"*Inquisitive?*" There was none of the usual pretence in Soffía's resentment. This time she was genuinely angry. "I'm investigating a criminal case! I have to ask the unpleasant questions."

Adam regretted touching this sensitive spot. Soffía was the most inquisitive person in Iceland, but could never bear to have it pointed out.

"OK. What sort of cancer is it?"

"The worst."

"What cancer do you call the worst?"

"In his head."

Adam grimaced. He agreed with Soffía. A brain tumour was the illness he would least want to get, except perhaps Huntington's or Alzheimer's. What all of these illnesses had in common was that they affected the brain.

"And how did Emil get to enjoy his inheritance?"

"On a Greek island. Then he came home because of the cancer."

"Do you know what he did in Greece?"

"Nothing, it seems."

"Did he get that much from his father?" It seemed to Adam that the late womaniser had been no small-time farmer.

"Loads. He paid off a bunch of debts. Spent the rest on ouzo and olives. Not bad."

Soffía banged the mug on the table as a sign that she had finished her coffee and would like more. Adam almost made the mistake of telling her to get herself a refill but then remembered the pandemic and got up from the sofa to do it himself.

"I'm not exaggerating. This is what his mother told me."

"Didn't you talk to him too?"

"Sort of. Emil won't leave the dog. I only talked to him on the phone."

"I feel sorry for him," Adam said without being asked. "Poor man. Forced to come home from Greece to the cold and wind, for cancer treatment. And this little gallery can hardly give him much of an income. After all, he scrounged the cocktail sausages from his brother."

Soffía took a sip as soon as coffee was returned to the mug.

"Scrounged? It was a few sausages!"

"Dóri and Sesselja seem to have managed their finances a little better than he has."

"They claim to be deeply in debt. This needle affair could do them real damage. On top of the virus."

"Not unless something related to Bar Three turns up." Adam felt the siblings had got off lightly in the matter of the toilet rolls, it could only become known if they were to tell the story themselves. The sausages business was worse. "Is there any more news about the dog?" he asked.

"He's not eating. It still looks dicey."

"The dog is the one who has come out of this needle affair worst." Adam shuddered. "But there was nothing to be had from the siblings? No competitor in the café business who could cross the line like that, or any disgruntled employee?"

"They don't have a clue."

"Wouldn't it be more sensible for them to close the doors while the worst of corona passes over? That's what I'd do."

In reality, Adam knew he couldn't run a business. He found it enough of a burden to be part of Sáló's activities, which consisted almost entirely of paying part of the rent and Gunninga's salary.

"They're determined to keep going. But Arngunnur has closed her shop for now. She still doesn't seem scared. It's incredible how unconcerned she is, in fact."

"She could offer home delivery."

Adam revelled in being able to have products from the unlikeliest companies delivered to his door, often at no extra cost. He saw this as the only positive consequence of the pandemic, apart from the big change that people had begun washing their hands more frequently.

"Home delivery? For such a small shop?" Soffía sniffed; she obviously thought the idea was absurd. "But Dóri and Sessí are concerned. That's because of the chatter around the dog, y'see. There's even a Facebook page for him!"

"Emil is hardly going to tell people where he got the sausages."

"They tried to talk to him. To make sure he'd keep quiet. The man's just barely functioning."

"That's understandable." Adam tried to maintain his calm in the face of what he thought was Soffía's shameful lack of empathy. "Emil is watching the dog fight for his life. You must realise that he can't imagine that his half-siblings' catering business is the most important thing in all of this. While nobody knows who did this, some other dog could be injured."

"Or a person," Soffía snorted, but Adam felt that she had taken his point.

"This dog is effectively his child," he continued, "and someone hurt the animal, perhaps fatally, by sticking broken needles into those little sausages. Intentionally! So the man's struggling with some very difficult emotions."

"All right. Feelings. Your area of expertise." Soffía stood up." Now we're going to see Bergsveinn. Big Svenni, as Dóri calls him."

"Is he an unusually big man?"

"No, but he's older."

Adam sighed as she nipped into the toilet before they set off. He would have to remember to sanitise the toilet seat and put the towel in the wash when he got home.

15

The hotel run by Bergsveinn Hansson surprised Adam. There was nothing about the exterior that indicated what lay behind, and it appeared to be just a perfectly ordinary residential building in the Laugardalur district. The only thing slightly different about the outside was a high white wooden fence that provided shelter from the wind and from curious passers-by.

Anywhere other than in Iceland, it would probably have been described as a boutique guesthouse rather than a hotel, Adam decided, as Bergsveinn showed them into a living room with a glass conservatory that doubled its size and greatly increased the available light. Much effort had been made to create a welcoming space, with elegant furniture, animal skins, mirrors and paintings.

Interior design was something in which Adam had no particular interest, but what he saw of the building reminded him of pictures of luxury ski huts in the Alps. Outside in the yard were two large hot tubs, each in its own corner on a platform that spanned half the yard. *Two tubs?* he thought.

A fire blazed in a hearth and thick altar candles burned on a chest of drawers in the conservatory, where the proprietor directed him and Soffía to brown leather chairs. Although the leather looked old, Adam suspected that it had been intentionally aged and the chairs were new, as they turned out to be well upholstered and comfortable.

Adam chose a chair that stood a little apart from the others, no doubt intended for loners who wanted to sit in privacy with a computer or a book and maybe a glass of cognac. Soffía sat confidently opposite him, in close proximity to the chair that Bergsveinn seemed to have been sitting in before they arrived, next to a small table on which lay an open paperback and the dregs of a cup of coffee.

Bergsveinn's hospitality did not extend as far as offering them anything to drink. He was obviously not going to do anything to prolong this visit, his sullen look indicating that he wanted nothing to do with any of this.

"As I told you on the phone, Soffía, I have not found any needles here. There has been nobody here since the end of February. So I can't help you."

Bergsveinn was very much like Dóri and Sesselja – good-looking, with the same high cheekbones, slim and tall. But his hairdresser was not as skilled as theirs, and he had been less fortunate with his skin. His face was pocked with the remnants of teenage acne. He stretched his legs over the chocolate-brown parquet, crossed them at the ankles and looked defiantly at Soffía.

"Doesn't your brother live here?" she began.

"Emil isn't a paying guest. I have a small basement room for staff who have night shifts, he can use it while there are no staff on site."

"Nice of you."

Soffía did not try to hide her sarcasm, and it had a tangible effect on Bergsveinn. Suddenly he was aggressively defensive.

"My siblings and I didn't know about his illness until a social worker at the National Hospital contacted us. We didn't even know that he was back in Iceland! Then he was discharged and the doctors didn't want him to go back to the gallery. Apart from that we probably still wouldn't even know that he was in the country, let alone that he was ill."

"What do you mean? Did he *live* in the gallery?"

"Sure," Bergsveinn said almost casually. "But he seems much happier now, apart from the thing with the dog."

Soffía looked calmly around the living room and Bergsveinn seemed to find the silence uncomfortable, judging by how he fidgeted in his chair. Adam would have bet everything he owned that the man had something to hide.

"So nothing happening here." It did not sound like a question, more like Soffía thinking aloud.

"What could happen in an empty house? Emil keeps to himself downstairs. I don't want to see any dog hair up here. There isn't even any junk mail."

"As you say... *no problem.*" Again, a statement rather than a question.

Soffía looked down at her lap and Adam could make out the smirk on her face.

"No."

"The unpleasant chatter online... Hasn't that caused any harm?"

Bergsveinn started but tried to hide it by pretending a mild cough. He was not a good actor.

"Unpleasant...?"

"You know what I mean. The pictures. The reviews." Adam had asked that Soffía not speak in riddles. Also, she should have told him what she wanted to talk about before they met the man. There was little point in having a psychologist with you unless he had that basic information to work on.

"Ah. That." Bergsveinn faked another cough. "Just part of the hotel business. It's to be expected, some wretched nerd messing around."

"Negative reviews about the guesthouse," Soffía explained to Adam. "On a bunch of booking sites."

"This is a hotel, not a guesthouse," the owner corrected, taking offence. "And it wasn't a bunch, just on three booking sites."

"Bad enough, though. Right?"

"Nobody wants lies about their business on the internet, it's a nightmare to get rid of it."

"What were these comments about?" Adam asked, unable

to keep quiet even though he knew Soffía did not want him to take part in these discussions.

"About gays in hot tubs," she replied quickly, without taking her eyes off the hotel's owner.

"Those pictures were from some porn movie, this was absolutely not filmed here." Sweat beaded on Bergsveinn's forehead.

"Guests couldn't sleep," she continued, as if the man hadn't opened his mouth. "Children were shocked. And people were warned about the place."

"There's absolutely no basis for any of this!"

Soffía watched Bergsveinn squirm in the elegant leather chair.

"Didn't you feel this was worth mentioning?" she asked.

"You asked about needles."

"Or other problems."

"This is nothing comparable," he objected stubbornly, like a child. "Nobody was hurt, nothing happened to me and no guest was in danger."

"But this was an attack on the company." Soffía did not give up.

"*Attack?*" Bergsveinn grimaced. "Yes, yes, yes, I suppose so."

"You complained about it. I found the statement you filed with us."

"Which did nothing whatever. The police are utterly incapable in this kind of matter." A look of contempt appeared Bergsveinn's face. "I had to hire someone for this, a guy who lives and breathes computers."

"What was the outcome?"

Soffía seemed to Adam to be taking a subtle pleasure in quarrelling with the man. He himself waited for the quarrel to end. He disliked arguments, especially when they had no purpose, and this was the case between Soffía and the hotel owner. She had obviously known everything about the case before they had walked through the door.

"With the computer guy? He found nothing." Bergsveinn wiped the beads of sweat from his forehead. "I also had to get a lawyer to contact those booking sites and demand that the comments be removed. It cost a fortune and took far too long. They're like weeds, almost impossible to get rid of. It can reappear at any time. A real nightmare."

"That said, the hotel was attacked ... your hotel."

"You don't really think that these fake reviews and the porn video are related to the needles at Bar Three and to Arngunnur?"

"I'm ruling nothing out."

"And also this sausage thing with Emil?"

"Yes, that too."

"Who has the energy to stir up all this trouble in the middle of the pandemic?" Bergsveinn seemed to expect an answer from Soffía.

"We're investigating exactly that."

"When this is over and I open again ... Could I expect to find needles in the breakfast? Or in the toilet rolls?"

"Could be. All of you siblings need to be careful. Until this is resolved." Bergsveinn frowned and seemed worried.

"Has anyone tried to do something to Haffí? Don't we need to take care of her, a helpless woman in a nursing home?"

"Hafdís is being carefully watched."

"By the police?"

"By the staff of the institution."

"The staff can hardly monitor a person around the clock. I demand – and I'm sure my siblings will agree – that you provide Hafdís with police protection until this is resolved."

Bergsveinn stood up, as if to indicate that their conversation was at an end, and to emphasise his demand concerning his sister's wellbeing. Soffía immediately followed his example, disinclined to let such a stuffed shirt try to dominate her.

"These actions are clearly aimed at business interests. Hafdís surely doesn't have a business. Unless?"

"What about Emil's dog? He had no business interests!" Bergsveinn spat out the final words.

"The needles were not in dog food. They were intended for the gallery visitors."

Soffía ended the conversation and gestured to Adam to make it clear that they were leaving.

16

"Wasn't that visit completely pointless?" Adam asked as they sat in the unmarked police car. "No new information, that's to say, nothing you didn't know before we went in there. But you could have prepared me better."

She started the car.

"It gives an investigator an advantage. Knowing more than you let on. But I wanted you to be more ... blank."

"Blank?" Adam felt weighed down. "I can understand that secret knowledge is useful to detectives, but the exact same thing applies to psychological consultants. They also benefit from knowing more, not less, when they monitor people's reactions."

"Sorry." She didn't sound remotely sorry, even though she forced herself to drop a cryptic apology. "How does the situation look to you now?"

"Well, I'd classify these complaints about gay parties as an attack on the company. And that changes a few things."

Soffía stopped before she was about to drive off, turned to Adam, and waited until he continued.

"These are no longer coincidences, none of these are pranks with a serious undertone. Now we know that there were these negative reviews on the internet, it's clear that this is a serious and deliberate attack on the siblings running companies." He paused for a moment. "Or more likely, an attack on companies run by these siblings. There is a slight difference between the two, I think. In other words, whether the focus is on the companies or on the siblings."

"What do you mean by focus?"

Adam had trouble explaining it. It was just a vague feeling. So he shifted to another aspect.

"Now, we see clearly that these attacks started earlier than we had thought. These lies about the hotel in February were clearly the first incident, the needles came later."

It came as a surprise to him when Soffía started laughing.

"What's so funny?"

"You're so gullible." Soffía wiped tears from her eyes." How do you know the comments were fake?"

"The hotel owner's hardly going to complain to the police over comments about his own place if he knew that boozing and group sex in the hot tubs had genuinely kept guests awake."

"Maybe he had to file a complaint."

"Had to?" Adam looked at her blankly.

"Because of the co-owners, maybe. So they don't believe this stuff about an orgy."

"Doesn't he have sole ownership of the hotel?"

"Dóri and Sesselja own forty-nine per cent."

"Why do I never get all the information?" Adam heard himself sounding petulant, but he was struggling to rise above it. "Are you including me in your investigation as just a joke? You clearly think that the matter of the hot tubs is well-founded and this has nothing to do with the needle attacks."

"I said *maybe.* I know no more than you."

"Didn't he submit photos when he filed a complaint? Evidence showing the pictures could not have been taken on his deck?"

Soffía drove off with a jerk.

"Not printed, no. Just a link to the comments. And the link no longer works."

Suddenly Adam remembered the room Emil had used and what Bergsveinn had said about it.

"Hey! If there was a night porter, he would probably have been aware of this nuisance and investigated it. Didn't

Bergsveinn mention that when he filed a complaint? And what was he up to, filing an official complaint, what did he expect the police to do? The guests had presumably left the country. If they really existed."

"Unfavourable reviews aren't removed, even if someone whines about them. Not from international booking sites. But if there's a police complaint... That's a different matter. And Bergsveinn got paperwork from us."

"That he had filed a complaint? I understand. But what about the night porter, wasn't he mentioned?"

"He took that shift himself. So he says. And heard nothing. So he says. Maybe he joined in."

"You and your maybes." Adam failed to understand why this had to be so complicated. "Couldn't Bergsveinn just provide the names, addresses and telephone numbers of everyone who stayed there that night? Even passport numbers? He must have had some data. Don't visitors have to sign in? I always have to do it abroad, even with a credit card pre-payment."

"The registrations were nonsense. Pretty much Mickey Mouse and Donald Duck. And all paid for through booking sites. Which are jungles."

"*Shit!*"

"Yes, some people just can't be trusted, Adam. Wake up and smell the coffee!"

Adam didn't get a chance to reply. A phone rang and a light on the car's touch screen flashed. Soffía tapped it with her fingertips and immediately a young woman's voice filled the vehicle. Steindór Hansson, a resident of Seltjarnarnes, had reported a burglary just a few minutes ago and specifically requested that Soffía come to the scene. He had said that she was involved in the matter.

"What idiot is committing break-ins now? Most people are at home all day. And on a Saturday afternoon."

"It wasn't in the house," the woman explained. "His car was broken into."

"What was stolen?"

"A sports bag."

"Any value?"

"No, clothes and a wet towel. He went to the gym this morning."

"Send someone on a routine patrol. Let them investigate this. And they can copy me in."

"Steindór demands that you come. He says this is related to a case you are involved with."

"The needle case?"

"I'm not sure. He said someone's been spying on him."

Soffía groaned.

"Doesn't he have security cameras?"

"Nothing to be seen on them. He had to park some distance from the house because the pipes in the street are being replaced, the pavement has been completely dug up. But he was going to check if any of the neighbours managed to get an image of the thief on their cameras."

Soffía finally gave up and told the young woman that she would go out to Seltjarnarnes and talk to Dóri. She didn't bother to ask Adam if he wanted to or could come along, she simply drove along Hringbraut instead of taking a left turn towards Kaplaskjólsvegur.

"Police officer kidnaps psychologist," he muttered to himself.

Deep down, though, he was not unhappy about coming along. This outing gave him, among other things, the opportunity to admire Esja for himself once again. He never tired of looking at this majestic mountain across the bay, it was beautiful throughout the year and every hour of the day. But Soffía managed to spoil his pleasure.

"Have you been up Esja?"

She had seen where his attention lay.

"You know I don't own a car. Maybe I can afford one if the police pay me well enough for my help."

But this wasn't sufficient to encourage Soffía to change the subject.

"There's a bus that'll take you to Esja."

"I know."

"*I* can't stop you now."

"Enough!"

Adam had dragged Esja itself into his arguments with Soffía when their marriage was ending. His complaint was that she did all her exercise indoors but never bothered to walk with him up Esja or go skiing. If she mentioned a word about skiing now, he would throw himself out of the moving car. Of course, their divorce had nothing to do with outdoor activities, and Adam had never before or since engaged in any activity other than a gentle walk on level ground.

17

Access to Steindór Hansson's home wasn't easy. A deep trench ran the length of the street where the pavement had been, and crude wooden bridges crossed it to each house. And with no access to garages, the street was crammed with cars.

"It's just as well that nobody in a wheelchair has to come here," Adam muttered as they carefully made their way over planks to reach Dóri's mansion. He was in a sour mood after Soffía had goaded him about the mountain hiking.

She didn't respond to his grumbling, but set a determined course to the house and ran straight into Dóri, who was dressed in a coat and winter boots. The man must have been watching from the window as they turned up. He slammed the front door hard behind him and led them back out into the street.

"As you can see, it's chaos here," he thundered without bothering with a greeting. "The geniuses who run the city had everything dug up before it froze last year. And now it's not possible to finish the work until spring."

"Do the Seltjarnarnes pipelines and roadworks fall under the purview of the city of Reykjavík?"

Adam made the question sound innocent, but he only asked to show the blowhard that he was mistaken. He had given up on keeping his mouth shut except when Soffía granted kind permission.

"It's the same shitbags behind everything," Dóri said dismissively.

Adam's comment had not affected the man in any way, and it seemed that he was keen to see Soffía. Maybe it would be wiser to just keep quiet.

"Look! It wasn't my imagination that someone has been spying on me."

Dóri stopped by a black BMW parked two houses away from his home. The driver's side window was broken and there were shards on the seat.

"Didn't the anti-theft system activate?" Soffía looked at the broken window with obvious indifference.

"The police should be aware by now that most people don't have the alarm armed. They're so damn sensitive, the slightest thing sets them off."

"What do the insurance companies say about that?" Adam let the question slip, despite his decision that it would probably be best to remain silent. The only response was a sharp glance from Dóri.

"Do you know when this happened?" Soffía looked thoughtfully at the car.

"I parked here almost two hours ago. Then my neighbour let me know half an hour ago."

"Was anyone seen near the car?"

"Not that I know of. I've knocked at all the houses around here but found nobody who saw anything. But not everyone was at home."

"And what was stolen?"

Soffía went to open the car door but Dóri caught her arm.

"You're corrupting evidence! Fingerprints."

The guardian of law and order was not amused. Soffía shook herself free, put her hand in a coat pocket and pulled out latex gloves. Adam suspected that she had used these gloves before.

"We're not looking for fingerprints. It's not that kind of case." She snapped on the latex gloves. "The thief undoubtedly wore gloves. It's freezing cold."

"Is nobody from CID coming?" Dóri seemed surprised.

"I'm here," Soffía replied curtly, opening the door and

sitting down without taking any notice of the shattered glass. "And you didn't get into the car yourself? When you realised that the sports bag was stolen."

"I didn't have to open it to see. The bag was on the back seat."

"Stuff in cars tempts thieves." Soffía opened the glove compartment and began rummaging through the contents.

"There was nothing in the bag but sweaty clothes and towels," Dóri grumbled, watching Soffía closely.

"The thief couldn't have known that. A bag of stuff is as good as a lottery ticket." She got out of the car, walked past him, and opened the boot. "Were there any valuables here? Or in the glove compartment?"

Dóri looked with interest down at the boot, as if expecting something surprising, despite having told them it was empty.

"Any neighbours with security cameras?" Soffía looked around intently and then answered herself. "They don't cover the street. And there's no pavement. So much for that!"

"There are very few who have CCTV, I checked when I was looking for witnesses." Dóri sighed heavily, as if endlessly disappointed by humanity. "It's ridiculous to have to rely on the surveillance cameras that were installed on the two routes in and out of town."

Adam looked questioningly at Soffía. He had not heard these cameras mentioned before. But she kept talking to Dóri without further bothering with explanations for her psychological consultant.

"They make no difference during the day," she agreed. "But they're useful when there aren't so many people on the move."

"Yes, it's probably pointless checking the recordings now. The thief might have been on a bicycle." Dóri slammed the boot shut when it was obvious that Soffía did not consider it part of her job. "Then he could have crossed Eiðistorg and through Mýrin over to Skjólin and bypassed the cameras."

Adam felt completely superfluous to the conversation, and

his mind was now beginning to wander. However, he wanted to know one thing and, when Soffía did not ask, he decided he would have to do it.

"What was in the gym bag, exactly?" He saw that Soffía had pulled a notebook out of her breast pocket and was jotting down what Dóri listed.

"Just the usual." The man seemed to find this tedious, but went ahead to list the contents. "Striped towel, blue and white. Dark grey tracksuit bottoms and a tee-shirt made of the same material. Yes, and grey sports socks and boxer shorts, all on the way to be washed. And black Nike sneakers, some stupidly expensive shampoo and a water bottle."

"It's probably possible to sell Nike shoes," Adam thought aloud. "Even used ones."

"No watch or phone? Or a wallet? "Soffía shot him a sharp look before barking this question at Dóri. She hadn't appreciated him being ahead of her in asking about the bag's contents.

"Nothing of that nature."

"Well, we'll file all of this." Soffía raised her hand in farewell and made to leave. Under normal circumstances, she would probably have shaken hands, but due to Covid, any greeting or goodbye no longer included physical contact.

It seemed to come as a surprise to Dóri that the police were leaving.

"Hey, are you just going to act as if nothing happened? Won't anything be done about it until you find me dead in a pool of blood?"

The man's voice trembled with emotion and Adam saw that the fear was no act.

"We're in the middle of a pandemic, Steindór. We are at the highest level of alert. A car was broken into, it's not exactly attempted murder."

"But... but... there's always someone *watching me*! Sometimes in the evening and in the night. You don't believe me? This is terrifying."

Dóri resembled a child about to be left alone at home. Despair and unease were plain to see in his eyes.

"And then the needles," he continued. "And ... and ... now this! And you're just writing this down in a tatty notebook! In what century do the Icelandic police belong?"

"I'm so sorry." Soffía changed her approach and tried to calm him down. "But we have nothing to build a case on. No evidence."

Dóri unexpectedly hauled open the car door, and dropped into the driver's seat. Without another word, he started the car. Then he accelerated away so violently that Adam had to jump quickly out of the way.

"You fucking lunatic!" he shouted. "I hope I'm insured as a police adviser."

"Insured?" Soffía scowled. "I'll check it out."

They did not say much to each other on the way to Kaplaskjólsvegur. She only asked if he thought there was a connection between the needles and the theft from the car and he answered by asking how she expected him to know. After all, he was a psychologist, not a clairvoyant.

Adam started planning dinner as soon as he walked through the door of his flat. He had found a clever idea in an interview with an English chef online. This was to bake risotto in the oven instead of standing and stirring in a pot for half an hour while the broth was slowly added to the rice. This was what he was planning to try out.

But he had got no further than slicing the shallots when Soffía called.

"I'm in the car. I'll be outside in three minutes."

"What is it now? Can't you go alone?"

"Dóri's home. Now he's completely hysterical. He says a there's a gun pointed straight at him."

"How is he calling the cops if someone's pointing a gun at him? That's rubbish."

"The gunman is out in the yard. He can see the red light on the curtains."

"What red light?"

"The one used to aim."

"*Come on!*" Adam thought he was caught up in some sort of farce. "These laser sights are only on large rifles used by snipers. Isn't that right? Does he really think that someone is sneaking around his garden in Seltjarnarnes with that kind of weapon? The man's seeing things. He's imagining this, you saw how worked up he was."

Soffía groaned.

"Be outside! I'm on my way."

052

18

"You are insured. I checked."

Adam failed to find this information particularly reassuring. He suspected that Soffía had looked into it quickly because she thought there might be something hazardous in all this. If she had cause for concern, then he could also have reason to be worried – instead of being convinced that this would be just some tedious wild goose chase.

There were two police cars at the scene and both had been parked across the street, blocking it off. Several imposing-looking older police officers were fending off curious neighbours, and a young woman in uniform spoke earnestly into a phone. She handed it to Soffía, saying that Steindór was on the line.

Soffía slammed the phone to her ear but then remembered Adam, removed the device from her ear and beckoned for him to come and listen. When he retreated rather than approach, she rolled her eyes but turned on the speaker.

"Dóri? This is Soffía. I'm outside. What's the situation?"

"The light is still there. The gun is aimed directly at the centre of the window. I'm standing up against the wall."

"Do you see or have you seen anyone in the garden?"

"I can see there's a gun aimed at me."

"But have you *seen* anyone? A shadow? Something?"

"Just the laser sight from the gun. It started moving around on the curtain as soon as I came in."

"Moving?"

"Well, it always moves a bit. It's never completely still, it's terrifying. This is clearly someone who's out of control. He could just suddenly snap and start firing."

"Can I get into the garden by the side of the house? Is there a wall? A fence?"

"No. Or yes, there's a wall. Well, there are two, but with spaces in them, alternating gaps. No gate or anything, nothing locked."

"OK. Stay standing against the wall. We're going to check the garden. But you stay on the line with my colleague. Don't end the call."

Soffía handed the phone to her colleague.

"I'm going behind the house. See what's going on."

She looked at Adam, who raised his hands as if he were at gunpoint.

"Are you off your head, Soffía? You two can go. I'll talk to Dóri, try to calm him down." Adam pointed to the phone the young woman was holding. "That's more my department."

"Maybe someone in the garden needs to be reasoned with. Come on."

Soffía took slow steps towards the house. As she reached the wooden bridge over the ditch, she looked around to see if he was at her heels, like a well-trained dog.

"Why is the Special Unit not here?" Adam whispered angrily, mostly at Soffía but also at himself for following her, contrary to any kind of good sense. "Are you going to barge unarmed straight into the range of a madman with a machine gun? And without even a bulletproof vest? We could both be stone dead in a minute. Who would Magga rely on, who's going to walk her up the aisle?"

"Maybe *Jenný*," Soffía hissed sarcastically but then changed gears. "Hey, calm down. There's no gunman."

Adam reeled. Had she really said *Jenný*? He had never heard her refer to Jenný by name before. No, he must have misheard. The tension was getting to him.

"How can you say there's no gunman?" he asked, as loud

as he dared. "You can't be sure."

"Ninety-nine point nine per cent. Come on."

Soffía slipped between the two high wooden walls with intersections, which together created an unbroken shelter for the garden from the cold gusts from the north.

"Hello!" she called without looking around the corner of the wall. "This is the police. Please show yourself."

They held their breath but no one answered. Soffía then repeated her request, giving the person an opportunity to identify themselves, and then waited a moment longer.

"He says the light is still on the window," said a low voice behind them.

Adam was so startled that he felt weak at the knees. He hadn't noticed that the young woman with the phone had followed them.

"Now we're coming into the garden!" Soffía called out. "This is the police. We are completely unarmed."

She walked slowly but carefully in front of the inner wall and stood still. Adam had no intention of following, but stood still behind the wall, even though he knew that bullets would easily pierce the thin wooden boards.

"I'm in the garden," Soffía now announced, loud and clear.

She took faster steps, but Adam waited in the shelter. The young woman went past him to accompany her superior to the scene, and when she also disappeared, he felt even more of a coward. Here he stood, the only man, cowering behind the wall, while the women valiantly rushed towards an alleged gunman. Soffía would tease him unmercifully about this.

"There's nobody here!" Soffía's voice was loud, clear and confident. "Not a soul! It's just a practical joke."

Reassured, he was now so curious that he hurried out into the garden.

"What joke?" he asked, breathless. "What are you doing?"

Soffía was taking pictures of a tree. In the brief light of the flash, Adam saw something tied to one of the branches. It looked like a laser pointer, of the kind used by teachers and conference speakers to point to slides and pictures on the wall.

"It was just to scare him."

Soffía put the phone in her pocket, put on latex gloves and tried to release the laser pointer without touching it. It did not go well.

"Do you still carry a pocketknife?" she asked Adam, and when he nodded she held out her open hand.

He dropped his red Swiss wonder device into her gloved palm without saying a word. Soffía had often made fun of him for using a pocket knife as a keychain, but he didn't let her ridicule have any effect on him. It was an ingenious device that could be used as nail clippers and a nail file. It could also open beer bottles, as Soffía knew very well. Even though she had teased him in the past about this gadget of his, she happily used it to saw through the twig to which the laser pointer was attached.

Now there was movement behind the picture window that spanned half the width of the house. First the white blind was rolled up, then the window concertinaed like an accordion and Dóri came out, shambling like a sleepwalker. He was pale, open-mouthed and staring.

"Is he gone?" he asked, his voice shaking.

"There was nobody here."

"But the laser?" Dóri did not sound convinced.

Soffía lifted a clear plastic bag. In it was the laser pointer, along with the section of branch onto which it had been attached with thin wire.

"Laser pointer," she said simply.

"Yes, but... but..."

"Now we need to talk," Soffía said with emphasis. "And you put all your cards on the table."

"I know nothing more than I've already told you." Dóri raised his hands as if in prayer and looked sadly from Soffía to Adam. "Don't you think I'd tell you everything I know if it would free me from this stalker?"

Adam did not doubt that the man was petrified and had been certain that someone had him in their sights. Now it also seemed clear that he was right. Someone was at least trying to scare the life out of the man, and the laser pointer demonstrated that. Unless Dóri had tied it to the tree himself...? But then he could hardly have simulated fear so convincingly.

"Do you want to chat here or at the station?" Soffía rested her hand on her hip while she waited for an answer.

"H-h-here," Dóri stammered and moved towards the house as if he had suddenly been struck blind.

"You can go," Soffía said to the uniformed officer. "We'll take his statement."

The young woman hurried away with relief, but Adam knew what she intended. Soffía had meant him when she said 'we'. He had not even been asked if he had time to attend another interview, never mind that his role in this investigation had become no clearer. This was more and more reminiscent of the final years of his marriage to Soffía. She kept going and simply expected him to follow.

When could he expect to get home?

Adam realised now how difficult being dragged away from isolation and tranquillity had been, like a baby being pulled from the womb under caesarean section. Long and boring days, which merged into one confusing blur, suddenly seemed an attractive option in comparison to this running around the city in a tug of war with the police.

But this stalking case aroused his curiosity as a psychologist. He was keen to hear what Dóri had to say to Soffía. The man seemed so shattered by all this that he was ready to tell the police about anything that could explain his fear of being watched. Adam was convinced that the businessman had withheld crucial information. Maybe Dóri also had suspicions about the perpetrator in the needle case.

So Adam decided to follow Soffía and Dóri into this smart house on Seltjarnarnes. Jenný and the risotto would have to wait a little longer.

19

Adam looked around keenly as Dóri closed the floor-to-ceiling window behind them and pulled down the white blind. The load-bearing walls had been replaced with steel girders, both vertical and horizontal, to create a living space that extended across the whole lower floor of the building. The expanse and the girders gave the building an almost industrial feel, and Adam thought of his childhood home in Wivenhoe, the quaint house where his parents still lived. The rooms were small, the windows glazed with small panes, the ceilings low and the floorboards creaked. This raw concrete villa on Seltjarnarnes was its diametric opposite.

The furnishings were also different from what Adam had been accustomed to in his family home, where there was a great deal of colour and packed, home-made bookshelves filled the walls not only to the ceilings but even extending to the wall spaces above the door frames. Here there were no warm colours on the walls, in the textiles or furnishings, with neither books nor potted plants to create a welcoming atmosphere. A single large painting hung on the wall and the furniture was like sculpture, apparently designed with looks rather than comfort in mind.

Adam looked around. Where could he sit without getting a pain in his lower back after five minutes or having difficulty getting up again? Finally he followed Soffía's example and perched on an upholstered, backless sofa with steel legs. It looked more like a bench than a sofa, plus it was as hard as rock.

Dóri fetched soda water for them from the double fridge in the kitchen part of the living space and placed a tray with two glasses on a smoky glass table in front of them. The home owner himself sat with the same kind of glass in a chair so low that he had to stretch his legs out along the floor, or else his knees would have been up at his chin. Adam did not understand how so tall a man could have thought of buying such ridiculous furniture.

"Well," said Soffía as Steindór's rear end met the chair. "What's going on?"

"I'm sure I don't know. The same as you." Dóri seemed to be on the defensive.

"I'm not going to drag this out of you by force."

Adam had to admit that Soffía was born to the role of interrogator. Although she was sometimes harsh, there was also something reassuring about her. She was a police officer, heart and soul, who went to work with a will. Steindór had practically no option but to tell her everything he knew or suspected – and she would do everything she could to solve the problem.

"No, OK. I understand, I understand." Dóri gulped soda water and placed the glass on the floor. "Look, of course I don't know for sure. As I said, I haven't seen the face or the licence plate of the man who has been following me."

"Or the woman," Soffía retorted. "You say you didn't see this person. Then you probably don't know the gender."

"These people don't use women for grunt work."

"Which people? And what grunt work? I meant what I said, Steindór. Talk, man!"

"I suspect this pursuit, or whatever it's called, is connected to a man who was chasing my sister."

"You have *three* sisters."

"Sessí, I mean Sessí. She was ... and still is, in fact ... going through a bit of a difficult time and this man managed ... well, he had a painful grip on her and he's ... well, not a man that anyone would want as an addition to the family, let's say."

Dóri was silent after stumbling through this description. When Soffía showed no reaction, he continued.

"Sessí never wanted to have children. I guess it's partly because ... well, we had no particular ... not a great childhood, in a manner of speaking."

He immediately seemed to backpedal as he hurried to add that they had been neither deprived nor abused.

"It wasn't that, no bad treatment. But Dad had a big farm and worked damned hard. A sharp businessman, even though he called himself a farmer. And he wasn't in trouble, not with booze I mean, nothing more than anyone else. But his private life was chaotic. Endless cheating and misery that affected us kids. Some of the women he was with were not quite right in the head. Some were real drama queens. Those were often the type that he fell for. So there was always some drama going on at home. Nonstop ... well, crying and gnashing of teeth, isn't that the expression?"

Dóri reached for the glass of soda water and rolled it in his hands without drinking from it.

"One also died in a terrible car accident, Hafdís's mother."

Adam thought back to remind himself who Hafdís was. The one who was in the nursing home, quite right.

"At that time my father was married to our mother, mine and Sessí's and Beggi's, but Hafdís's mother lived there too. You can imagine how that was."

"Are you talking about bigamy?"

"No, Dad had never married her, y'see. Hafdís's mother, that is. He didn't acknowledge her until after her mother died. And then my mother went crazy because he had sworn blind up to then that the child wasn't his. Then Mum and Dad split up and we moved with her to Borgarnes. But she never could get rid of her anger, she's still furious and bitter, decades later. And her hatred of Dad poisoned all our lives when we were younger."

Dóri groaned.

"Why did I start talking about *this* again? Yes, *Sessí!* This screwed-up childhood didn't exactly give her any incentive to start a family of her own. None of the three of us have really done that, not the stable nuclear family thing. We don't really know how a family like that functions."

"You had a cohabiting wife and children." Soffía's words sounded like a combined question and an accusation.

"Yes, I tried to go for the whole package. But it didn't last long. The kids now live in America with their mother and her new husband." Dóri looked at her for a moment. "We are six siblings, I am the only one who has had children and they live on another continent. That tells you something."

Soffía shrugged her shoulders and Adam saw that she wasn't inclined to swallow Steindór's self-pity.

"But then Sessí began to approach forty," Dóri continued, "and then she felt she was missing out on something. This completely overwhelmed her, an almost uncontrollable urge to have a child."

"With the man who was after her? That you dislike?"

"Not necessarily with him, she just wanted a child. Women can fix it themselves nowadays. But this man had been sniffing around Sessí when this started to eat her up, they were in an on-off kind of thing, and I just didn't like the look of it. It was hard enough to know that she was entangled with him and worry that he would drag her into something ... well, something illegal. But if she'd also had a *child* with him! I just couldn't stand by without doing something."

"What could *you* do about it? And who could be that undesirable?"

Adam saw and heard that Soffía was deeply interested.

"I have eyes and ears, and Sessí and I are very close, both as brother and sister, and as business partners. So I knew a lot and could guess more. And I decided to share that knowledge with people who are on the lookout for such information."

"Be clear." Soffía emphasised each word, pointing unexpectedly at Adam, who had not expected to be involved in the conversation. "Adam here is a great crossword puzzle solver. But not me. I *cannot stand* riddles."

Dóri straightened himself in the elegant armchair and seemed to be in the grip of an internal struggle, presumably about how much he should tell them.

"I have a very hard time talking about this," he said at last. "Both because I provided information anonymously and ... and because Sessí doesn't know about this. I can't take the chance that you're writing a report that might be quoted. It was all very secret."

"Was the information about this on-off boyfriend?"

Dóri nodded.

"And the ones you squealed to..." Soffía thought. "Financial crime or the drugs squad?"

"I can't say more, I'm stressed out enough already." He took a deep breath. "I'm just trying to explain that there is a certain person who got into some trouble and if he has any suspicion ... even a slight suspicion ... that any of his troubles might be connected to me in some way... Well, then he'd definitely be behind this."

"This *what*? Stealing sweaty tracksuits? A big fish in the underworld? Attaching a laser pointer to a tree?"

"Not in person, of course." Dóri sounded like a petulant child. "He left the country after I ... after what I was telling you. Sessí hasn't heard from him. I guess he believes her phone will be tapped. So he's hardly likely to be here in person to stalk me, I didn't mean that. But this is a man with connections. He has people on his payroll, staff. He certainly hasn't stopped all his business dealings in Iceland, even though he's been forced to go overseas."

Soffía was quiet for an oddly long time. Adam, however, could see that she was doing this to stop herself from laughing. She didn't seem to have much sympathy for Dóri, but Adam did. He found it admirable of the man to have protected his sister from a criminal despite being now terrified, convinced that he had been found out.

Despite this, Adam found Dóri's theory dubious. He agreed

with Soffía that the theft of a sports bag and this joke with a laser pointer could hardly be traced to the city's underworld. Additionally, he was convinced that the needle affair was unlikely to be connected to Dóri's revelation about the man who had known Sesselja. That had to have wider implications.

In Adam's opinion, however, what both cases had in common was that they were far from over. Something more was surely going to happen. And sneak attacks had a tendency to escalate.

20

They sat for a while in the car outside Adam's home, talking things over. He sensed that she wanted him to invite her in ... and she knew he knew. All the same, he didn't. The small apartment on Kaplaskjólsvegur was his refuge and shelter. The more often Soffía came in and spread herself out in it, the more time Adam had to spend rebuilding the atmosphere he had created for himself.

Not that there was any point trying to explain this to her. In Soffía's mind, an apartment was just an apartment and a house was just a house. She did not understand the *soul* of homes and hotels, let alone in an even larger context, as in entire neighbourhoods. As far as she was concerned, this was artificial nonsense. As well as that, she would be offended by Adam feeling that she was somehow invading his private realm.

So they sat still and talked with low voices, and Adam insisted on keeping two windows open to reduce the risk of infection. But it did not matter how long they discussed it, or how hard he tried to convince her that the needle case and the prank aimed at Dóri were not related. Soffía was fixated on the idea. She was convinced that the same person was behind all of this, and was certain that this would all now fade away.

"Attacks on all the siblings' companies. Tick. Scare Dóri shitless. Tick. No obvious motive. No attempts at extortion. What else could there be?"

But Adam was adamant that these were unrelated cases. He pointed out one was focussed on business and was more dramatic than appeared at first glance. The needles could have caused serious harm to people and also to businesses. In addition, copycat strikes could spread like wildfire. It had been pure luck that things hadn't been worse than they had turned out. Plus, this could be just a first phase. There could be more serious incidents to come.

Adam felt that the pranks against Dóri were in some ways more innocent, at least so far. Someone seemed to be enjoying shredding the man's nerves by stalking him. But no attempt had been made at a direct assault. It had been a complete coincidence that it was Dóri who hurt himself on the needle in the toilet roll rather than a guest at the café.

These pranks could also intensify, Adam maintained; he did not let it bother him when Soffía rolled her eyes. The so-called stalker's activities had already escalated. He had stepped up from watching Dóri from a distance and had not only broken into his car but had been poking around in his garden.

"The great sports bag robbery!" Soffía burst out. "I don't think so. Theft from cars is a daily occurrence."

One of the few things that they agreed on was that the criminal Dóri had removed from his sister's life was certainly unrelated. If an influential underworld figure had wanted to pay Dóri back, he would be in the National Hospital by now with shattered kneecaps.

"So what do you think will happen then? If this isn't over?"

Adam did not find it easy to answer that question.

"Of course I can't predict that precisely, Soffía. This is not a known process. But Dóri isn't free of this."

"Good thing you didn't say that to *him*. The man's petrified."

"Is there no way to get him some protection? Even if it's just a police car driving past from time to time? But it would have to be a marked car, otherwise he'd just be even more frightened."

"Sorry, no way. I can't... Covid, you understand. They'd just laugh at me."

Soffía seemed thoughtful though, and Adam felt that she

was less certain of her theory than she was prepared to admit. After all, she was the one who kept going through this instead of saying goodbye and driving home.

"But *why* would some person do this?" she asked. "Or persons. What does psychology have to say about that?"

She had asked this a hundred times before and had never been satisfied with the limited theories that Adam put forward about the root causes of such crimes. But Soffía was a person who never tired of squeezing rocks in the hope of getting water out of them.

"As you know better than most, Soffía, psychology can't answer this. Not at this stage, I simply don't have enough material to work with." Adam took a deep breath in an attempt to stay calm. "But I've told you before, and I'll say it again now. I'm convinced that these attacks on the siblings' businesses have personal roots. I discussed this in confidence with Brian, my classmate. You remember him, don't you? The one who said he worked for the police but was still certainly with the intelligence services, he just couldn't admit it. And he agrees with me. But I don't have a more detailed analysis at the moment."

"Personal roots?" she repeated, gnawing her upper lip thoughtfully.

"Yes. I think so. So there's reason to look into the background of the siblings and this Hans, their father. He doesn't seem to have created a particularly stable home life for his children, except perhaps for financial security. And then there's the missing Danish husband Arngunnur would like to divorce. Could he have grievances against his in-laws? I'm just saying."

"OK, OK." Soffía slapped the dashboard three times with her palm. "I'll try to dig something up. I'll probably find nothing but obituaries. I don't know what I'm looking for."

"It's Saturday night," Adam pointed out gently. "You need to rest just like everyone else. Just look into it tomorrow or Monday."

"By then someone could be dead," she growled. "Considering you thought both cases could escalate."

"And yet I'm still going to take it easy tonight. You should do the same."

The sentiment was well meant but rubbed Soffía the wrong way.

"Meaning you can't be disturbed tonight?" she asked coldly, and added in a mocking tone, "Or the two of you?"

Adam decided to ignore the remark. Soffía had no right to interfere in his private life and he owed her no explanation.

"Although I'm sure this will continue, Soffía, I don't see any indication these cases are heading for murder." He opened the car door. "I'll do a little digging in the morning and check if I find anything more concrete about stranger stalking cases. It's often the case that the victim knows who the stalker is. A former boyfriend or girlfriend is, for example, a common perpetrator, but Dóri hasn't suggested anyone except this criminal Sesselja had a relationship with."

"OK. Let's talk tomorrow." Soffía had become very brusque.

Adam was satisfied that he had managed to conceal from her just how intrigued he had become in Dóri's case. He could hardly wait until the morning to flip through the academic journals he had access to online.

Although he had handled all sorts of cases in his career as a psychologist, none of his clients had been persecuted by a stranger. On the other hand, he knew many examples of people who had not had a moment's peace from ex-lovers or spouses. But in all these cases, it had been clear from the beginning who was responsible and why.

One of the fascinating aspects of Dóri's problem was the secrecy surrounding the perpetrator and what drove him or her to behave in this way. It was also possible that more than one person could be behind this. That made it even more intriguing. So many aspects of this case made it fascinating for a psychologist with a crossword addiction.

During the conversation with Dóri in Seltjarnarnes there

had been a question Adam had asked. He wanted to know if any of the man's romantic or business relationships had ended on bad terms. By this he meant fighting, damage to possessions, or other physical outbursts.

"People don't last in business if they can't handle losing ... but don't all romantic relationships end on bad terms?" Dóri had asked in return, seemingly with the utmost sincerity. "At least in my experience. When *I* end things, women are usually furious. And if *they* end things, it's always because I'm impossible – and that's why *they're* angry. I mean, *I'm* always the bad guy and it's always a hell of a mess."

However, Dóri had not wanted to tell Soffía about any of his former girlfriends when she asked for more details to follow up Adam's question.

"It's been more than two years since I was last in a relationship," he said, sounding almost proud. "So there's no angry woman coming after me, that's for sure. I've experienced enough of that to know exactly what I'm talking about, all the fucking turmoil that goes with splitting up. The same goes for this constant commitment that women always want while they're in a relationship."

"Constant commitment?"

Soffía had failed to understand – she was far too independent to be the clingy type. Adam could have told Dóri all about it. But Adam recognised his complaint clearly from clients who had sought his help.

"Yeah, couples who have to be stuck together all day long," Dóri explained petulantly. "You have to account for every single hour you want to be alone or spend time with someone else, understand? Let alone a whole weekend away. The suspicion and the tantrums get cranked up so high that it isn't even worth going fishing or taking a trip to a football match in Britain with the boys, because it causes so much argument. So I've been a free man for two years and it suits me perfectly."

Something in Soffía's expression had made Dóri continue.

"I'm not saying I'm a monk, because I'm certainly not. But

nothing solid, no commitments. Nothing like that. And my ex-wife got full custody and remarried in California. So there is no crazy bitch on the warpath after me, let's be completely clear on that score."

21

Instead of immediately sitting down at the computer, Adam decided to tidy up quickly. The place was already clean, apart from a little dust on shelves and windowsills, but dusting was a way to wind down after the dramas of the day. Then he mopped the bathroom floor and polished the sink and the mirror, seeing as he was already doing some cleaning. He scrubbed the toilet every morning and evening, so it was still sparkling from its treatment earlier that day.

Here on Kaplaskjólsvegur he could be sure that everything was in its place, unlike when Soffía and he had lived together. That was the biggest difference. Everything he needed to clean the bathroom, for example, was available in the bathroom, sprays and the clean cloths. Now the scales also always stood close to the bathtub, not at an angle where he could stub a toe on it, and the toilet brush was hidden as far behind the toilet as possible. Soffía had practically left the brush standing in the middle of the floor. Nothing changed even when Adam pointed out to her that the brush was encrusted with germs and filth, and was no ornament to be proudly displayed.

His ex-wife had never seen the point in putting the toaster in a cupboard when it was not being used, closing the lid on the washing up liquid so that the nozzle did not clog, or putting the forks in a separate section from the spoons in the cutlery drawer.

"We have eyes in our heads," she had said. "Or can't you

tell the difference between a spoon and a fork? Maybe I don't want to have these *right* places and *right* methods. Why do *you* decide what system is *right*? This is also *my* home. Maybe my idea of *right* is different to yours."

Certainly she had a point. The only problem was that according to Soffía's world, there was one place and one method today, but then there could be another set of ideas tomorrow. As Adam always pointed out to her, this chaos resulted in a constant search for things they needed to use every day.

He preferred to spend his time on something other than having to search through four kitchen cabinets to finally find a can of kidney beans, vegetable stock or green peppercorns. He also wanted to avoid turning the fridge inside out because it was impossible to know if the butter was on the top shelf, in the vegetable drawer or in the meat compartment – or just a slimy puddle on the kitchen table.

And that time the power went off and Soffía had been alone at home with a newborn Magga? It would have been ideal if the torch had been in its place in the top drawer to the right of the fridge. She could at least have admitted that.

Adam sighed as he put the glass polish back in the bathroom cabinet and threw the rag into the basket with the dirty clothes. Why was he, a highly educated psychologist, still focussed on his and Soffía's conflicts, many years after their divorce, considering he had helped many clients nurture gratitude and focus their thoughts on the positive rather than hanging on to endless bitterness over things long in the past that could never be changed?

Adam himself was thankful for so much. But sometimes this just flared up and he did not realise where his thoughts had gone until he felt the tension in his clenched jaw. This was how old differences could come between people even when they thought they had settled things like mature people. The past was like a coat that fluttered behind you on a brisk walk but could slip down, tangle around your feet and even trip you up if you didn't maintain your pace.

After this burst of cleaning, Adam was hungry but was also even more excited to get online. He settled for a grilled sandwich with salad rather than cook anything more complicated. All the same, it didn't cross his mind to eat on the run, let alone standing in the kitchen, as a certain woman he knew often did. In his home the table was set and a candle was lit, with a napkin artfully folded.

Afterwards Adam made a pot of tea, a habit since his youth in Wivenhoe. Then he got comfortable at the computer and began searching for scholarly articles about people who had been stalked by strangers.

When statistics from the UK appeared on the screen, he understood why he had never had a client in this predicament. The numbers were not completely up to date, but according to these figures, ninety-seven per cent of victims were stalked by a former spouse, friend, or acquaintance. This meant that only three per cent of those who were subjected to some form of abuse or persecution had not been familiar with the stalker.

In fact, the classification of such crimes had become more challenging in recent years, one article after another discussed it and he knew this from experience of the clients who came to Sáló.

Stalkers were increasingly bringing technology into their efforts, and it was obviously more difficult to find these individuals online, let alone to define their relationship with their victims. According to the latest information, more than half of stalking offences seemed to take place, in whole or in part, online.

Adam burst out laughing. So the person sitting outside Dóri's home was out of touch, spending all that time hanging around the man! He knew he shouldn't be laughing at this. Serious again, he sipped his tea and wondered if this approach revealed something about the perpetrator. Maybe this person was on the older side and had limited knowledge of the nooks and crannies of the internet?

No matter what keywords Adam entered, he could find no

descriptions that matched Dóri's case closely enough – assuming the man had told them the complete truth. There was one possibility to keep in mind, which was that Dóri could be considered something of a celebrity in Iceland, even though his existence had up until now passed Adam by. Even a glimmer of fame could lead to a disturbed person developing an obsession. This so-called celebrity stalking had many times been in the news in other countries, including in connection with famous actors, musicians and TV personalities He recalled Björk having been stalked at the height of her fame.

Maybe this was the price Dóri would have to pay for having been in the spotlight over the years? If a middle-aged woman like Gunninga knew all about this man and his home, then a large proportion of the population could be considered potential perpetrators.

Adam had read enough by now but still did not quite know what to do. He was on annoying middle ground where he was too tired to read or watch TV but not tired enough to sleep. While he paid close attention to BBC News, he did not turn up the volume, preferring not to release the flood of reports and interviews about Covid into his space.

He was about to get up to see if the tea in the pot was still hot when the phone rang. He started cursing Soffía for her selfishness, but then saw someone else was on the line, a number he did not recognise. Hopefully nothing had happened to Margrét. That was always the first thing that came to mind on the rare occasions when the phone rang in the evenings, and especially at weekends.

"Adam."

He hoped the trepidation was not discernible from his voice.

"Yes, Adam, hello. Forgive me for calling so late. But you said I could call if there was a problem."

"Who is this, please?"

"Björn. I came to your office the day before yesterday. Rebekka Rósa's father."

"Yes, that's right, of course! Hello, Björn. What can I do for you?"

"It's Rebekka, of course. My whole life revolves around her. I finally managed to get her to sit down with me and talk things over. Not for long and not in any depth, but it's at least a start and... Yes, better than nothing."

Björn was silent but Adam did not prompt him, and waited patiently for him to speak again.

"And as I said, not much has changed now but ... well, she's ready to talk to someone. A psychologist, she said. She feels she needs help. But... Well, she would rather meet a woman than a man. I hope you understand... Nothing personal. She just finds it easier to talk to a woman, she says."

Adam quickly said that it was entirely understandable, and that the main thing was that Rebekka was asking for help in this difficult situation. He did not resent her preference for a female psychologist.

"But we just don't know where to start," Björn continued. "So I was hoping ... maybe you could point me to a good psychologist. A woman, that is. Someone who might have time to meet Rebekka tomorrow. I'm concerned she's going to change her mind. Strike while the iron's hot, you know? So I was hoping..."

Adam suppressed a sigh, not prepared to tell Björn that it would be hopeless to try to find the right person for this task at such short notice, a woman who could familiarise herself with Huntington's disease in a hurry and meet the girl tomorrow, all during a frightening pandemic during which the authorities urged everyone to stay at home.

"Yes, I understand, I understand, yes," he said slowly, mentally treading water. What on earth could he do for the man? Two of his co-owners at Sáló were women and skilled in their field. But one of them was out of the question, he thought. She was simply not the type for this task and flexibility was not her strong point. She would want time to prepare herself, and that could take until at least Monday or Tuesday.

Pandóra, who was the undisputed leader of the group at the practice, would be able to handle this extremely well and she was certain to give her full attention to such emergency. The only problem was that Pandóra had brought her elderly grandmother into her home two weeks ago and now only did appointments via video call. It would be out of the question for her to consider endangering the old lady by meeting Rebekka in person, whether it was at the clinic on Síðumúli or anywhere else – especially if Adam were to tell her the truth about Rebekka frequently dating strangers.

No, he could not ask Pandóra to take this on. But neither could he deny Björn help in this urgent situation. He had to help the man, now his daughter had finally agreed to meet a psychologist.

"OK, I know a woman who can definitely meet Rebekka tomorrow," he said, without really having decided what he meant to say. The words popped out of his mouth before he could stop them. "Her name is Jenný."

DECEIT

SUNDAY 05.04.2020

More than one thousand individuals infected with corona virus are currently being monitored at the Covid-19 Outpatient Department at the National Hospital, of which about one hundred are children.

Eighty patients have been admitted to the National Hospital since the beginning of the pandemic, of whom twenty-two have needed intensive care and eleven have been intubated.

22

Adam barely slept that night. What had he got himself into, he who never did anything without the most careful consideration? He was the least impulsive man in Iceland! What madness had befallen him?

No matter how sorry he felt for the father and daughter and how difficult the situation was, there was no justification for the ridiculous idea of presenting Jenný as a fully-qualified psychologist. He had never before done anything so foolhardy. This was completely wrong, and madness to think it could work.

What if Björn or Rebekka tried to look up this woman Adam had recommended? To do so would be perfectly normal. But they would find no Jenný registered with the Association of Independent Psychologists. Adam broke out in a sweat at the thought.

In the morning he prepared himself for a call from Björn. Did the man not want to call and ask about this woman who could not be found on the Association's website, but who was supposed to help his daughter through the most difficult time of her life? In Björn's place, Adam would have checked. But how could he answer this desperate father?

However, despair seemed to have blunted Björn's suspicious nature. He had not even been surprised when Adam said that Rebekka had to meet Jenný at his own home in the western part of the city. The man's main worries were about payment, whether Jenný could take a card payment or would Rebekka have to go to a cashpoint?

This was what had almost tripped Adam up. In his haste he hadn't even considered payment, any more than other practical aspects of what he was doing. The only thing he had been clear about was that Rebekka would have to come to Kaplaskjólsvegur, Jenný could not meet her anywhere else. Jenný was never seen out of doors in Iceland, only abroad.

He had solved the problem by explaining that Rebekka could simply transfer payment to Jenný's account after their meeting. That would be most convenient. Jenný would give her an invoice with bank details and an ID number. What had he been thinking? Jenný did not have a bank account.

This was now a colossal mess. Soffía would laugh herself to a complete standstill if she knew what Adam was up to. For her, all this would be beyond hilarious. But only to begin with, after which she would be irritated with him for walking into this with his eyes wide open, a grown man with his fair share of common sense.

The clock ticked past eight, and then it was nine o'clock, but there was no call from Björn to enquire about this mysterious psychologist. About half past nine Soffía called, and she was agitated.

"The guesthouse was set on fire. Emil was asleep in the cellar. The dog was put down yesterday and now the poor man is suffering from smoke inhalation."

"You mean Emil?"

"That's what I said. Emil. Think about it. The man has a brain tumour. Had just lost his dog. And then he almost gets burned alive." She sighed. "Can you come to the hospital?"

"Almost burned alive? You said he had smoke poisoning."

"People can die from smoke inhalation. Those who are inside a burning building, understand? Bodies don't necessarily burn."

"Is he very seriously ill?"

"I'll be outside in fifteen." Soffía did not wait for an answer. This hadn't been a question.

Adam checked the time. He did not feel in a stable enough condition to go with Soffía to the National Hospital. Wouldn't it be more appropriate for another police officer to go with her rather than a psychological counsellor? Did she expect him to give the man trauma counselling or what was his role supposed to be?

Rebekka was not due to arrive at his flat until four o'clock. Maybe it would be fine to simply be Soffía's sidekick once again, rather than spending hours pacing the floor until the time came, and becoming increasingly stressed. But Adam would have to be sure to be home by two o'clock. Jený would need at least an hour or two to get ready.

He stepped out of his pyjama trousers, slipped into black jeans and put on a grey wool sweater with a large turtleneck that his parents had given him at Christmas. They were still worried about the cold in Iceland, even though they had visited several times, even during the winter. The winters were no colder here than in Britain, just a lot longer and darker.

He had just finished lacing his shoes and was winding a scarf around his neck when the phone rang. Soffía was outside. On the way to the hospital in Fossvogur she told him what little she knew about the fire.

"I just heard about this by chance," she began. "There were other officers at the scene. Nobody connected this to the needle case."

"You think there's a connection?"

"I'm not sure. This is Bergsveinn's business. I want to at least keep tabs on the investigation."

"When did the fire start?"

"The security provider called Bergsveinn at half-past two. They also alerted the fire service. It was put out by the time Bergsveinn arrived. He lives in Mosó. Or maybe out in Kjalarnes."

"Is there much damage?"

"Yes and no. Part of the ground floor is badly damaged. The

fire seems to have started at the front door. It burned through and the hallway is gutted. Then it spread into the kitchen and living room. But there's less damage there. All the flooring is ruined. And some of the furniture. It's going to be expensive."

"Did it start in the hallway? Do you think it was deliberate? And maybe the perpetrator is the same person as the one who made the comments on the booking sites and put the needles...?"

Soffía interrupted him.

"The fire brigade's guess is arson. No formal conclusion has been reached. That takes time. But probably burning material was pushed through the letter box."

"A Molotov cocktail?"

"A bottle wouldn't fit through a letter box. Possibly rags soaked in oil. Followed by a lit match. Something like that."

"I see."

Adam had almost forgotten the existence of matches, he always used a large lighter to light candles. On the rare occasions he saw smokers these days, they all used neat little lighters. Matches had to be available in every shop, although they weren't something he would notice.

"The fire reached one of the guest rooms on the first floor. The others only have smoke damage. And nothing on the upper floors or down in the cellar. The shared areas got the worst of this."

"How did Emil inhale smoke, if he sleeps in the cellar?"

"He went upstairs to try and put the fire out. Maybe Bergsveinn called him. Or a smoke detector woke him up."

In the car park outside the hospital, Soffía opened the glove compartment where she kept boxes of masks and latex gloves that they put on. Adam had been beginning to worry about going unprotected into a hospital in the middle of a Covid pandemic.

"But wait... Can we go in?" he asked. "Aren't visits prohibited?"

Soffía rolled her eyes above the light blue mask.

"This is a criminal investigation. Not a friendly visit."

"Yes, but ..."

She had left the car behind her so he had no choice but to run after her.

When they arrived at the front door of A&E, Soffía waved her police ID, like an actor in a crime film, and a security guard let them into an empty waiting room. People presumably tried to avoid going to the hospital if they could help it or find support elsewhere.

From the waiting room, electric doors opened onto a long hallway without Soffía having to say anything. The security guard saw to that. Otherwise, she would have had to call to the staff, as security grilles had been installed to make sure that nobody came closer than allowed under civil protection regulations.

Inside the corridor, Soffía showed her police ID again and said she needed to talk to Emil Hansson, who had been brought in an ambulance that night suffering from smoke inhalation. She and her assistant would need to talk to the man in private, she added.

"He's in a private room," said a woman with broad face, the lower half of which was obscured by a large white mask, as she regarded them gravely. Clunky glasses with thick, black frames made her seem even more severe. "But does it have to be both of you? It would be better if only one of you goes in to see him. You know that there's a strict ban on visitors."

"We're not here for the fun of it. We're investigating a crime."

The woman shook her head, obviously dissatisfied. But she refrained from arguing, instead pointing the way while explaining that Emil would not have the strength for a long conversation with the police. They could stay with him for a maximum of ten minutes.

"We've decided to admit him and are trying to find him a bed," she explained, her forehead furrowed with concern. "It's difficult when people with a serious illness get smoke inhalation as well. Of course, it would be best if he could go to the oncology ward as he's been there before. But everything has been shifted around in here, as you know, so I'm not sure it's going to work. Covid-19 has disrupted every department in the hospital."

The doctor knocked lightly on the door and opened it.

"Emil? There are some people here from the police who need to talk to you. They've promised to be here for only five or ten minutes. But if you get tired sooner, just say so or ring the bell. All right?"

Emil lay on an examination bench and had pulled a large yellow cotton blanket over his head, presumably to hide his eyes from the strong ceiling light that someone had been so thoughtless as to leave on. Without seeing the face under the blanket, anyone would have imagined that a child lay on the bench, considering how emaciated the man was.

"From the police?" he asked, looking at them in confusion. He had an oxygen tube in his nose and was hooked up to an intravenous drip.

The doctor promptly disappeared to take care of other urgent tasks and carefully closed the door on the way out. But Soffía was neither as quiet nor as considerate. She grabbed a plastic chair from by the wall, dragged it rattling against the floor to the bench, and sat down heavily.

"We're investigating arson," she said, focussing her gaze on him. "You were lucky. It could have been worse."

Adam wondered if it was possible to have started this conversation in a more undiplomatic way. Did Soffía really think that Emil believed himself lucky, lying here hooked up to oxygen and waiting for news of whether there might or might not be a bed for him on the cancer ward?

"Was this definitely ... arson?" Emil asked, and coughed so badly that he had to sit up to catch his breath.

Soffía waited until he had almost recovered from the coughing fit.

"Looks like it."

Emil sat and leaned forward, which seemed to help him breathe more easily.

"First Mango... And now this was supposed to ... to finish me off," he wheezed, gasping for breath.

23

Soffía suggested a late breakfast at Bar Three after the visit to Emil. But Adam immediately recoiled at the thought of the virus.

"And eat food that someone else has prepared and use cutlery, glasses, and plates that other people have handled? No thanks. We don't know how the people who work there observe infection precautions, Soffía, it's like playing Russian roulette."

"But there's plenty of space separating the tables."

"What difference does that make? I'm talking about the kitchen where staff can sneeze onto the food or into a hand and then handle the crockery."

Adam hated being in the role of the person terrified of infection, but he was sure that Thórólfur, Alma and Víðir would behave in much the same way. He couldn't imagine them sitting in a café and letting strangers serve them food and drink. He shouldn't have to feel that Soffía was being brave and that he was the chicken. But that was exactly how he felt.

"Jesus, Adam! I'm starving. Just come with me. You can drink something from a bottle." Soffía headed in Bar Three's direction without waiting for an answer.

Adam fumbled in a coat pocket and found a packet of disinfectant wipes and a small plastic bottle of sanitiser. He knew these things were there, as he did not leave the house without them, but touching them gave him a sense of security. If he bought himself a soft drink, he could clean the bottle thoroughly and drink from it.

After Soffía ordered eggs Benedict with mashed avocado on grilled sourdough bread, she pulled out her notes of the conversation with Emil.

"Strange." Soffía stared at the pad. "None of the siblings invited Emil to stay. At home, that is. Dóri and Sesselja both have plenty of space. Bergsveinn no doubt as well. Maybe not Arngunnur in Grjótathorp. But all the others do."

"Maybe he didn't want to impose. I'd much prefer an entire hotel to myself."

"You're a recluse," Soffía snorted, still scanning her notes, and Adam decided to ignore her comment.

"What's this list?" he asked.

"Those people who knew where Emil was."

"You don't really think that the arson was because of him?"

"I can't rule anything out." She shrugged her shoulders. "But I think it's pretty unlikely."

"He told us the siblings knew he was staying there," Adam recalled. "And his mother. Yes, and the oncologist and the girl who sometimes works in the gallery. It's quite difficult to imagine that any of them intended the man to burn alive. After all ... why? Even if one of them hated him so intensely... Doesn't he have just a short time left, or am I misunderstanding the seriousness of his illness?"

"I don't know about how long he has. But it's incurable."

A young man with a ballet dancer's build brought Soffía a cafetière, while Adam accepted an unopened plastic bottle of sparkling water and swiftly declined a glass.

"Emil's accountant also knew where he lived." Soffía looked impatiently at the coffee. The waiter had told her to wait two minutes before pushing the plunger down.

Adam cleaned the bottle carefully.

"An accountant?" he murmured thoughtfully. "Maybe Emil is really filthy rich and nobody except the accountant knows."

"And what does he have to gain from Emil's death?"

"Maybe they're secretly married?"

"Really?" Soffía grinned. "I suppose the accountant could be a woman?"

"Just saying."

"Emil lived in the gallery," she thought aloud. "A wealthy man could have rented an apartment. All the Airbnb apartments are empty."

"That's right." Adam unscrewed the cap from the bottle and took a sip of soda water. "I think you can write off the possibility that someone intended to kill Emil. I agree with what I thought you were saying on the phone earlier. This is very probably the same perpetrator as in the needle cases."

Soffía sighed and slowly pressed the plunger down.

"And where does that leave us? Will he start all over again? Set fire to all the siblings' houses?"

Adam felt that she was not fully convinced that they were on the right track.

"I really hope not." He was aware that this was not what she wanted to hear – she wanted certainty and facts. "But it's a possibility. In your position, I'd ask the other siblings to be very alert. Yes, and preferably provide them with some protection, even if it's just a security alarm or something like that."

He was going to be funny and suggest cardboard cut-out cops but gave up. This was not something to joke about.

"The perpetrator has clearly upped the stakes," he added. "The needles were more ... well, certainly dangerous, but with a subterfuge about them. And it was just random chance if they would cause any harm and what kind of harm. Arson is a totally different matter."

They paused the conversation when the lithe waiter brought Soffía's food to her. Adam's mouth watered when he saw the slice of bread and everything that had been stacked on it. Still, he couldn't be persuaded to eat a single thing.

"What about the security cameras? At the hotel, I mean. Guesthouses must have these things."

Soffía chewed for a moment before she answered.

"There was a system failure."

"I don't believe it!" Adam slapped his thigh. "A system failure? That's hardly a coincidence."

"The corona pandemic."

"That doesn't affect security cameras."

Soffía pointed at him with her fork and spoke with her mouth full. This habit of hers had been one of the things about their daughter-in-law that Adam's parents had never been able to get used to. According to their English standards of politeness, speaking with your mouth full was the height of vulgarity.

"Minimal staffing levels right now. And a Covid surcharge for every call-out."

Adam was shocked.

"Customers pay a fixed monthly fee for systems that have been installed. You can't have people paying for a security system that doesn't work."

"They get a discount." Soffía sipped coffee with obvious pleasure, far from overcome with sympathy for people having trouble with their security systems.

"There's not much point in a discount when something like this happens."

"Bergsveinn made a choice. He chose to wait and get a discount."

"He must surely regret that now."

"I'd have done the same," Soffía admitted. "The hotel was empty. Burglaries are at an all-time low. And Emil was on site."

Adam drank his water in silence while Soffía finished eating. He was as concerned as she was about where this was going. Since he was the psychology consultant on this peculiar case, which seemed to be escalating, he needed more detailed information about the siblings against whom this vague threat seemed to be directed.

Maybe the police would have to call someone in for

questioning and then he could demand to be present. He would prefer Soffía to have a video connection with him, so he could take part from Kaplaskjólsvegur. But first he would have to give Rebekka all the time she would need today, so he could only help Soffía until two o'clock and then not again until later in the evening.

His stomach lurched at the thought of Rebekka, and Soffía stared at him inquisitively.

"What are you pulling faces for?"

"Faces? Can't a man pull a face? I was thinking about our next steps. We need more information. Or I do, at least, if I'm going to be of any use to you."

"Like what?"

"Everything you can provide about the siblings and their childhood on the farm."

"Who should I be talking to? Who should I be looking for? Some enemy who lived on the next farm along? Do we know an arsonist in Borgarfjörður?" Soffía sighed. "This pandemic is screwing everything up. I don't get a team. Not a clear enough threat."

Adam screwed the cap onto the bottle.

"Not a clear enough threat? Even if a terminally ill person could have been the victim of a house fire?"

Soffía's phone rang before she could answer. Adam could hear that this was a work call and saw from her reaction that this wasn't good news.

"Hell," Soffía groaned when she hung up the phone. She looked at Adam as if the bad news were his fault. "More needles in fruit."

He shuddered.

"Where?"

"Three supermarkets, all in Reykjavík." Soffía wiped her mouth and got up from the table. "In Breiðholt and in the west of town. Found last night and this morning. Minor injuries. But the retailers are panicking."

"Any known connection to the siblings?"

"I need to find that out. Do you want to come?"

"Down to the police station? No, I'm busy today, probably until seven o'clock. I'll call you if I'm free earlier."

Adam had no idea how long Rebekka needed. He wouldn't limit himself to the usual fifty-minute session time, in case she needed to talk for longer.

"Can't you change it?" Soffía scowled.

"No, sorry." Adam followed her out of the café. "Of course I have nothing to go on, it's just a hunch, but I'd guess that these aren't the original perpetrator but a copycat. One individual, but possibly more," he said as they stood on the pavement outside.

24

Adam had seldom been as anxious as when he came home to Kaplaskjólsvegur. His main focus was the intolerable situation facing his future client. Compared to what Rebekka was struggling with, his own problems were insignificant.

He had even found a solution to what had been preying on his mind. Jenný would not ask for payment for this appointment – nor for a follow-up appointment, should the girl want to come back. This ensured almost no risk that Adam could lose his licence to practise. If no money were to change hands, the Association could hardly censure an individual for chatting in their own time with someone who needed help.

While he had an early lunch, he turned up the television volume and watched the panic that had gripped Britain, where the government had taken longer to take measures than Iceland had, so now the nation was dealing with the consequences. Each news item was bleaker than the last.

Doctors complained about the lack of protective clothing, masks and gloves, and relatives of nursing home residents told horror stories about the wellbeing of their loved ones. Grocery store shelves looked like a field after a plague of locusts, with not a single remaining toilet roll or loaf of bread. Exhausted health workers were left empty-handed when they went to the shops on their way home after long and draining shifts, weeping in disappointment on live TV over the selfishness of their hoarding fellow citizens.

Adam resolved to call his parents, preferably today but

otherwise tomorrow. Fortunately, they lived in a well-heeled neighbourhood and were sensible academics. He knew they would take care. But they were in their seventies, and he realised that they found it hard to bear that he and Margrét, their only descendants, lived in another country.

He'd have to make another attempt to get the girl to apply to the University of Essex, close to Wivenhoe. It would make her grandparents so happy if she could spend even a few years with them, not to mention assuaging her father's conscience. But she was reluctant to humour Adam. She was worried that the old couple would stay up waiting for her late into the evenings and generally pry into her private life.

After lunch, Adam took the time to check for further online coverage of the needle cases. There certainly was, with both news media and social media ablaze with speculation about this new home-grown menace, right in the middle of a global crisis. Not only was there concern about the food security of the nation at a time when there was little traffic between countries, but also about the safety of the food that was available.

For some reason, there was always talk of perpetrators, in the plural, and the spokespersons for the supermarkets where the products had been purchased had harsh words for those responsible in interviews with the media. All of them claimed to have the best security cameras and that surveillance footage was being analysed. It would not take long for the police to catch these dangerous people who had behaved so abominably during this terrible time.

"You believe that, mate?" Adam retorted to one of them. He sometimes talked to the computer and the television when he was alone.

Although the retailers claimed that they could identify the perpetrators by checking surveillance footage, Adam knew that it wasn't that simple. They did not have clear close-ups of the fruit and vegetable sections, just wide-view cameras mounted overhead in the supermarkets. It was therefore hopeless to expect conclusive evidence with video sequences of tiny needles being inserted into bananas, broccoli, cucumbers or oranges.

All that could be seen on the footage was people handling fruit, as people typically did. Adam usually avoided grabbing the topmost peppers in the pile for himself, he would rummage for the ones he liked best. That was how customers usually behaved when picking fresh produce. If someone was going to insert a needle into an apple or aubergine, it would be easy to sneak it in without arousing suspicion.

He knew that Soffía was under a lot of pressure because of this latest development. The only positive thing about this was surely that she would get some additional manpower. The police would have to take the needle case more seriously, and it would have to be linked to the fire at the guesthouse.

One cop with her ex-husband in tow was not enough of a team and never had been. If the pandemic had not spread around the world and if part of the police force hadn't been in isolation, Soffía would never have been left to single-handedly investigate a case that clearly could quickly take on a much greater significance. Adam was relieved that he had warned Soffía about the possibility of copycats right from the start.

He was immersed in a respectable online academic article when the doorbell rang. His heart pounded and he hurriedly checked the time. It was barely even one o'clock. Was it possible that Rebekka had arrived three hours before the time agreed?

"Who were you really expecting? It's like you're expecting to be taken out and shot!" Margrét squeezed past him, even though he stood in the middle of the doorway. "I'm on my way home, I stayed with a guy on Meistaravellir. But I've nothing in the fridge, so I thought of scrounging some bacon and eggs from you."

"Magga, love..."

"Isn't that the bonus of having an English dad? English breakfast."

JÓNÍNA LEÓSDÓTTIR

Adam sent her to the bathroom to wash her hands and made
a start in the kitchen.

"It would be polite to ask if you're interrupting," he scolded
when she returned. "I'll do you bacon, eggs and mushrooms.
But I only have half an hour. Then I have work to do and I must
have complete privacy. OK?"

"Are you still enforcing the two-metre rule or can I make
myself toast and coffee?"

"Have you been notified that the pandemic is over?" he
asked. "You sit down. I'll see to the food."

"But we've met loads of times since it started. Well, maybe
not all that many, but a few times."

Adam did everything at once as he talked to Margrét – put
water in the kettle, slid bacon and mushrooms into the pan,
got a carton of eggs and butter from the fridge, opened a can
of baked beans and put a bowl in the microwave, and dropped
two slices of bread in the toaster.

"And in between visits you're out meeting all kinds of
people," he huffed. "And now you've just got out of bed with
some guy who could be infected."

"There was nothing wrong with this one, Dad." Margrét
winked at her father. "He was well fit."

"He could get sick tonight or tomorrow. He'd be at his most
infectious today."

"Dad, try to relax. I know that stuff like this can be stressful
for someone like you. Just be careful not to have a stroke or
something."

"Someone like me?" Adam raised his eyes from the pan.
"I'm no more frightened than other people. But I follow
foreign news stations and..."

"Just the BBC," Margrét retorted.

"OK, I watch the BBC," he agreed, "and it goes much deeper
into all the data and talks to world-class scientists, and this
pandemic is just much, much more serious than Icelanders
generally seem to realise. There are all kinds of aspects that
still need to be researched properly, such as this thing with

152

the blood types and why black people are affected much worse than white people and all kinds of possibilities."

"I'm sure there'll be a vaccine soon and then everyone can live happily ever after."

This comment upset Adam even more.

"*Vaccine?* A working vaccine won't be available until at least the end of the year, Magga. At the earliest. It's much more likely that it will take even longer, and then the virus could have mutated, and then you have to start all over again. Even Thórólfur has said that."

"Mutate? Is that what happens in this next wave that you've already started to worry about?"

He arranged the food as neatly as he could on a large plate and placed the toast on a smaller plate with a pat of butter.

"Look, let's stop talking about Covid." He placed the plates quickly on the table in front of her. "I have to do some very important work later and I don't want to go into it straight from some virus argument. I need to be calm."

"OK." Margrét looked longingly at the food. "I just find it funny that a person in your profession can be so short of self-awareness."

She wolfed down her meal, while her father scooped coffee into a cafetière that was only used when his daughter or Soffía were visiting. Then he poured boiling water into it.

"How's it going with the distance learning?" he asked to change the subject.

"It's no problem. It's worse at work, both places I worked for are closed. I've become almost disgustingly broke."

Adam knew what was coming next.

"Same here," he said. "Clients aren't knocking down the door these days."

"I can't really afford the rent anymore." Margrét showed no reaction to what her father had said about his own finances. "I may have to move in here for a while."

Adam froze. Although he loved Margrét more than anything, it would turn his life upside down if she were to move in with him.

"It was such a big deal for you to get away from home."

"I'd prefer not to invade your space, but what else can I do?"

"Your mum has more space."

"She lives at the end of the world, Dad! At least it's possible to walk to a party from here."

This was the last thing Adam needed, just before Rebekka was due to arrive. He took a deep breath and silently counted to ten.

"Don't do anything in a hurry, love. Your mum must be able to help you with the rent until the summer. Government employees are being paid full salaries, no matter what. Maybe I can also help a bit. There's something in the emergency fund."

Margrét burst out laughing.

"You're so transparent, Dad. Do you think I don't know why you don't want me to move in here?"

Adam held his breath as she wiped egg yolk off the plate with a piece of bread, popped it in her mouth, and chewed.

"You're totally on edge. You'd be running to disinfect the toilet every time I pee and wouldn't dare to eat anything in the fridge that I might have touched."

He was so relieved that he unexpectedly started to laugh, as if she had tickled him.

"All right... Right... you are," he hiccoughed when his nervous burst of laughter had faded away. "This pandemic is stressing me out."

"It's not just the pandemic." Margrét looked at him inquisitively. "Mum says you've always been weird."

25

As soon as Adam had cleaned up after Margrét's visit, he headed for the shower. The hot water softened the muscles of the back of his neck and shoulders, and as usual he was filled with appreciation for the Icelandic heating system, remembering how small the hot water tank at home in Wivenhoe had been. He stood for a long time under the powerful jet of water before using lemon-scented shampoo on his hair and then an expensive conditioner that he only used on special occasions. Next, he carefully shaved his legs and jaw until they were silky smooth.

A few minutes later, Jenný stepped out of the shower refreshed, wrapped herself in a thick bathrobe, and carefully dried her shoulder-length hair with a towel. Because her hair was naturally curly, she used the hair dryer sparingly so as to avoid looking like a lucky troll. She applied moisturiser from head to toe, filed her nails and finally removed the polish from her toenails. After that, she went into the living room with the make-up mirror.

The bathroom faced east and was a little dark. When Jenný put on her make-up under electric light, there was a risk she could use too much or apply colours that were too strong. This couldn't be allowed to happen today. That was why she chose to be in the living room, facing south, where the light was more suitable.

To begin with, she was unsure and trembled a little, like a young girl getting ready for her first date. But as she progressed, her movements became steadier and her self-confidence increased. After applying light make-up, fine powder, dark brown mascara and ultra-thin eyeliner, she decided to skip highlighting her cheekbones. She needed to not go overboard, and to keep things looking natural. There would be nothing conspicuous but bright red lipstick and matching nail polish.

Jenný had already decided what she would wear. She felt it was important to be feminine, as Rebekka had emphasised preferring to talk to a woman. All the same, she did not feel a dress was the right choice. So she chose a dark grey denim skirt and a shirt of the same colour.

She wore thick black tights and around her neck she fastened a necklace of red coral and grey lava beads which she thought pulled the outfit together. She also made sure to wear a bra with B-cups. C-cups would leave the pendant dangling like a pendulum between her breasts.

After loosely combing her hair, she finished her efforts with red nail polish. It was only three o'clock, and now she had an hour to compose herself. That preparation had actually been in progress, both consciously and unconsciously, every minute of the day and night, since it had been decided that Björn's daughter would meet Jenný.

She used the time until four o'clock to listen for the third time to online interviews with young people with Huntington's disease. It was obvious that the condition affected each individual very differently – they became unwell at different ages, the symptoms varied, as did the progression of the illness.

Jenný felt she did not have a sufficient overview of the symptoms that Rebekka was struggling with. Björn had mentioned depression, anger, lack of concentration and stiffness of movement, but that was not necessarily a conclusive list. This made it difficult to decide what would be the best course of action for this delicate task.

She would let the girl lead the conversation to an extent, to be flexible and ready to follow in whichever direction the conversation went. This first session might be all about Rebekka feeling her way and reassuring herself that Jenný was trustworthy. This was nothing unusual for a new client, no matter the reason for seeking help from a psychologist.

There was one thing that the sick young people online had in common, and knowing this must weigh heavily on Rebekka. Gradually, they lost the ability to lead an independent life, as they needed increasingly more support and assistance, before their inevitable admission to an institution.

Abroad, there seemed to be plenty of institutions for young people in need of round-the-clock care. Jenný assumed that in Iceland young people in this position would be placed in hostels. What kind of future was this for a young woman who had been a university student when diagnosed with Huntington's? Could there be any heavier blow?

By the time the doorbell rang, Jenný had largely shaken off her tension. She was ready, mentally and physically, and walked confidently to the door to let in this new client. All the same, there was still one glimmer of anxiety, at this critical moment, and it revolved around Rebekka's immediate reaction to meeting a person like her. But she put all her faith in the new client being a modern, open-minded, girl.

Young people in Iceland had grown up around much more diverse lifestyles than Jenný's generation had. One could never automatically assume that everyone had the same attitudes. Hopefully, her client would simply assume that Jenný was trans and find no particular reason to discuss it.

This was what transpired. The girl standing outside made no comment. In fact, she was so obviously preoccupied with her own problems that Jenný doubted that she would have blinked an eye even if a bright green alien had come to the door.

"Hello, I'm Jenný. You must be Rebekka Rósa. Please, come in."

Neither of them made an attempt to shake hands, and Jenný moved away from the door so that the girl could easily pass by. Rebekka walked into the apartment like a sleepwalker and looked around confused.

"You were probably expecting a consultation room," Jenný guessed as she politely directed the girl to the coat hooks. "I'd rather see you in peace and quiet here at home. And I hope you won't be offended if I ask you to wash your hands first. There's a white towel by the sink, which is completely clean, and there's sanitiser here on the table."

She stopped herself from repeating the 'we are all civil defence' mantra. As a young person with an incurable illness she must feel like she was all alone and exposed, rather than aligned with the general mood.

Rebekka hung up her coat, shook off her fur-lined boots and went into the bathroom without saying a word. She took some time to wash her hands, until Jenný began to wonder if she was ever going to be finished. Maybe it was too much of a challenge to start by sending the girl off to wash. Maybe sanitiser would have been enough?

"Would you like to sit at the table or on the sofa?" Jenný asked when Rebekka finally returned to the living room. It would be more comfortable for the girl on the sofa, but it was lower than the dining room chairs and some people found it uncomfortable to be literally looking up at someone. But Jenný did not trust herself to sit with her in either place.

"The sofa's fine," Rebekka said in a low voice.

"Please help yourself to some water, I sanitised both bottles just before you arrived." Jenný pointed to two plastic bottles of water standing on the coffee table, one still and one sparkling. A similar pair of bottles stood on the dining room table, in case the girl had chosen to sit there, while Jenný went to the sink and got herself a glass of tap water.

Rebekka dropped down on the sofa. She reached for the sparkling water, unscrewed the cap, and downed almost half the bottle.

"I'm just here because of Dad," she whispered as she put the bottle down. "Nobody can help me."

"It's very understandable that you see it that way, Rebekka. I've learned a little about the condition you were diagnosed with, and it must be devastating to get such a diagnosis. That's a normal reaction. But no matter how bleak the outlook, there are always ways to make oneself feel a *little* better. For example, just talking about how you're feeling and the difficult emotions that people in your situation experience. People often understand things better when they can express them with words. There are also medications which can help with some of the physical symptoms, at least for a while, although there's no cure yet."

Jený did not know if Rebekka had heard a word of what she had been saying. The girl stared silently into space from where she sat on the sofa.

"I do not want to be more understanding of anything," she finally said without making eye contact. "I wish I didn't know *anything*."

"I meant that it can help people to put their emotions into words, to better understand their own feelings."

"I don't have to shout out loud that I'm angry to know that I am." Rebekka's voice became a little louder. "That I am angry, have no hope and everything seems black and horrible. It's not complicated. I *hate* the man I got this fucking disease from. I want to find him and kill him and then kill myself. That's the only thing that matters to me. Absolutely the only thing. There's nothing to look forward to. *No life*. Not for me."

Jený took a deep breath. She felt as if she were feeling her way through a minefield. It was crucial to step in precisely the right places, and with the utmost caution. The last thing she wanted was to do or say something that would make Rebekka storm out.

"And how has the search for your biological father progressed?"

Rebekka shrugged her shoulders.

"I have found out a few things. But I've been too smashed to do much."

"Have you been drinking a lot?"

Rebekka stared into space.

"This isn't something you can deal with sober. The moment I straighten up, my mind goes to this death sentence that some shitbag is responsible for ... and then I need to find something to take my mind off it."

"What are the "few things" you found out about your biological father?"

Jený had immediately sensed that Rebekka had neither interest nor stamina to discuss her emotional turmoil. A conversation on those lines would have her heading for the door, so Jený instead chose to approach her through the practicalities of finding her biological father.

"His name starts with S." Rebekka closed her eyes again and tried to concentrate. "And he lives ... or lived ... in Borgarnes."

"Do you draw these conclusions from the letters your father found after your mother died? I mean Björn."

"No, not *just* from that."

While the girl seemed to be under the influence of some substance, Jený suspected that this lack of concentration was also a symptom of the illness. She decided not to push, but waited instead to see if Rebekka had any further information about the man she blamed for her condition.

"I found an old friend of my mother's who knew something." The girl put her index finger to her lips. "Shhh, not a word to Björn. He doesn't know anything."

26

Jenný looked at Rebekka for a long time and hoped that her expression showed encouragement and a deep understanding. When that didn't appear to work, she reiterated the mantra from before their conversation began.

"Remember, everything said here will be entirely between the two of us, Rebekka."

The girl still held her finger to her mouth, as if to indicate that she had taken a vow of silence. Jenný tried again to break the silence with a question instead.

"Tell me, Rebekka, where did you find this old friend of your mother's?"

It was as if the girl on the sofa had been released from a spell.

"Well, where all the old people are," she said, as if Jenný could have figured that out for herself.

"In a nursing home?"

"On Facebook!"

"I see." Jenný couldn't help smiling. "And what did this woman know about the man you think wrote the letters, and who you believe is your biological father?"

But Rebekka had her mother in mind.

"My mother was only *forty* when she died." She sounded offended on her mother's behalf.

"I understand."

"She got pregnant at eighteen and had me when she was just nineteen."

"Was she considerably younger than your father?" Jenný did not know Björn's date of birth, but reckoned he had to be in his fifties.

"Fifteen years between them." She leaned over and asked innocently, "Do you think that's a lot?"

"Not at all. Every couple is unique, there's no hard-and-fast rule."

"Some people thought he was too old for her. But, then, she still died before him! Who'd have thought it?"

Rebekka had become ebullient and Jenný was concerned that she might lose control of the conversation. It was easier said than done to try to help a client who was facing such a cruel fate. Not least because it was difficult to understand the girl's behaviour – what could be attributed to the illness and what to substance abuse? And what had Rebekka's personality been like before the illness began to take hold?

"What new information did your mother's friend give you?"

Rebekka sighed, snatched up the water bottle and drank until it was empty. Then she put it down, rolled it across the table and belched.

"Sorry."

"No problem." Jenný desperately wanted to stand the bottle up so that no drops would fall on the table, but she stopped herself.

"Do you remember what your mother's friend knew about the man who might be your biological father?" she repeated.

"There's no 'might be' about it. Mum had no other boyfriends, just him and then Dad right after."

"Do you know if this man still lives in Borgarnes?"

"No." She sniggered. "I mean, no, he doesn't live there any longer."

"What was your mother doing in Borgarnes? Did she live there?"

"She was only there one summer to look after some kids. But he lived there then. The shit. *The Big Shit.*"

Jený suppressed a sigh. The conversation had made progress and she wanted to avoid the girl losing her thread and becoming distracted with this childish nickname. It could wait until later.

"Did your mum's friend know the boyfriend's full name?"

"Well ... my mum sent her a few postcards over the summer." Rebekka paused for a moment. "It was a private joke between them, sending each other postcards, understand? It wasn't the olden days. There were telephones and everything."

It took very little for the girl to lose track of what she was saying.

"And?"

"Yes, and Mum just referred to him as S. Maybe to save space. There's so little space on postcards, y'know? And then anyone could have read it, someone at her friend's house or just the postman, because it wasn't in an envelope."

"But when she came back to town in the autumn? Then they could have talked in private, as friends do."

"Yeah, no. Then they broke up and my mother didn't want to talk about him. She didn't talk about him to anyone, she didn't even want to talk about him to Dad. And he just accepted it. That's typical of Dad. Anyone else would have demanded to know about the guy who got his girlfriend pregnant. I mean, I could have been born black and it would have taken him totally by surprise."

Rebekka reached for the other water bottle and unscrewed the cap before continuing.

"I've asked everyone who knew her. The whole family, if it can be called a family, as there are so few of us, and everyone she worked with, the whole sewing club. This woman was the only one who knew anything."

"And it wasn't much," Jený said, bursting with sympathy for the girl, even though there was nothing positive behind her search for her biological father. In fact, she harboured a faint hope that if a meeting with her father could be engineered, the anger might be softened and some sort of reconciliation could be reached. But maybe that was too optimistic.

"She told me one more thing, though. Maybe this S-guy was Hansson."

Jenný felt a shock run through her.

"Hansson? How did the woman know that? S. Hansson and he lived in Borgarfjörður?"

"Not Borgarfjörður. Borgarnes. But Borgarnes is of course in Borgarfjörður, that's where it is. So both are correct. Or..." Rebekka looked at Jenný as if she had no idea why these places had been mentioned. But after a moment's consideration, she continued. "And this Hansson thing could be a joke, but I still don't think so. There was something on one postcard, about S being 'a chip off the old block', something like that. Like a puzzle. She did not quite remember, the woman. But it totally helped me out."

Rebekka took a gulp of water.

"Right now I know of someone this could be. I'm almost completely one hundred per cent sure. There's a Borgarnes group on Facebook. Or maybe a Borgarfjörður group. Now I'm completely confused. But, *anyway* ... I asked about him there. S. Hansson. Bingo!" Her laughter suddenly bubbled up. "I've been kind of following him for a while."

Jenný waited for a further description that did not come. Then she cleared her throat politely. When the hint wasn't taken, she asked straight out, "And how has that turned out?"

"Ach, I'm not cut out for spying. It makes me want to go for a spliff or check Tinder. But he's not getting away. Nobody's leaving the country or anything right now, because of the virus. Everyone's just *grounded*. So I'm in no hurry."

Jenný's heart pounded in her chest as she made an effort to remain impassive. She had stumbled across the person who was frightening the life out of Dóri at Bar Three – Dóri whose full name was Steindór – whether he was Rebekka's biological father or not. But this wasn't exactly good news. The principle of confidentiality between psychologist and patient meant that this information could go no further, least of all to the police.

That, however, was not the only problem here. Jený had doubts that the girl had the right man in her sights. But could she somehow involve herself, without breaking confidentiality?

She was startled out of her musings as Rebekka mentioned murder.

"I'm sorry, I was miles away," she quickly apologised. "What did you say?"

"I'll kill him as soon as I'm ready to kill myself." Rebekka was agitated.

"Really?"

"It's miserable enough to have this fucking disease, I'm not going to jail as well! That's why I'll kill him first and then myself immediately afterwards. But I'm not quite there yet."

Jený felt she had to tackle this immediately, but she was still in the middle of a minefield. There must be no question of taking any false step.

"Have you thought of something, Rebekka?" she began. "If you got the illness from your biological father, which seems pretty certain, then ... well, could he actually be dead? Have you considered that possibility? Because he'd also have had this flawed gene and it's been more than twenty years since he spent the summer with your mother."

The girl on the sofa hesitated for a moment.

"Of course I've thought of that. He has the gene, I know that. That's what this is all about. But it varies so much how old people are when they are diagnosed. Maybe he's luckier than me, maybe he's had more good years. Decades, even! It's not certain that he has even started to get sick yet."

Jený thought this unlikely, but had no counter-argument.

"This is a genetic condition," she said. "He must at least be aware it affects his family."

"Exactly!" Rebekka seized on this. "That's why he

shouldn't have had children! That's why I'm so furious with
him! He should have had the snip before he started having
sex."

This gave Jenný an opportunity to mention the promiscuity
that the girl's father worried about.

"What am I supposed to do, become a nun?" Rebekka
shrugged. "I'm living life as much as I can while I can."

"Do you think sex with different, new men is the best use
of the time you have left, Rebekka?"

"A person with no future can't commit to a relationship.
That would be unfair."

This gave Jenný a clearer understanding of her feelings.
Everyone has a need for physical intimacy, not least when
they feel unwell. Not necessarily sex, but at least touch and
warmth. This was the path that Rebekka had chosen rather
than connecting closely with just one man. These were brief,
shallow acquaintances that protected both herself and the
men concerned from any pain that would be part of a closer
relationship and deeper feelings.

"I can't do any more," Rebekka Rósa said suddenly and
leaned back on the sofa.

"What do you mean?" Jenný replied, wondering if she
meant her life with this diagnosis, the conversational therapy
or something else entirely.

"Talking. Now. No more today. Can you call a cab for me?"

"A taxi?" This contradicted the theory that Rebekka had
hung around in a dark car outside Dóri's place.

"Yes, there are plenty still at work."

Jenný did not ask how using a taxi would comply with the
two-metre rule.

"Would it be good for you to come back?" she asked. "It
won't be as stressful now you know what to expect. And I'm
not going to accept any payment for these sessions so you
don't have to worry about the cost."

When Rebekka said she was prepared to come back, Jenný
was taken completely by surprise. But the girl failed to thank

her for her time and declined to make an appointment, saying she would book one later.

Jenný obviously had no registered phone number, so she wrote down a Gmail address that she said Rebekka was welcome to use to get in touch. Fortunately, she had set this email up in the event of an emergency.

A few minutes later, the taxi was outside.

"Don't you have a car, Rebekka?" Jenný asked as Rebekka Rósa stooped to pull on her boots.

"Nope."

With that, she was gone before Jenný could ask any more questions about access to cars belonging to her father or her friends.

27

Jenný kicked off her black suede shoes and threw herself on the sofa. She did not have the energy to mix a gin and tonic, which she certainly deserved, or to turn on some soothing music. She was shattered. The nervous tension had been off the scale.

She had been in contact with another person. She had! Jenný! And not just in some bar abroad, where nobody knew her. This had not been a trivial chat about everything and nothing. Jenný had been through a session here in Iceland and started vital conversational therapy with a very vulnerable client, in which there was no room for error and...

Wonders of wonders! The world was still turning!

Rebekka had not asked any questions and made no comments. Could this have happened? Had the girl accepted Jenný at face value? Had this been a turning point? Had Jenný overcome what she feared most, almost as if nothing had happened, despite letting the fear build up for years?

Although she had good reason to celebrate, Jenný found this difficult. This personal victory of hers was intricately linked to Rebekka's and her father's tragic circumstances, circumstances that cast a shadow over everything. Jenný had no reason to break out the champagne, even if there had been a small chilled bottle waiting in the fridge. This was no time for celebration.

She also allowed herself only a moment to lie down on the sofa. She had promised to let Soffía know when she was free.

That is to say, Adam had promised. Soffía had meant to dig out further information about the siblings from Borgarfjörður, at Adam's request, and pass it on to him when he gave her the green light. This meant that Jený would have to get her skates on.

She took off her tights, skirt, sweater and bra. She removed the necklace, make-up and nail polish. Then she tied her hair in a bun and with that, the police's psychological consultant was ready for action. Or as ready as he could be under the current circumstances. It was not just that the relief was still flooding through him, there was still the concern about possibly knowing who Dóri's stalker might be – without being able to do anything about it.

Adam sent Soffía a text message telling her she was welcome to call.

Maybe she had now been given more manpower and had less need of his help. The situation had become much more serious after the discovery of needles in supermarket produce, which had triggered a broad-based emergency situation. And then, of course, Bergsveinn's hotel had been set on fire, so the aspect of this case concerning the siblings was also a worrying development.

It only took a few seconds for the phone screen to light up, Adam had forgotten to take it off the silent setting. It gave him a warm feeling to know that Soffía still seemed to need a psychological consultant. He also had to admit that he found the needle problem fascinating.

"It's getting worse. More needles found. In Akureyri and in Stykkishólmur," Soffía rattled off without saying hello. "No major injuries so far. Scratches and pricked fingers. No mouth injuries. All thanks to your advice. Very smart."

"What advice? I have given you so much smart advice." Adam had not yet begun to think clearly after his transformation.

"To not mention that the needles were broken. The original needles. That made all the difference." Soffía sounded more positive than she had been since the needle case began. "All the needles in Reykjavík were whole. The same up north and in Stykkishólmur. Like you said, copycats. And whole needles are usually discovered before they end up in anyone's mouth."

"Good to hear." Adam was relieved that he had been able to make a valuable contribution. "But how can you take advantage of the knowledge that these are copycats? Is it time to let this news leak out?"

"Considering it."

"Have you got any manpower for the case?"

"A little. I need it. Dóri calls every hour."

"Is he still scared?"

"Terrified."

"Has he experienced anything new, such as this afternoon?" Adam waited anxiously for an answer.

"Nope. Not that I know of. Listen, now I know more about the siblings. Can't I bring food over? I'm dying of hunger."

Adam was not clear-headed enough to cook, but he also could not imagine eating food bought elsewhere, or having Soffía cook anything in his place.

He didn't respond straight away.

"I'll buy a couple of frozen noodle ready meals," Soffía continued. "The ones in little boxes. They were definitely made long before Covid."

All of a sudden, he longed for noodles. It was a brilliant idea.

"OK, bring noodles. Can you get three or four varieties? I don't know what I want and we can try more than one dish."

"Do you have soy sauce?"

"Yes, and also chopsticks in sealed packaging, if you prefer them to a fork."

"Nobody but you!" Soffía giggled. "New chopsticks! You're one of a kind," she said and ended the call.

Adam prepared everything ready for dinner while waiting for Soffía, laid a place mat and a plate on each of the two tables, neatly folded napkins and put ice and water in a jug. Even though it was Sunday night, Soffía was still at work and driving, while Adam had stopped drinking alcohol a few years ago. On Kaplaskjólsvegur, only two people drank alcohol, Jenný and Margrét. One stuck to a pink gin while the other occasionally liked a beer.

Soffía made no comment as Adam sanitised the noodle containers, but she didn't appreciate sitting apart.

"You sat next to me at Bar Three. And in the car. This is illogical." She was both surprised and put out.

"I'm not going to sit next to you here," he said calmly, as if she were a small child in need of clear boundaries, and the tone indicated that the matter was not up for discussion. "I also need to use the computer so I can take notes."

Soffía couldn't contain herself.

"I have this." She waved the phone. "I can send you the document."

Adam pretended not to hear. Two types of noodles were ready and he put the other two cartons in the microwave.

They were both very hungry. Soffía immediately started shovelling food onto a plate and Adam did the same when she sat down. When they had taken the edge off their hunger, Soffía started reading from the document on the phone and Adam wrote down the main points.

"This Hans was a proper big salmon," she said.

"Big salmon?" This was a phrase Adam did not recall hearing before.

"Like a big shot. Powerful. Maybe even a bully. The main man in the district, in his own opinion."

Adam understood what she meant and gestured for her to continue.

"And a philanderer. We knew that. Eight kids with four women. And the relationships overlapped."

"Is that a good word for adultery?"

"Write this down. Arngunnur is the eldest, she's fifty. Her mother was from Reykjavík. She couldn't cope with country living. Gave up on shovelling horse shit. Moved with the girl to town and went on to study."

"What did she study?" Adam interjected.

"Study? The first woman? Wait. I didn't do all this myself." Soffía scrolled back and forth in the document. "A teacher training course. She was a primary school teacher. Now she's retired. OK?"

"So Arngunnur was not brought up in Borgarfjörður," Adam thought aloud. "But she spent time there every summer. They all did."

"Got you."

"But now it gets complicated. Hafdís is next, forty-seven. Daughter of a woman who worked on the farm."

"Why is she in a nursing home?"

"The document states Parkinson's/Alzheimer's. And Hans didn't acknowledge Hafdís. All the same, the farm girl stayed on at the farm. With the baby, that is. The old man was then married to the mother of Bergsveinn, Sesselja and Dóri. And she had a temper. So they say, I mean. I gather he was scared shitless of her. But he cheated on her later. With Emil's mother. And then the marriage exploded."

"How old are the three full siblings?"

"Between forty and fifty. Bergsveinn is forty-six. Sesselja forty-four. Dóri forty-two."

"Was Hafdís already an adult when Hans admitted to being her father?"

"No. Her mother was depressed, or at least something of a loner, and she died in an accident when Hafdís was just a small child. That was when he recognised her as his child. That was when I reckon the witch went nuts."

Adam felt he had to defend the woman.

"It can hardly have been pleasant for her to be cheated on twice. She must have been tough. In the countryside everyone knows everything about everyone, and that makes things like this more difficult."

"Isn't that just a myth?" Soffía sniffed.

"So Emil is the youngest," Adam said to keep them on the subject. "He'll probably be the first of the siblings to die.

That's tragic."

Soffía peered again at the document on her phone.

"He's the son of this woman who lives in Tenerife." She sharpened her gaze on Adam. "Does this help?"

"This isn't much additional information." Adam was immediately on the defensive. "It just puts them in order of age. Plus the old man's messed-up private life. What did this temperamental mother of the three do when the marriage ended?"

"Hmmm ...?" Soffía took a moment to go through the background information she had asked for. "She moved to Borgarnes. But the children were in the countryside a lot."

Adam stretched out on the sofa and his eyes widened.

"Did Dóri live in Borgarnes at some point?"

"It seems so. His mother was there. And those siblings were all at school there. But still very connected to the farm. Why do you ask?"

He sighed. Could he be breaking some law by withholding information about a case the police were investigating?

Rebekka spying on Dóri was admittedly not a particularly serious crime, at least not when one was aware that the perpetrator was just a desperate young girl who drank heavily, smoked dope and was most unlikely to embark on anything dramatic. So far, at least... It did not change the fact that Adam could not possibly share what he knew with Soffía.

But it was always possible that the girl could take a drug that would have a negative effect, leading her to take action that could injure her alleged father. Adam tried not to think about how that would make him feel.

28

"These are actually three separate issues," Adam said, thinking aloud. "The attacks on the siblings' companies, both the needles and the false complaints about the guesthouse. And then Dóri being stalked, and the copycat needles."

"Don't forget the fire," Soffía said. "And why keep Dóri separate?"

"What?" Adam had lost the thread.

Soffía counted on her fingers.

"The needle man ... or woman. The online complainer. The stalker. The arsonist. These could all be the same perpetrator."

"No, y'see... I don't think so. I have a strong feeling that this stalking affair isn't related to everything else." Adam hoped that Soffía would not expect justification for his intuition. "But the arson, on the other hand... And maybe the complaints on the booking web sites. Well, it's quite likely that is the same perpetrator. But it's hard to tell whether or not this is also the needle person."

"I'm just worried about how this is going to shape up. What do you think?" Soffía was neither reticent nor entreating, but was close to it – and clearly anxious. "Haven't you written down something that gets to the heart of the matter?"

Adam looked at the notes he had taken. Most of it quoted her. They would need something more solid before they could have a better basis for theories. He glanced through his list.

Hans's children:
Arngunnur, 50, shop owner (mother: teacher, Reykjavík)
Hafdís, 47, patient (mother: farm girl, died in a car accident)
Bergsveinn, 46, hotel owner (mother: the witch, Borgarnes)
Sesselja, 44, business owner (mother: the witch, Borgarnes)
Steindór (Dóri), 42, business owner (mother: the witch, Borgarnes)
Emil, 37, gallery owner (mother: with new husband, Tenerife)

"How long has it been since Hans died and how did he die?"

"Six years, almost seven," she read. "Was in the stable when he suffered a stroke. Found the day after."

"Do you know if anyone wanted to take over the estate? Or were they all happy to sell up?"

"Not Emil's mother."

"But she was not a beneficiary, since she and Hans were just cohabiting?"

"She wanted Emil to take it over."

"And maybe she was the only one who felt that way?"

Adam could not see the dapper gallery owner stepping into the shoes of a farmer in Borgarfjörður. But that could be prejudice on his part. Widespread mechanisation meant that modern farmers no longer relied on sheer muscle power, and Emil might have been very interested in farming. On the other hand, he probably lacked the business acumen of his half-siblings, as he had been in debt when their father died.

"All the heirs wanted to sell. The six siblings."

"And everyone got an equal share, presumably?"

"Of course. This isn't like it is in Britain. People can't give their whole estate to the Elf Society."

"Does that really exist?"

Adam regretted asking when Soffía burst out laughing. He hurried to distract her attention by asking how Hafdís had been doing when Hans died.

"Quite right." Soffía looked again at the document on the phone. "She went to an old people's home shortly before."

"Nursing home," he corrected, although his suggestions seemed to have a limited effect. "But there must have been some money that came her way. Who do you think has her power of attorney?"

"There's nothing about it here. But you're right. It was a lot of money. More than she could spend. Not for her own benefit. And I know she's childless." She looked intently at Adam as if trying to read his thoughts. "Do you suspect something?"

"Nothing in particular, no. I'm just speculating."

"I'm going to check on the power of attorney."

"On a Sunday night?" Adam glanced at his watch.

"Don't you want to know?"

"Yes, but ..." He gave up. When Soffía had her teeth into something she would never let go, and of course it would be useful to know who was in charge of all of Hafdís's money.

When the officer who had compiled the information for Soffía turned out to be clueless, she hung up on him as quickly as possible and called another number.

"Hello, Sesselja. This is Soffía. From the police."

Adam's eyes almost popped out of his head. Was she really calling Sesselja to ask this?

"No, I'm sorry. Nothing to report. But there's one thing you can help me with. Who holds power of attorney for Hafdís's affairs?"

"All right, I understand." She frowned at Adam. "Yes, that would be good. Please do. Look, thanks for this. And I'll get in touch ... if anything new comes up."

"What did she say?" Adam asked as she hung up the phone.

"Some woman in Sweden. Someone called Tove. She takes care of Hafdís's finances. They're cousins."

"You don't hang about," he said, slapping his thigh, full of admiration and a little taken aback.

"Well, the psychological counsellor needed the information," Soffía shot back. "Sessí didn't have the woman's phone number or email address. But she can get it. Does this change anything?"

"Don't you have to talk to all the siblings again and go a little deeper into this?" Adam asked.

"Can you be present?"

Adam escaped answering because Soffía's phone started ringing in her hand. It was clearly a work call and she went into the bedroom. Adam felt uncomfortable. Something of Jenný's could have been left out. Soffía shouldn't be wandering around the apartment like this. She was also putting her hands on things he would need to sanitise after she had gone.

He tried to calm himself down by making some tea. When evening came and he was agitated, he chose the green tea that Margrét had given him. The taste was actually reminiscent of seaweed, which he did not like, but it was better than nothing. He would have preferred a cup of Assam tea, but lately black tea had started to keep him awake. Or maybe it was his age, as he would be turning fifty later that year.

"Yes!" Soffía came triumphantly out of the bedroom, punching the air. "They've nicked the needle guys. Both in Akureyri and Stykkishólmur."

"Guys?"

"Three pals up in Akureyri and a pair of brothers in the west. They aren't finding this funny right now. The brothers are little kids but the three friends are teenagers. The whole lot of them have been detained. With the parents, naturally."

"Can children be questioned at police stations?"

"It's just a chat. It's more effective at a police station."

"Were they seen on CCTV?"

Soffía nodded.

"The young lads didn't realise there were cameras. Absolutely clueless. But the teenagers attracted attention because they were so interested in vegetables, and then they went and only bought sweets and pop. Idiots!"

She perked up even more at the sight of the teapot.

"Could I have some coffee?"

"Can you sleep if you drink coffee so late?"

Soffía rolled her eyes.

"It's not that late. And I can always sleep."

"No problem." He tried not to show his envy. Soffía had always been tougher than him, in every way.

"There'll be a press release," she said. "No mention of how old the boys are. Just that they were brought in for questioning. Scare tactics. But it's out there. Everything ends up online."

Adam scooped coffee into the cafetière. Soffía always wanted it strong.

"So the copycat thing is now just here in Reykjavík. No doubt that's kids as well. But it's still bad if someone gets hurt."

"Bloody kids," Soffía growled. "They should be at home. And Dóri keeps on calling. Even if a leaf flutters in his garden."

Adam placed the coffee pot on the table in front of Soffía, along with a mug and the milk carton.

"Dóri?" he said thoughtfully. "Is he never called by his full name?"

"Steindór? Yes, could be. Why?"

"Oh, just something I'm mulling over." Adam sat down on the couch with his tea. "And the brother ... Bergsveinn. Is he sometimes called by a nickname, do you think? Svenni, maybe?"

He was sure he had heard one of the siblings call Bergsveinn by that name, or he could have been mistaken. He seemed to recall that someone had also referred to him as Beggi.

"Don't most people have a nickname? Unfortunately. I refuse to answer to Soffa."

"You tried to call me Addi when we first got together. It's not as if that was any shorter. Both names are two syllables." Adam had completely forgotten this until now.

"I thought Adam was so formal. But why have you started thinking about this?"

"It's nothing."

"Hey, I know you. You never ask about nothing."

DECEIT

MONDAY 06.04.2020

Boris Johnson, the Prime Minister of the United Kingdom, has been admitted to a London hospital. He was diagnosed with the coronavirus ten days ago.

Helicopters from the Coast Guard have transported ten nurses and paramedics from the back-up teams to the Westfjords today.

Six people have now died in Iceland due to the pandemic.

29

Before Soffía left Adam's place, she had decided to bring in the siblings who were not in hospital or a nursing home to talk to her at the police station, even though only Bergsveinn and Emil had any connection to the hotel fire and they had all given informal interviews before. She had tried hard to persuade Adam to be present, but he refused to budge. It was out of the question for him to sit in a small room while two police officers interviewed four civilians, one after the other.

"We're the police. We follow the two-metre rule. Otherwise Víðir would be livid," Soffía told him repeatedly. "Everything will be sanitised. Yes, and you can wear a mask."

While Adam was not inclined to give way, he felt it was important to both see and hear how these people expressed themselves. Therefore, he planned to miss the meeting with his co-owners in Sáló, which had been arranged a long time previously, and asked Gunninga to postpone appointments with two clients. That would give him an opportunity to follow the police interviews with the siblings remotely.

Soffía found this idiotic. She doubted that these people would agree that under these circumstances a psychologist was like a fly on the wall. Explaining his presence would be very different if he was in the room.

Adam reminded her that he was not just some stranger, he had met all the siblings before, and that he would be visible on the screen so they could see that he was just sitting quietly in his house drinking tea. His indirect presence was perfectly normal in these strange times when grandparents read bedtime stories to their grandchildren over FaceTime and friends met in Zoom sewing clubs.

Eventually, Soffía became impatient to get home and gave in.

After she left, Adam racked his brain for a long time concerning Rebekka's search for her biological father. He did not understand how she could have narrowed the search so that Steindór was the only man under consideration. The mother's friend must have given her some information that the girl had not told Adam, something that led her to Dóri.

But could Adam make the girl understand that she might have the wrong man in mind, that there could be other candidates? That was demonstrably not his role. Besides, it was just a guess – but a guess that could save someone's life. The problem, however, was that by pointing Rebekka towards Bergsveinn, the danger was simply transferred from one brother to another. It was even possible that she might aim her barbs at both of them. Did Adam want to be the cause of that?

He also considered the possibility of discussing the matter somehow with Dóri and Bergsveinn. It would then have to be hinted at, and without compromising Rebekka's confidentiality, otherwise such an intervention would only make matters worse. Dóri could simply report the girl to the police or take some other measures for which Adam had no desire to be responsible.

He tried to look at the matter as if he were involved at a personal level, not simply as a professional. If his daughter were struggling with Huntington's disease, he would want her to accept all the help that medical science had to offer, such as antidepressants and possibly physical and occupational therapy. Quite simply, every bit of help from every direction that could alleviate some of the symptoms of the illness, even if only for a short time.

Adam wanted to help Björn support Rebekka in this way. In doing so, he would also have to defuse her obsession with wanting to kill her biological father. Because as the girl herself had pointed out, it was even harder to be sick in prison than as a free person.

He had fallen asleep during this speculation about Björn and his daughter, overwhelmed by the feeling that he had never been more powerless as a psychologist. After a few hours of shallow and restless sleep, Monday morning came much as Sunday evening ended – but this time with a phone call from Björn at half-past eight.

He was obviously distressed at having troubled Adam, apologising repeatedly, and Adam did what he could to calm him down, reassuring him that the time did not matter. He had had nightmares last night and had difficulty sleeping. That was true enough.

"Has something happened?" he asked. "What's wrong?"

"Rebekka's friend says she stole a DNA sample from a man she thinks is her biological father. She's going to have it analysed. It's something she took without his knowledge."

"How could she steal a DNA sample?" Adam rubbed his eyebrows. "Had a sample been taken from him for something else?"

"No, it's not like a Covid sample, not taken with a swab. She stole his clothes and means to have them analysed."

"Clothes?"

"Sportswear that the man had worn. She plans to have the sweat from the clothes tested for DNA."

"I understand." So it had been Rebekka who broke into Dóri's car and stole his sports bag. Had she just been pretending to be numb and stoned? There seemed some pretty clear thinking behind breaking into his car to steal clothes with traces of genetic material.

"Didn't she mention this to Jenný yesterday?"

Björn's voice was quivered with emotion.

The mantra of every psychologist's duty of confidentiality to their clients, let alone colleagues, was on Adam's lips, but he did not have it in his heart to follow this up under such circumstances.

"I'm pretty sure Rebekka didn't mention anything of this nature," he said softly, as if it made the breach of trust somehow less bad.

"Her friend says that she called deCODE Genetics, but there's only an answering machine on the weekends. It seems it's also possible to send samples to laboratories abroad. But of course the post offices are closed and there are almost no flights. She probably wants to check the local options first." Björn sighed. "What should I do, Adam? My daughter is committing crimes. It's so unlike her, so completely wrong."

Adam had managed to stop himself from telling him that breaking a car window was not a serious crime. But Björn had not mentioned a car, and maybe he had no idea of how Rebekka had stolen clothes from her alleged biological father.

"Do you know what she did?" Björn asked, as if he had read Adam's thoughts.

"No."

"She went to some shop and got a friend of hers to vacuum-pack the clothes!" Björn gasped.

"What?" Adam asked, barely awake and without taking Björn's words in fully.

"She had them packed in an airtight container! In a shop. Like chops or salami."

"Right. Why do you think she did that?"

"So the genetic material would not evaporate, I guess. Which I naturally don't know if genetic material does. Do you know?"

No, Adam did not know.

"But imagine the despair. Her determination to find the man." Björn sniffed. "I'm at the end of my tether, don't know which way to turn. What if she... If she...? I was hoping that this was just something she was messing with as part of the grief and despair ... and maybe to piss me off. But when I heard this about the stolen clothes last night, then... Well, I felt like this had reached a new level."

Since Adam needed very much to go to the toilet, he asked

Björn if it he could call him back, as soon as he had read up on DNA and had time to consider this latest development over a cup of coffee. Björn almost seemed relieved. He had found a certain reassurance in sharing with Adam, whom he trusted, the news of what Rebekka had in mind.

Adam made tea, not coffee, and when it was ready, he switched on the computer and read about DNA. He was relatively quick in finding reliable information claiming that almost no genetic material could be found in sweat. That did not mean, however, that Rebekka's efforts would necessarily have been in vain, if she were to find someone to examine the sweaty, vacuum-sealed sportswear in the middle of a pandemic. The garments probably contained skin cells that could provide information about the genetic material of the wearer.

Adam also found a newspaper article from several years previously in which the deCODE Genetics CEO Kári Stefánsson had said he would be happy to research genetic material for people who needed such help. But now things were different and the majority of the staff were no doubt busy doing screenings for coronavirus. No matter how much he searched, Adam found no information about the effects of vacuum-sealing on genetic material. Maybe nobody had thought of doing that.

After his second mug of tea, he called Björn and explained what he had discovered.

"I just don't understand how she can focus on just a particular individual," muttered Björn, as though to himself. "Those letters her mother had kept were just signed with an S. Her flatmate says she doesn't know who Rebekka has in her sights or how his name came up. But she could be not telling the full story to protect Rebekka."

Adam knew what was coming next and prepared to disappoint Björn, just as Rebekka's friend had done.

"Did she tell this Jenný who this is?"

Adam was fortunate that the question was phrased this way.

It allowed him to provide a negative answer with a clear conscience. Rebekka had not mentioned any name during the session with Jenný, he assured him.

But now he had far overstepped all limits of the professionalism which he had previously put every effort into keeping. His only reservation was that Björn talked about 'this' Jenný both times he mentioned her. Did he suspect the truth about the psychologist Rebekka had met? Maybe Adam would, after all, get into trouble because of Jenný?

One thing, however, had become quite clear. Adam had been left in a difficult situation after the call from Rebekka's father. He now knew for sure who had been stalking Dóri and had broken into his car. Could he conceal this information from Soffía, considering he was supposed to be her consultant in the case of Dóri and his siblings?

30

"Can I run something past you?"

"Good morning, Soffía! I hope you slept well."

Soffía paid no attention to his sarcasm or tone.

"Arngunnur Hansdóttir's partner is in intensive care. It's life-threatening."

"Does she have Covid?"

"She was injured. At their house. Just before the guesthouse fire. At or around midnight yesterday. But I only just heard about it now."

"Was she attacked?"

"She slipped on ice. On the steps by the front door."

Although Adam obviously felt sorry for the woman, and for Arngunnur, he didn't see any great relevance in this.

"Don't people get hurt slipping on ice all the time? Maybe not so many now that there aren't so many people out and about."

"Maybe Arngunnur was the one who was supposed to be injured." Soffía put a dramatic emphasis on the name.

"You said nobody attacked her. But anyone can have a fall."

Adam had become irritated. It could be heard in his voice, and he no longer tried to hide it. He was worried about Rebekka and all the complications associated with her, including the possibility that he was breaking the law by withholding information. His patience with Soffía, who was clearly only giving him information in bits and pieces instead of saying outright what was going on, was at a low ebb.

"Listen." Soffía perceived his impatience. "I talked to Arngunnur earlier. She is, naturally, very upset. She said she had cleared the steps. All the way down to the bare concrete. Not so much as a snowflake on them. Then Katrín went out at midnight. To call in the cat. Then the steps were like glass. Bam, she fell over backwards. Severe head trauma and a broken elbow."

"And you think... *what?*"

"Well, I didn't see the scene. So I just have Arngunnur's description. But she thought ... she's adamant ... that water must have been sprayed on the steps. It was below zero. A thin layer of water would have frozen immediately."

"Jesus, Soffía."

"Are you thinking the same as me?" she sighed. "Or could it have been kids?"

"Of course it's possible. Then these must be bloody dangerous kids." Adam thought about it. "No, you know, my first reaction is that this is the person behind the needles, who moved on to arson and breaking bones."

"You're not including Dóri's car? Or the laser pen?"

"No, that's work of a different nature."

Adam trusted that Soffía, whose mind was on the steps at Arngunnur's place, would not ask for his reasoning.

"She didn't report this," she growled angrily.

"She's probably had the shock of her life, having to call an ambulance for her wife. And because of the pandemic, she's not allowed to go to the hospital and has had to phone to get any idea of what's going on. People don't think clearly under those conditions."

Adam guessed that Arngunnur would have come across Katrín in a pool of blood on the steps. It must have been a huge shock that would take a long time to get over.

"And the partner's condition is life-threatening?" he said.

"That's what Arngunnur says. I haven't called the hospital myself. But I sent an officer to check on the steps. It's just too late now."

Adam agreed. Arngunnur had probably scattered the steps with salt to dispel the ice so that nobody else would be injured.

"Arngunnur didn't connect the ice on the steps to the needles?"

"Nope. I just called her to ask her down to the station. And she sounded so depressed. Then out came the whole story."

"Are there any security cameras nearby?"

"On the next corner. Not by the house. It's being investigated."

Adam tried to visualise the course of events.

"The person who did this could simply have had a water bottle in their pocket," he said. "Maybe two. Then he could have quickly splashed water on the steps, almost in passing. That would hardly be picked up by a camera at the next corner."

"The time frame is also quite wide. The video needs to be watched. Arngunnur cleared the snow at seven-ish. The accident happened around midnight."

"Hadn't the cat come home at twelve o'clock?"

"Jesus, Adam. You're such a square. This is not a child. This is an animal that wanders at will."

Adam did not take the bait. Soffía was welcome to make fun of his habits and well-ordered ways, if she got anything out of it. It had long since stopped bothering him.

"Like the other attacks, this is premeditated," he continued. "The perpetrator certainly intended to cause harm, as with the needles, and there was also some uncertainty over who could be the victim. Do other people live in the house?"

Adam remembered that there were two floors above the health food shop on the ground floor.

"Arngunnur owns the whole house," she said. "She rents the attic floor to some young lads. They were at home, she says. As everyone is now. Always. *Home sweet home.*"

"Someone might have intended to prank the boys, not Arngunnur," Adam muttered, mostly to himself. "Or they simply did it out of childishness or cruelty, without having any idea who lives in the house. Visitors could also have been at risk. Or someone delivering papers."

"Did the perpetrator keep an eye on the steps, do you think? Let's have your ideas, Mr Psychologist." This time Soffía wasn't joking. "Did he hang about at the next corner? And maybe took pictures? Would he get a kick out of this?"

Adam thought about it and then decided to take a risk by presenting a theory.

"Right, I consider this to be the same perpetrator as in the needle case. It focusses on the business interests of the siblings. The arson was not at Bergsveinn's home but where he has a business. But now he is ... this same perpetrator ... shifting up a gear and becoming more personal with this death-trap on Arngunnur's steps."

"You say he?"

"The perpetrator. This could just as easily be a woman. Or even more than one perpetrator, although I find that less likely. But I don't think he would have hung around to see if anyone fell. He's not crazy. I don't believe this is some teenager fooling about."

"So this is a clever criminal?"

"Maybe it didn't matter to him who was injured." Adam was on a roll. "If this was directed against Arngunnur, the intention was successful, even though she didn't suffer a fall herself. She must be in a state of shock and beside herself with worry. And she would also have been devastated if a tenant or a courier had been injured, all because of someone wanting to hurt her. So this was a clever plan to harass this woman, which seems to have been the purpose."

Adam heard Soffía flipping urgently through papers.

"Could this be the Dane?" she asked. "The missing husband? This Morten?"

"Then why would he attack her siblings' companies?" Adam asked in return.

"Some old dispute?" This was a theory rather than a

189

question. "I'll ask her that. She's on her way. Will you be ready for Zoom in a moment?"

"No, Soffía." He sighed. She never listened to him properly. "I already told you I don't have Zoom. But I created a special Facebook profile, just for this, and sent you a friend request. You just have to accept it and then we go from there."

"Do you have two Facebook accounts? The social media hater himself!" Soffía burst out laughing, either unaware of or indifferent to his irritation.

"Send me a text message when you want me to connect," he added dryly. "Then I can start a video call."

"OK. See you soon."

Adam used this break to make a full pot of tea and open a packet of biscuits. He had no idea how long the conversation with the siblings would take, if they would be one after the other or whether there would be a break in between them.

It was lucky that he had been so quick to get ready because the message from Soffía came much sooner than expected. He hurried to Facebook, saw that she had become *Adam A. Adammada's* first friend, and clicked on video call.

"Hi."

Hi? He thought Soffía very informal, considering this was a formal session.

"Hello."

"You don't have to be so stiff. Arngunnur's not coming."

"No? Why?"

"An exception was made. She was allowed into the intensive care unit."

"Isn't intensive care packed with Covid patients?"

"Not where Katrín is."

"I thought no visits were allowed. Not intensive care or anywhere else. Is the woman dying?"

"Could go either way."

"Poor Arngunnur."

"I feel more sorry for Katrín. She's the one who could be dead."

"If she dies, this will be a murder investigation," Adam said, and an ice-cold shiver ran down his back.

Maybe he should withdraw from this advisory role. Until now he had felt that helping Soffía had been almost like a puzzle to pass the time during the pandemic. If Arngunnur's partner were to die, then this would become a matter too serious for his liking.

31

It wasn't long before Soffía sent a message to let him know the meeting with Bergsveinn was about to begin. Adam hurried to make the video call and then he just sat and listened. However, he didn't relax on the sofa, and made sure he was ready with a comment or question, in case Soffía wanted him to be an active participant in the conversation.

The first thing that caught his attention regarding Bergsveinn was his outfit, and how tense he appeared to be. He wore a dark suit, a light yellow shirt and a beautiful tie. A handkerchief matching his shirt, artfully folded, peeked from his breast pocket. Anyone would have thought that the hotel owner was on his way to a smart reception, although if that were the case he would undoubtedly have been more cheerful. Bergsveinn was restless, his eyes flitting around the room and his hands never still.

Soffía asked him to tell her a little about Hafdís. The question surprised Adam and seemed to take Bergsveinn off guard.

"Why?" He gripped the edge of the table. "Has something happened?"

"I want to get a clearer picture of you all. And Hafdís isn't able to tell us much."

The man in the suit relaxed slightly.

"Why is someone persecuting *us*? We're not even regular siblings. Only Dóri, Sessí and I. The others were just a bunch of kids we used to see at Dad's farm, mostly in the summer."

"What about your mothers?"

"Do you really need to ask?" He glared at Soffía. "Of course they weren't friends, there was all kinds of trouble. We kids instinctively picked up on it, even though we didn't understand it until much later."

"What do you mean?"

"Well, you were always aware of malicious gossip. Yes, and saw your mother in tears. Then your anger would flare up … sometimes at Dad and sometimes at the other women. Or the other kids."

"But there was only one woman after your mother. Emil's mother."

Bergsveinn loosened the knot of his tie, as if he was having trouble breathing. Adam sensed that Soffía had touched a sensitive spot there, although there was no knowing if this had been accidental or intentional.

"Only one woman?" Bergsveinn sneered sardonically. "Maybe only one the man lived with, yes, and had a child with. But he shagged anything with a pulse. While he was with my mother, I mean. She got to hear constant gossip about this or that woman he'd been screwing, young, old, unmarried, married. He never left any woman in peace. And while not every one of them spread her legs for him, there were plenty who did. But don't ask me what they saw in him. I have never understood what they found so attractive about that man."

Adam wondered which of the siblings was most like their father. Maybe Dóri and maybe Sesselja too. Those two seemed to live colourful lives and Dóri had spoken briefly about his relationships with Soffía. But it was possible that their lives just seemed eventful because they ran popular bars.

Soffía seemed to be digesting the tale of the farmer Hans's amorous adventures for a moment. Then she repeated her request that Bergsveinn tell her about Hafdís.

"Yes, and her mother's relationship with your father," she added.

"Dad's and Greta's relationship?" He spread his hands

wide. "It started before I was born and was over before my earliest memories!"

"But what have you *heard*?"

Bergsveinn sighed.

"Well. Rúna, my father's first wife, can't have been suited to running a rural household with a horde of labourers who needed feeding and looking after. That was understandable. She was a young girl, a proper city kid, and suddenly found herself thrown in at the deep end. Then she became pregnant with Arngunnur, and could no longer stand the smell of the cowshed and food, that kind of thing."

Bergsveinn shook his head and sighed.

"The old man wasn't strong on patience. He never tolerated whims, as he called any kind of emotions. So Rúna definitely didn't have a happy time of it during her pregnancy. Then she went to Reykjavík to have Arngunnur and refused to come back to Borgarfjörður."

"How does this relate to Hafdís's mother?"

Soffía asked so harshly that Bergsveinn was startled.

"Because ... you see, because of all this, Dad went and found this Swedish woman, Greta."

"Greta?" Soffía looked as if she had lost the thread, but this had to be a pretence.

"Greta, Hafdís's mother. She worked in some embassy or a hotel but Dad got her to come up to Borgarfjörður. She'd been raised in the countryside and was very hardworking. So she became a kind of housekeeper. And then Rúna came back with Arngunnur and everything got better for a while. So I was told."

Bergsveinn scratched at the table with a fingernail. "Greta was probably something of an introverted type. I understand that she never wanted to talk about the pregnancy or any personal matters, and she never named him as the father of her child."

Soffía jotted something down on a piece of paper.

"Everyone says she was as tough as old boots," Bergsveinn

added. "She tied the kid to her back, like in Africa, and continued taking care of this large farm, no fuss, no bother."

Soffía did not ask another question, knowing that most people found silence uncomfortable, and he soon continued.

"Around the time Greta gave birth to the child, Rúna demanded a divorce and went back to Reykjavík for good with Arngunnur. I think she'd just had enough of the countryside."

Soffía flipped through the notes she had in front of her.

"Rúna could also have left because of your mother?" Despite the questioning tone, Soffía knew the answer. "She didn't waste time moving in with your dad."

"The old man's affair with our mother must have started before Rúna moved to Reykjavík." Bergsveinn bowed his head for a moment, as if some of the blame were somehow his.

"Rúna took her daughter back to town. Your mother turns up. Tough Greta dies in a car accident."

"Greta could have been more sensitive than she looked," Bergsveinn said, unprompted. "I once heard my mother say she was depressed, but that could have been because of being disappointed in love."

"And then Hans accepted Hafdís?"

"It's my understanding that there was some fuss. I think the child was supposed to have been sent to Sweden. Either to relatives or to foster care, as Greta had family there, I'm not sure about that. But my father put an end to that, acknowledged paternity of the child and got custody."

"Was he good to Hafdís?"

"Good to Haf...? Not specially. But nothing bad either. Dad just wasn't big on kids, no hugging or reading bedtime stories."

Bergsveinn sniffed. The handkerchief in his jacket pocket was clearly too classy to be put to practical use.

"Not until Emil was born," he added, the bitterness creeping into his voice. "Emil was the only one of us the old man had any time for. The farm was doing well. He had bought more land nearby and modernised the buildings. I think money had often been tight when we were little. But we never knew anything about that."

Soffía looked at the papers for a moment but then looked up.

"So just Hafdís and Emil grew up on the farm?"

"That's about it. But we all spent time on the farm every summer, Dad was adamant about that. Cheap labour, you see."

"Then Hafdís moved to Sweden?"

"Yes, she was about sixteen years old, I remember. Until then, she just visited her mother's family once a year. But they felt it was important for her to learn Swedish, they didn't want her to completely lose touch with her mother's homeland."

"It seemed to have worked out well."

"Yes, in a way. Yes, yes. But that's actually a problem now, now she *only* speaks Swedish and the staff at the nursing home have a hard time understanding her. Most of the women who work for her are from Poland or Asia."

"What brought her back to Iceland?"

Bergsveinn was quick to answer.

"It was the *farm*. She finished school in Sweden, went to agricultural college and came home to run the farm with Dad."

32

Next, Soffía tried to get a clearer picture of Bergsveinn himself. He was first asked to describe his mother. The image Adam had built up of Signý indicated that she was volatile and demanding and Bergsveinn confirmed this, although he used gentler terms. He said Signý was proud and a determined woman who had been poorly treated by Hans.

"My mother felt the man humiliated her by endlessly chasing women. She took it badly and she became temperamental and strict, not least with us kids. But she never let Dad suffer for it while they lived together."

"Oh?"

Soffía seemed amazed by this, but it didn't strike Adam as surprising.

"Well, maybe during those last months ...when she saw it was a losing battle. Then she began to lose her grip. She's a one-man woman, my mother. She never looked at another man, neither before nor after they were married."

"But still she left him?"

Bergsveinn sighed.

"Left? Yes, when that man announced that another woman was expecting his child. Then my mother finally packed up and moved with us to a two-room apartment in Borgarnes. She got a job as a cleaner and never again set foot on land owned by my father."

"That must have been a change."

"Just a bit. Mum slept in the living room and the three of us had the little bedroom, the other two in bunk beds and I had a camp bed that was folded up during the day. But we were at the farm during the summer and there was plenty of space there for us."

"He must have paid child support."

"I expect so. But my mother got into a mess. The child support no doubt ended up in the till at the State Alcohol Monopoly or this or that bar in the city when she was on a binge. And sometimes she took taxis each way. That must have cost something."

Adam felt ashamed that he had mentally nicknamed the woman 'the witch'. Farmer Hans had treated her badly, and this had done their three children no favours.

"In the autumn we always went with my dad to Reykjavík," Bergsveinn added, as if he wanted to adjust the family picture. "Then we would stay a night at Bændahöllinn, have dinner at Grillið and then Dad dressed us up."

"Dressed you up?"

"The clothes, shoes and other things he bought for us on these trips lasted all year. School clothes, pyjamas, underwear, winter shoes, coats, hats and mittens. All the things kids need. For us it was a big adventure, all of us together."

"And the cramped flat in Borgarnes. Didn't you miss the house at the farm?"

"My brother and sister were so young when we moved. They don't remember being on the farm except over the summer, and they didn't realise the situation when our parents' marriage was falling apart. I was eight or nine and I knew what my mother was going through. I bore the brunt of it. It was hell."

He saw the man's mouth twitch, as this was clearly a sensitive point. But Soffía did not follow up on Bergsveinn's revelation, as Adam would have liked her to, instead rummaging through papers, running her finger down a closely written page.

"Primary school in Borgarnes. Then what?"

"I had no idea what I wanted." Bergsveinn carefully unscrewed the cap from a bottle of sparkling water in front of him on the table. "Except I didn't want to be a farmer or go to high school. I was never much of a one for studying."

"Did you go out to work right away?"

He took a sip of water before answering.

"No, the old man sent me to school in Britain. This wasn't Oxford or Cambridge, just a school with all kinds of courses to help confused kids figure out where their interest lies. And business administration appealed to me. *Business.* I took a few courses and then got a job with a company on the south coast of England that organises all kinds of events – conferences, anniversaries and birthday parties. I then moved into the hotel business and ended up running a popular boutique hotel in Brighton."

Now Adam would have liked to ask if Bergsveinn had been in Britain all year round or if he had spent the summers in Borgarnes – and then maybe slept with a girl and wrote her postcards, signed with an S? But of course Soffía did not ask about that.

"Why did you then move back home?"

"When the inheritance from my father came through a few years ago, I wanted to invest in something of my own. And Iceland was recovering from the financial crisis and starting to get noticed."

"Get noticed?" Soffía repeated.

"Become fashionable," he explained. "It was all going so well, until this damned pandemic wrecked everything and the bottom fell out of the tourist industry."

"Those pranks can't have helped," Soffía reminded him. "Negative comments on the booking sites. And now the arson attack."

Adam noticed an instant change in Bergsveinn the moment Soffía mentioned the booking sites and the fire. His facial features became hardened and his gaze sharpened. This was another sensitive point, although of a different kind.

"Yes, well…" Bergsveinn scowled. "Do you know what Emil's situation is?"

"No. Why do you ask?"

The unexpected change of tack took Soffía, and Adam, by surprise.

"I just wondered…" Bergsveinn was silent for a moment and seemed to sense that he had moved the conversation in a direction that surprised the investigating police officer. "Because you reminded me of the fire. Contractors will be working on the hotel soon, carpenters and painters. That's why I was wondering … well, if Emil is likely to be discharged soon."

Soffía muttered something that Adam did not hear.

"The carpenters will start early in the mornings and there will definitely be a lot of noise so… Let's say it won't be a good place for a very sick person."

"I understand. You don't want him back."

This was the side of his wife that Adam remembered. Former wife. She said it straight out. It was Bergsveinn's turn to be caught off guard, and he half-heartedly made an attempt to steer the conversation elsewhere.

"You know. It could well be that he … doesn't have much time left, do you know?"

Adam would have given a lot to know what the man was thinking. Would he let Emil stay with him if he was sure his brother would soon breathe his last?

"I don't have this kind of information." Soffía spoke slowly and clearly, as if addressing a child. "You're his brother. Hasn't there been a family meeting?"

"None that I've been invited to." Bergsveinn held up his hands, as if taking an oath. "And not Dóri and Sessí, as far as I know. Maybe Arngunnur, although I find that hard to believe. We brothers and sisters aren't all that much in touch."

"Is it correct that Emil has neither a spouse nor children?"

"Yes. His mother must be his next of kin."

"Isn't she in Tenerife?" Soffía obviously knew the answer.

"So you think Emil isn't dying, otherwise his mother would come from abroad?"

"I didn't say that. But Emil recently opened a new exhibition. So he must have been in good spirits. And no reason for his mother to come."

"Until now? Do you think she's coming now?"

Adam could not understand why Bergsveinn kept returning to the same thing. Soffía had clearly stated that she had no detailed information about Emil's health or future prospects. There had to be something behind this.

"I know nothing about Emil." Soffía sounded tired of the refrain. "You're one of the man's closest relatives. Ask the oncologist! You need to discuss housing issues directly with your brother. Not with me."

33

Soffía switched off the video connection as soon as Bergsveinn got to his feet. Moments later, Adam's phone rang and she was on the line.

"Don't you think he was strange towards the end?" she asked.

Adam agreed.

"He has Emil's illness on his mind. Is this a fear of death?" she continued.

"Emil is his brother, who isn't even forty and seems to have only a short time left. Bergsveinn may be into the grieving process. It can start long before the patient dies, when the cause is known. And..."

"I didn't find him sorrowful," Soffía interjected.

"No, exactly. If you'd let me finish? Bergsveinn seemed almost impatient rather than apprehensive. It's almost as if he *wanted* Emil to have only a little time left."

"Isn't that overthinking?"

"I'm just describing how it appeared to me."

Adam felt the familiar frustration well up inside him, a reaction to Soffía's tendency to ask him his opinion only to then immediately sweep aside his contribution. She had habitually done this during their marriage, in major and minor matters.

"Why should he *want* Emil dead? They have virtually no contact. Alive or dead, it shouldn't make a difference to him."

Adam wasn't happy with Soffía's interpretation, although

she was right about this. Bergsveinn and Emil were more like acquaintances than brothers. He pointed out that taking this into consideration, this abiding interest in Emil's life expectancy was surprising.

"Maybe it's about money?" Soffía suggested, before answering her own question. "No. The inheritance issues have long been settled."

"Who inherits Emil's property? His mother?" Adam asked.

"I imagine there are only debts. The gallery is a rental space and Emil slept there. I wonder if he has enough to cover the funeral?"

"Ach, Soffía." Adam groaned.

"Then there's being childless." Soffía was getting into her stride. It took more than a groan to put her off.

"What about it?"

"Dóri has kids in America. The other siblings are all childless. It must be an Icelandic record. Imagine if the old man was alive. All that shagging, and six children. But only two grandchildren."

Adam was aware of a possible third grandchild, but couldn't mention that to Soffía. This promise was weighing heavily on him now. But he could not break Björn's and Rebekka's confidentiality to tell her that Dóri maybe had a daughter as well. Or Bergsveinn.

There was still the possibility that neither of the brothers had got a young girl pregnant in Borgarnes just over twenty years ago. Paternity had not been confirmed, whatever might happen later. Rebekka's biological father could have been a completely different man who had no connection with Hans the farmer.

"Maybe the siblings had enough of family complications when they were kids," Adam guessed, feeling that Soffía was waiting for a further response from him.

"Problems in childhood can leave deep scars. You probably saw Bergsveinn getting tearful when he talked about his parents' stormy marriage."

Soffía did not respond but instead put forward another theory.

"The old man also had a positive effect," she said. "He clearly thought big. Bought land. Erected buildings. Became wealthy."

"You mean, they inherited some business genes from him, don't you? Not just money?"

"Something like that."

"Yes, of course they all run companies, all except Hafdís."

"She ran the farm with her father for a while."

"That's right."

Adam had to admit that Soffía had focused on two important points. Even if Rebekka turned out to be farmer Hans's granddaughter, this was still an unusual family.

"How does the psychologist interpret this?" she asked.

Adam had been waiting in trepidation for this question.

"Soffía." He thought for a moment. "I can't read anything more than you can from what we already know. For example, it tells us nothing about who might want to harm the siblings."

Adam felt he had to say something more, in a powerless attempt to meet the unrealistic expectations of the woman who would have to approve the invoice he would be sending to the police.

"But I've been thinking about the mothers of the siblings," he added. "Whether any of them could be taking revenge on children Hans fathered with other women. But then, of course, the person in question would be very dangerous and would be endangering her own child – or even children."

"I see."

He sensed that the theory had struck a chord, so he continued.

"The first, Rúna, Arngunnur's mother. She didn't seem to have any fondness for the old man or the farm. I can't see a retired teacher seeking revenge now that Hans is long dead."

"Agreed."

"Number two, Hafdís's Swedish mother, is dead. And I think we can rule out a ghost."

"Agreed." Soffía was apparently still interested.

"Signý, on the other hand ... the third, the mother of three, the one I'm ashamed to have named 'the witch' in my notes. She got into no end of a mess after Emil's mother usurped her. I don't know if she's still drinking or is in a state of sobriety. Could she be behind the needles, the arson and the ice on the steps?"

"*Usurped her*...! And *a state of sobriety*! Sometimes you have an incredible vocabulary."

Adam tolerated such remarks even less than the corrections. Anyone would think that Soffía was a teacher encouraging a child to do well. He never praised her for her varied vocabulary when she spoke English. He simply assumed that she was good at it after several years of studying in Britain. On the other hand, she thought it was a miracle that he had managed a reasonable command of Icelandic.

"These terms are frequently used," he explained curtly.

"But could this Signý have placed the needles at Bar Three? The place her children run?" Soffía's mind was again on the siblings' mothers as possible perpetrators.

"The needles were in the bathroom for customers." Adam felt that this maternal theory was running out of steam, but he needed to take it to a conclusion. "Maybe she expected her son to use a staff toilet."

"But the needles in the sausages? How could Signý plant those?" Soffía continued to muse on the idea. "And if the needles were to harm the companies, would she do that to her children?"

Adam had to admit that this seemed unlikely.

"I'm dubious concerning the complaint about drinking in the hot tubs at the guesthouse," he said.

"Exactly. Do old ladies know about booking websites? And how to send photos as attachments?"

"Soffía! This woman's probably about seventy. There are

fully active people of that age who have used computers for decades."

"Then what makes you dubious?"

"Just that the complaint was about gays. That some gay people were behaving badly in the hot tubs in the middle of the night."

"What about it?"

"Maybe it was something for Bergsveinn from his mother, some indirect message. Maybe the woman is prejudiced."

Soffía immediately picked up on this.

"You mean this young, playful, computer-savvy woman?" she teased. "But really, this is far too far-fetched. What do gays have to do with it?"

"Well, Bergsveinn is gay. Or so I think."

"I'm not sure you're right about that."

"Maybe he's marketing the guesthouse as a retreat for BDSM and has some kind of dungeon in the cellar," Adam continued, even though Soffía seemed unconvinced. "His mother might be unhappy about it."

"But the place caught fire! Did the owner's mother do that?"

Adam sighed.

"No, probably not. But what about the last woman, Emil's mother, whatever her name is? Is she definitely in Tenerife?" he asked.

"Her name's Halldóra. And answered a phone registered in Tenerife."

"Haven't most Icelanders returned home because of the pandemic?"

"I can go over the passenger lists."

Adam said he thought it was unnecessary. But knew that Soffía would have the lists reviewed, whatever he thought.

"Emil could easily have eaten a sausage containing a needle," he said. "Would his mother have taken the opportunity to harm her cancer patient son? And would she really have set fire to a building where he was sleeping? If that's the case, then there has to be something seriously wrong with this person and it would have been noticed before now."

"This is where the mother theory collapses!" Soffía did not seem too unhappy with the outcome. "Hey, Sessí's on the way. I'll start a video call in a moment."

"Would it have killed you to say goodbye?" Adam asked the phone's blank screen.

34

While Adam was out of contact with the police station, he once again pondered the possible connection between Rebekka and the siblings from Borgarfjörður. Since her mother had not had Huntington's disease, as far as was known, the girl must have inherited the gene from her paternal line, as she had clearly assumed herself. But her biological father had to be a carrier, while both Dóri and Bergsveinn were in their forties and seemed in good health.

Adam looked again at an article online to review what was known about the ages of the people who suffered from Huntington's.

"The more often the defective gene is inherited, the greater the number of recurrences and, as a result, there is a greater risk of developing symptoms earlier in life. In families where the condition occurs, individuals inheriting the defective gene become younger and younger when the condition appears..."

Did this mean that a child could possibly be diagnosed ahead of the parent from whom he or she inherited the illness? Could Rebekka have been diagnosed before her father? No such examples were explicitly mentioned in the article.

Adam hurriedly tried to find answers elsewhere but was unable to find exactly what he was looking for, although one scholarly article by two reputable doctors stated that in ten per cent of cases, there was no family history of Huntington's in people diagnosed with the condition.

No family history? The simplest explanation in such cases must be an incorrect attribution of paternity. Alternatively, the parent from whom the patient had inherited the gene could have died of something else before exhibiting symptoms of the illness. It was also possible that the gene had come from a deceased parent who had been misdiagnosed with another serious illness.

Was it possible that Björn's wife did not have cancer but Huntington's disease? Adam found it very unlikely that such an error could have occurred in the modern Icelandic health system.

Perhaps Rebekka was one of the very few people diagnosed without the origin of the gene being identified. Adam did not think that likely. After all, he had been brought up by scientist lecturers who believed that explanations could be found for anything, if only things were researched in sufficient depth.

He had just stood up to stretch when the computer pinged a notification of a video meeting. Sesselja Hansdóttir must surely be at the police station.

This turned out to be right, but something more seemed to be happening. Soffía's face was much more serious than when they'd talked a few minutes previously. Adam felt a knot of anxiety in the pit of his stomach. Had the police become aware of his communication with Rebekka? In such a small community he should have known that it would come up, with him sitting on both sides of the table.

But the serious mood at the police station, which was almost tangible even through the internet, was due to something other than Adam's concealed information about Steindór's alleged stalker. Soffía looked directly at the webcam and informed her psychological consultant that this had now become a murder case. Katrín, Arngunnur's partner, had died from the head injuries received when she had fallen on the front door steps.

Adam felt a chill. Could people really die after missing their footing on the steps of their own home? Of course he knew that a blow to the head could be life-threatening, but it was just so tragic: a woman goes out to call her cat in … and dies.

"There's an aircraft on the way to collect her organs," Soffía added, not seeming to notice that Sesselja, who was sitting opposite her, grimaced. "I thought that was all suspended for the moment."

"I would have thought so," Adam agreed. "Aren't the organs usually taken to Sweden, where coronavirus is rife?"

"Has Arngunnur really had a request for *organs*?" Sesselja asked, her voice shaking, and looked anxiously at Soffía from beneath a thick fringe that reached below her eyebrows.

"Consent is no longer required. The law was changed." Soffía sorted a pile of paper on the table, apparently getting ready for the interview.

"Isn't consent needed?" Sessí sounded so frightened that it was as if she expected a surgeon with a knife and an organ donor bag to appear at the door at any moment.

"These days we're not just all civil defence. We're all organ donors." Soffía shrugged her shoulders. "Unless we specifically opt out."

Now Adam would have discreetly nudged Soffía if he had been sitting next to her. She did not always realise that what she took for granted would not strike others the same way.

"Do you know if there's anyone with her? Arngunnur, I mean?" Sesselja pulled a tissue from a box on the table and put it to her face.

No, Soffía didn't know that.

"Can I text Svenni about going to the hospital?"

"Svenni?"

"My brother, the one you were talking to. Bergsveinn, Svenni, Beggi! We met in the lobby earlier, he's definitely just in the car on the way home."

Adam was glad that Soffía could not see the flush of his cheeks, or she would immediately have realised that Adam was hiding something.

As Soffía explained to Sesselja that while visiting was not

DECEIT

allowed at the National Hospital, Arngunnur had only been allowed to rush in to say goodbye to her partner, Adam wondered about the nickname and the possibility that Bergsveinn could be considered likely to be Rebekka's biological father, even more so than Dóri.

The brothers could each have signed a letter to a girlfriend with an 'S'. But if Dóri had done that, the signature would not have been related to his nickname and thus more formal. Or so Adam felt. Therefore, it was even more likely that Bergsveinn had used 'S' as a signature.

It was also a problem that both brothers seemed to be in good health and that Adam was almost certain that Bergsveinn was gay. The latter, however, did not have to be an issue. Homosexuals could have had heterosexual relationships in the past, especially those who became adults before the struggle of gay rights campaigners caused a shift in societal attitudes.

Adam scribbled numbers down on a piece of paper and became a little thoughtful. Bergsveinn had been about twenty-two or twenty-three when Rebekka was conceived, in 1996 or 1997. Could a gay man have been sleeping with women at that age? It was possible. Civil partnerships had not become law until '96 and Pride had not begun to become properly visible until the turn of the century. Bergsveinn could well have been deep in the closet when the girl was conceived.

"Hey, Adam?"

He was startled as a loud voice from the computer called his name.

"Sorry! I was miles away. Ready now."

"We'll keep it short. Sesselja is going to meet Arngunnur. She's on her way home from the hospital."

"OK."

"Let's get into it." Soffía looked intently at the woman with high cheekbones and tousled hair. "These attacks on your siblings. The needles. Trying to undermine the guesthouse. Ice on the step that resulted in a fatality. Who could be at work?"

Sesselja crumpled the tissue and stretched at the same time. "Don't forget Mango."

It took Soffía a moment to realise what she meant.

"Yes, the dog. But this was not an assault on him."

"And whoever broke into Dóri's car."

"If it's part of it. We don't know. But, Sesselja, what's going on?"

Adam both saw and heard Soffía's impatience with Sesselja's irrelevant responses. She drummed her fingers on the table. But her restlessness was not helping.

"How the hell am I supposed to know what's going on, if the *police* don't know?"

Sesselja seemed to direct the question to herself rather than Soffía, who answered immediately.

"The root of it is with your brothers and sisters. That's clear. Maybe something that happened in childhood. Maybe something to do with money. Inheritance, perhaps?"

Sesselja leaned forward so that her fringe covered her eyes.

"I just can't think of anyone or anything. I mean, of course, there was often all sorts of trouble while Dad was alive and then after his death. The inheritance mess wasn't the most fun I've ever had. But we just got tough lawyers onto it. They sold the land and took care of everything."

"It was a lot of money."

"Sure. But the state took a large slice. Do you know how high inheritance tax is?"

"Wasn't it possible for Hafdís to continue to run the farm on behalf of your siblings?"

Sesselja seemed surprised.

"Hafdís? No, she was already ill by the time Dad died." Sesselja sighed. "Poor Dad had to take care of everything. It hit him terribly hard."

"Everything?"

"Yes, to get Hafdís to let it go. She loved the farm, loved the animals and she ran it extremely well. Dad was a little biased against her for a long time, just like many of his generation.

But he couldn't have had a better person with him. That's to say, while she had her health."

"Tragic."

"Incredibly tragic," echoed Sesselja, who had become very upset. "Dad had to take it all over and it was like taking sweets from a child. He was completely overwhelmed having to do this, the poor old guy. He also had to sort out all sorts of chaos Hafdís had caused without anyone realising."

"I understand." Soffía waited for more information.

"This was just as Dad had taken a step back due to his health. It wasn't because he was that old. It was just stress. Coronary artery disease and high blood pressure, you see. The workaholic had started to follow doctor's orders and relax. He even got into golf."

Sesselja smiled suddenly, but not for long.

"The tension around this turmoil with Hafdís definitely contributed to his death. It was absolutely devastating. You couldn't miss seeing it. His face had turned purple."

"How was the relationship with Hafdís? After she was persuaded to let go and moved to town?"

"There was practically none. She felt like we were all in some kind of plot with Dad. But we were just trying to lighten the burden for him." Sesselja sniffed. "It was only her illness that made her so suspicious. We knew that. But it wasn't pleasant to hear what she said about us."

"Who supported her at that time? Before she was admitted to the old ... the nursing home? She can't have had to cope with this alone?"

Adam mentally gave Soffía a point for this question. The months leading up to a dementia patient being admitted to an institution were often a difficult time. Hafdís could hardly have lived alone during that period. It must have been painful, transferring her to a nursing home, no less than persuading her to relax her grip on the operation of the farm. Had all this fallen on the father?

"Her cousin from Sweden," Sesselja replied curtly. "I

already told you about her, their mothers were sisters. Tove moved to Iceland temporarily to take care of Hafdís. But now she only comes to visit once or twice a year. Or maybe she just comes to collect a slice of the inheritance. It must be difficult to spend the money in Sweden for the benefit of its owner, who's in an institution in Iceland."

"What are you suggesting?"

"Of course I have no proof." Sesselja shrugged carelessly. "But she could probably buy all sorts of things when she's in Iceland, so it looks like it's for Hafdís. Clothes and jewellery, even furniture and white goods ... which she could then have shipped to Sweden."

Suspicion begins at home, thought Adam, listening in from Kaplaskjólsvegur.

35

Adam was relieved to get a break, which Soffía called a piss break, after the session with Sesselja. He got to his feet quickly and paced the floor to get his circulation going. It was such a short walk in this small space, so he took a few laps. When Covid broke out, it had troubled him that he had neither the space nor the equipment to exercise. A treadmill or an exercise bike would have allowed him to watch the BBC with fewer guilty feelings.

He wasn't just physically stiff. It had also been mentally draining to follow Soffía speaking to Bergsveinn and Sesselja. Adam's work at Sáló could also be tiring, especially when clients were on the lookout for compassion and cure-alls that required no effort on their part. But the procedures detectives had to go through in order to gather information were no less tiring. He could not understand how Soffía could do it.

The phone rang just as Adam turned up the volume on the television to watch a BBC report about a possible group infection in a nursing home. He quickly turned it down again.

"Hello?"

"Can you come with me to see Arngunnur?"

"*Hello, Soffía.*"

"What got into you?" She was not amused. "We are in the middle of a job. You can see my name on the screen. Should I have introduced myself?"

Adam switched tack.

"Isn't Dóri coming for an interview?"

"Afterwards, I mean. When he's done."

"Aren't you going to give Arngunnur some time to recover? She just lost her wife."

"That's exactly it. This is murder. She must want to help."

"Okay. I'll come along." He wanted to make sure that Soffía would not be too hard on Arngunnur. "But that does mean that Gunninga will have to postpone my clients again."

Adam did not expect thanks, he had expected Soffía to hang up without warning. But she unexpectedly posed a question about the session with Sesselja.

"What did I think of her?" He spoke slowly. "Well, much like I expected ... a lot of focus on money."

"She runs a business. She's that type."

Adam thought he could sense respect in Soffía's voice.

"Yes, but the insinuation about the Swedish woman at the end..." he muttered. "I think money just worries these siblings. Emil may be the only one who has really *enjoyed* his legacy."

"*Enjoyed?* A chunk of it went into paying off debts. He's hardly enjoyed it."

"No, all right. But he spent years living by the Mediterranean. That must have been enjoyable. He seems to be interested in the arts and is helping Greek artists to establish themselves in Iceland."

Soffía sighed.

"Adam! Emil spent the lot. The inheritance went to his creditors. Then he took it easy for a few years. What's cool about that? Or fun? Then he was forced to come home. And he's dying."

"I didn't mean..."

"And that gallery is a cubbyhole," she went on, without giving him an opportunity to continue. "He slept on a camp bed in the back room. And these Greek tapestries are crafts, not art. Even I can see that, and I know nothing about art."

Adam had no opportunity to protest. The call ended and moments later they connected via Facebook. This time

Steindór sat opposite Soffía at the police station, and she was about to start, with a statement rather than a question.

"You have a bodyguard." She jerked her head, presumably to indicate that the guard in question was on the other side of the wall.

When the sentence had hung in the air for a moment without Dóri replying, Soffía continued.

"What's going on? Has something happened?"

"Something else, you mean? You could say that."

Dóri put his elbows on the table and rested his head in his hands, as if it had suddenly become a great weight.

Adam saw that Soffía hurriedly moved her chair back from the table. In her place he would have worn a mask, as the police surely had to have sufficient supplies of safety equipment. But she was too much of a tough guy for that.

"Needles, spies, my car broken into, and now... a cyber-attack." Dóri emphasised the last words, like it heralded the end of the world.

"A cyber-attack? On you personally?"

"On mine and Sessí's company."

"She just left here. She didn't mention anything."

"I didn't tell her about this until just now in the corridor. I was trying to deal with the problem so she wouldn't have to know about it until everything was sorted. But everything is still in a mess and now Sessí is rushing down to Bar Three in a total panic."

"Aren't you going to see Arngunnur? Your sister-in-law just died."

Dóri puffed out his chest, as if an outburst was coming, but it quickly faded away.

"*Sister-in-law?* I met her three times at most! And we siblings aren't close, you know. We were just kids who met up at the farm every summer. Then Arngunnur moved to Denmark." He coughed. "But we'll definitely go to see her later today."

Soffía shook her head but did not follow up on this, as it was hardly the job of the police to examine family communications.

"This cyber-attack. When?"

"Last night. It's a terrible setback." Dóri gathered his strength and gestured emphatically. "Our website, accounting, shift schedules, online banking, communication with suppliers, orders from abroad. Nothing is accessible. So now I must insist that you take this seriously. I know there's a pandemic and all that, but we have the right to be taken seriously in this matter by the police. Naturally I didn't know what was going on when this needle business began, but... Well, now Arngunnur's wife is dead. And Emil's dog. And... and... and my brother's hotel almost burned to the ground ... and Emil with it!"

"But is there any business at the moment? The hospitality industry is paralysed."

Adam was sweating. Soffía had a unique way of sprinkling salt on wounds. Now it was as if she had put a firework under Steindór's chair and lit the touchpaper, as he rose from the chair seat and slammed a flat palm so hard on the tabletop that Soffía's pile of documents trembled.

"*Paralysed?* Yeah, everything is certainly shut down. Except for home deliveries! The demand to get food delivered is off the scale! People are bored to tears with cooking for themselves, day after day. They want to get the feel of eating out, at home. That's why Sessí and I were about to open Bar One and Bar Two as well, to take advantage of this opportunity. And then the computer system crashes! How do we get supplies, receive orders or payments, or make sure we have enough staff and cars?"

Although Soffía had quickly moved her chair away from the table, Steindór's saliva must have sprayed over her. If the man had the virus, she could hardly fail to be infected.

"Don't you have a systems analyst? Or a computer consultant? Someone who set up the system?" She was calm, but the response to this calm and logical question was like pouring oil on a fire.

"Computer consultant? Yes, we have a consultant! But where is he? I'll tell you where. He's in the hospital and is probably dying! So yesterday I was searching for someone else to help me. On a Sunday night and the whole world in quarantine. You can imagine just how easy that was."

Adam had been about to lift his mug to his lips but put it back untouched on a coaster on the table. Was Dóri's and Sessí's computer consultant at death's door? What could have happened to him or her? Was that possibly part of this strange case?

"Who's dying? Why didn't you mention this before?" Soffía spoke heavily.

"Mention it? You know all about it. It's Emil. He's been managing our computer system since he moved home from Greece."

"Is Emil a systems analyst?"

"Not formally, no, but the boy has been deep in computers since he was barely out of nappies. He can find his way around almost anything digital."

"I understand." Soffía scribbled something in a notebook.

"We had just that moment decided to change computer systems when he came back from Greece, shit broke as usual. So we got him to do it. Paid on the black. I'll admit that. But what don't you do for a sick man? It's hardly a crime to help your brother."

"Didn't Emil come home to have cancer treatment? Was he able to work?"

"It was inoperable and he didn't want chemotherapy. The doctors also said that it wouldn't be much help. But he was given an implanted port and regularly went to the hospital for treatment. It's some kind of morphine, I think. And he went for some radiation therapy, part of pain management. Then he takes all kinds of medicines for the side effects. It's a non-stop cycle."

"Did it ever occur to him to go to his mother in Tenerife?"

"It would have been too expensive. He had never registered

in Greece and was still legally a resident here, so this was the most cost-effective way of getting medical care and treatment." Talking about Emil's difficulties calmed Dóri down. "His mother's trying to get home, but travel is so complicated. Then she'll definitely need to go into quarantine and even after all that effort, it's not certain that she will be allowed to visit him."

An expression of concern appeared on Soffía's face.

"Emil doesn't have long left?"

Dóri shrugged indifferently.

"I have no idea. The hospital doesn't allow visits."

"You can make a call."

"I haven't had time to do that. There's so much going on right now." Dóri puffed out his chest, as if he had been pumped up.

Adam shivered in his warm living room on Kaplaskjólsvegur. The lack of connection between these siblings was chilling.

"But you're close relatives." Soffía's outrage was unmistakeable. "Considering his mother's not here."

Dóri started counting on his fingers.

"Look, I have a company that I can't keep open because of this virus, and a there are a lot of people working there. I can't get into any computer data related to my own business... or whatever's left of it. Our businesses have been under attack by this needle business, my brother's hotel was set on fire, my other brother almost lost his life in the fire and now my sister-in-law is dead! And then someone is stalking me day and night, God knows why, and the police ... are completely useless!"

Soffía opened her mouth and was about to say something but Dóri did not give her a chance.

"So I don't just have a bodyguard. I've also hired a lawyer who you are going to hear from today. It's a scandal how you've gone about this investigation. A scandal!"

Dóri finished by banging his clenched fist on the table.

"So you think you need a lawyer?" Soffía growled.

"Yes. If that's what's needed to light a fire under your arses and get you to do your jobs. He's drafting a formal complaint that you will get later today, and a copy to all major media outlets."

36

"If you were stuck in a lift with one of these *siblings*," Soffía made quote marks with her fingers, "who would you prefer to be stuck with?"

"For how long?" Adam asked in return.

She popped some chocolate-covered liquorice in her mouth and thought about it.

"Two hours. And there's no light in the elevator."

"Probably Emil. He could tell me about Greece. Or maybe Arngunnur, I'm sure there's a lot she could say."

"Not Sesselja and her legs-up-to-here?"

"No thanks. Better her than Steindór, however. That man is all ego, with a capital E."

"But he would break his way out. He's a big, strong guy."

Adam understood that Soffía would prefer to be locked up with Dóri for company, even though she talked about him practically with contempt. Human beings were strange creatures.

"Can you help me out a bit?" Soffía had parked the car half across the pavement, but remained in the driver's seat and ate more sweets without switching off the engine.

"Help you out?" he echoed. Had she thought him pushy for asking for access to the day's interviews? He had sat absolutely silent on his sofa at home and just watched.

"Yes, with Arngunnur." Soffía was awkward, which happened very rarely. "Y'know. Grieving people."

Adam understood. It must have cost Soffía a considerable

effort to ask this favour. Despite years as a police officer, she found it difficult to deal with newly bereaved people. In particular, she felt uncomfortable watching people in tears. As a psychologist, Adam, on the other hand, had endless experience of this. Of course, he found it more pleasant to hear people laugh, but crying was also a natural expression of emotions and there was no reason to be at a loss when someone shed tears.

"Absolutely," he said quickly. "Why have a paid psychologist if you can't make use of him in such a situation?"

"Thanks. You can take the lead. You know Arngunnur as a customer in her shop. Then I can throw in the odd question."

She handed him a box of disposable face masks, as if offering him a fancy box of chocolates, and indicated a similar box of latex gloves between the seats. She preferred to just sanitise her hands instead.

Adam turned down a mask as the chief epidemiologist kept insisting that these provided little protection, merely encouraging a false sense of security. But he sanitised his hands and put on gloves. That should be enough. A visit from the police would be enough of a trial for Arngunnur, even without the caller being hidden behind a mask. He would also try to not touch his face, although that was easier said than done.

The front door steps had been so thickly salted that it crunched under their boots, and two bags of industrial salt stood in a corner. Nobody would lose their footing here any time soon. A large outdoor candle had been lit by the door, even though it was still daylight. Adam knew why the candle was there but hoped that no bouquets of cut flowers in cellophane would be added. He felt it an unfortunate custom to let expensive flowers rot in places associated with tragic events.

A dark-haired, dark-eyed young man let them in, and a boy of a similar age, red-haired and freckled, was sitting in

Arngunnur's living room. These were the pair who rented the flat above. Nobody else was there, to Adam's surprise. He had expected an apartment full of relatives and friends, mostly women, but he had forgotten to take coronavirus into account. It went without saying that people were reluctant to visit those mourning under these circumstances.

"Our deepest condolences, Arngunnur." Adam felt that it was better to speak for them both, then Soffía would not have to extend her own sympathies. "This is Soffía Sigurðardóttir from CID and as you no doubt remember, I'm a psychologist. My name is Adam."

"Psychologist?" the red-haired boy repeated and looked curiously up at Adam.

Arngunnur looked up slowly, completely expressionless, and regarded them silently. Her eyes were swollen, empty and staring, and her cheeks were mottled red. She was curled up on a brown sofa covered with cushions in all the colours of the rainbow, wearing a patterned dress under which she had tucked her legs.

Adam had never seen her without jewellery before, without a single necklace, ring or bracelet. She had probably had to remove all of it for hygiene reasons at the hospital when she went to see Katrín for the last time.

"Yes, I'm advising the police on this case," Adam replied to the boy on the sofa. He and Soffía had not been offered a seat, so they stood in the middle of the floor, she a little behind him.

"This was no accident, someone poured water on the steps to make them slippery." The dark-haired boy was very upset. He also stood and looked at Soffía and Adam alternately as he spoke. "Róbert and I came home about an hour before Katrín fell, around eleven, and then there was no ice. Nothing at all, clean steps, just bare concrete. But when we heard Katrín cry out we ran down to check what was happening, I fell straight on my arse and Róbert only just managed to grab the doorknob, otherwise he would have landed on top of me. But

Katrín had rolled down the steps and must have hit her head, maybe more than once. There was a lot of blood and ... and the way she lay was somehow so strange."

The dark-haired boy was silent to catch his breath after blurting all this out.

"Ómar was lucky, he just broke his coccyx," his housemate added.

At this remark, Ómar, having caught his breath, seemed to forget for a moment that there was a woman who had lost her life partner that day sitting in the living room.

"It's not *just*, it's insanely painful. I had to buy an inflatable swimming ring to sit on, to protect the...it'll probably take weeks to mend."

Adam was about to gesture to Ómar how inappropriate it was to complain about pain in the arse under these circumstances, but then Arngunnur spoke suddenly, in a low voice.

"I had gone to bed, the bedroom's on the other side of the house," she whispered. "Katrín never wants to go to sleep until Púrra has come in."

Adam noticed that Arngunnur still talked about her partner in the present tense, which was common so shortly after a death. He glanced quickly at Soffía, ready to stop her if it looked like she was going to try to correct the use of tense. But Soffía was still standing in the middle of the room as if nailed to the floor, her mouth shut tight.

"It was really lucky that we heard her," Ómar continued when Arngunnur said no more. "Katrín, I mean. Our living room window is directly above the front steps and it was open while we were watching TV. There was a corny straight love scene with nobody talking just as she fell, so we both heard her call and rushed downstairs."

Adam sat down on a chair and motioned for Soffía and Ómar to follow his example. In a situation like this, it was important not to talk down to people – quite literally.

"Did you see anyone around, after you came out on the steps?"

He directed the question to Ómar and Róbert, as it was very unlikely that Arngunnur's attention had been focused on anything other than Katrín, in a bloody heap at the bottom of the steps. All three shook their heads.

"It was so late," Róbert explained. "The city's almost always deserted now. Everyone works at home and there are no tourists."

Ómar nodded his head in agreement, while Arngunnur stared silently into space. Adam suspected that she had taken some kind of sedative. Three glasses of red wine stood on the sofa table, of which two were almost empty, but the glass in front of her seemed untouched.

"Arngunnur."

He cleared his throat and waited for a moment to give her an opportunity to focus on what was going on in the living room. Her thoughts were obviously elsewhere.

"Hm?"

"I'm sorry, but I have to ask you a few questions, even though you've just returned from the hospital and Katrín has passed away. It's so important for the investigation."

"Dead. Kata's dead, "murmured Arngunnur, as if she were repeating foreign words she did not understand. "It hasn't sunk in yet."

"It's very understandable, it all happened so quickly."

Róbert and Ómar, sitting either side of Arngunnur, held her hands tenderly. Adam was glad she had the boys, considering there would be little support from her half-siblings.

"Did you or Katrín notice anything unusual in the last few days? Be sure to mention anything you can think of, anything could help. Anyone hanging around the house, anything through the letterbox, any weird phone calls?"

"Nothing." Arngunnur answered as he dropped the last word. "Well, the needles in the fruit. But you know all about that."

The red-haired boy, Róbert, sighed.

"Have you found this needle maniac? I saw online that needles have been found in all kinds of shops, all over the country. You don't think that the ice on the steps is related to all that stuff? Is everything going wrong in this country or what?"

"Or the whole world?" Ómar added. "The US President is in total denial and says corona is a chemical weapon from China. I think it's going to end in war, it's crazy."

Soffía gestured quickly to the tenants that they should take a step back. This was her first interaction with what was going on in the living room and the boys fell completely silent. Soffía had an authority about her, when she wanted to use it.

"Arngunnur, do you remember anything else apart from the needles?"

Adam tried to drag her back into the conversation, although he didn't agree with Soffía about completely shutting the boys up. Since they lived in the house, it was possible that they had important information.

"Yes... There was a strange phone call," she said, and her voice sounded like that of an automaton. "From Svenni."

"Do you mean Bergsvelnn, your half-brother?" Adam guessed, and he heard Arngunnur whisper *yes*. "Was this unusual? What did he want to talk about?"

"I don't think he's ever called me before," she said, and looked at Adam as if the sentence were a riddle it was his job to solve.

Silence.

"And what did he want from you, Arngunnur? Why did he call?"

Adam saw that Soffía was starting to get restless on the chair next to him but hoped she would let him finish. If she were to pressure Arngunnur with a careless choice of words, she'd retreat back into her shell.

"Who?" The grief-stricken woman had lost her thread.

"Svenni. Bergsveinn, your brother. What did he want?"

"I don't remember." Arngunnur's forehead furrowed as she thought. "It was something I didn't understand. Something about Emil, I think."

"About his illness, the cancer? Or maybe about the fire?"

"What?"

"Was this before or after the fire in the guesthouse? You remember, the fire at Bergsveinn's place. Was this after it? Or before?"

"After. Because Katrín was in the hospital but I wasn't allowed to be with her and didn't want my phone to be busy if the doctors needed it... I didn't want to talk about Emil and ... and ... whatever it was. The fire."

Adam tried as gently as he could to get Arngunnur to remember something more about Bergsveinn's message. When he had lost hope that he would succeed, he turned to the young men but that was also fruitless, although they both did their best to remember anything that might be relevant to the investigation.

He finally gave up, with Soffía's tacit agreement. They asked Arngunnur and the boys to stay put, as there was no need for them to show them to the door.

But as they were lacing up their shoes, Arngunnur came into the hall, tottering as if she had aged many decades.

"It was something about the needles. And computers. What Svenni was talking about on the phone. Computers and ... yes, no, wait ... letters ... I think. Or was it a door?"

"And do you remember why? Was he telling you something or maybe asking about something, or asking for something?"

"I don't remember. Can't you just ask him?"

37

"Computers and letters," Adam muttered. "Could it be about an email?"

Just outside Arngunnur's house, Soffía strode through the ankle-deep snow of the unfenced plot, the shortest way to the car. Adam had taken the rutted street.

"One side of a triangle is shorter than the sum of the other two." Soffía pointed her index finger at Adam, as if he had failed a maths test by not wading through the snow to save himself a few steps. She did not respond to his email hypothesis.

"Don't we have to talk to Bergsveinn?" Adam got into the car, took off his gloves and sanitised his hands carefully. "You, I mean. Can't you just call him now?"

"Aren't you a psychologist?" she asked. "Face to face is better than on the phone. We go to his place."

Naturally, she was right. But Adam wanted both to hear what Bergsveinn was saying and to get to the clinic as soon as possible. He needed to check whether anything important had been decided during his absence from that morning's meeting, and to go over notes about two clients who had appointments today.

He also felt he couldn't wait in uncertainty over how Rebekka was doing and whether she had taken the clothing to deCODE Genetics. How long would a DNA analysis take? Most of all, however, he had to somehow let the girl know that Dóri now had a bodyguard. It wouldn't be easy, since he – that is, Jenný – was not supposed to know who it was Rebekka suspected of being her biological father.

His only reassurance was knowing that she did not seem to have reached the point of wanting to end her own life. That meant Dóri was in no immediate danger of death, although she could continue to harass him. But if the bruiser Dóri had hired to defend him were to get a hold of Rebekka, her life could be even more difficult than it already was. That was something that Adam wanted to try to prevent happening.

"You could start with a call to Bergsveinn to find out what he has to say," he suggested to Soffía as she started the car. It was a shame that it was such a short journey from Grjótathorp to the western end of town, he was too tired to tag along with her to see Bergsveinn, based on Arngunnur's vague recollection. The man lived all the way up in Mosfellsbær.

"You could go and see him if you don't get enough out of him on the phone," he added.

"We, you mean," said Soffía, quickly correcting him.

It was clear that she had no intention of letting him go straight away. The invoice for the police would be a hefty one, evening rates, weekend rates, pandemic surcharge, plus anything else he could dream up.

"Stop!" Adam called out suddenly as Soffía reached for the bag of liquorice she kept between the seats.

But his warning came too late, her hand had already dipped into the crackling plastic bag. Adam snatched the sweet bag from her without thinking, rolled down the car window, and tipped the contents on the pavement.

He then dropped the bag on the rubber mat in the footwell. Even in this situation, dropping a plastic bag on the street didn't occur to him. But the liquorice was organic. Even if it did not rot there on the street, it would probably end up in a seagull, or a rat. The thought ran through his mind that chocolate-covered liquorice might be dangerous to animals, but this was no time to worry about that.

Soffía stared at him for a moment, frozen, her mouth open in a silent cry, too surprised to utter a word.

"Sanitise your hands!" He pointed to the bottle of alcohol gel next to the liquorice bag.

"Are you crazy?" she finally groaned. "Throwing away my sweets?"

"You can't just grab sweets without sanitising your hands and then stuff them in your mouth, Soffía. Not after just leaving a stranger's house, in the middle of a pandemic."

"That's my problem, Adam! No business of yours."

"It is! When we have to meet every day and be together in a car and spend time with all kinds of people. If you get infected, the chances are I am as well." Adam sighed. "And maybe Magga," he added. "Don't forget her."

"I used sanitiser before we went in." Soffía rolled her eyes, unmoved by his logic. "And didn't touch a single damn thing."

"You touched the knob on the front door three times and leaned against the wall in the hall, both when you put on and took off your shoes."

"Christ! Do you keep tabs of everything I touch? And so what? Was there a nasty virus on the wall? Exactly where I put my hand?"

Adam had no answer to this, but picked up the bottle, and aimed the pump.

Although Soffía heaved an ungrateful sigh, she accepted two generous splashes of sanitiser, and massaged it carefully into her hands, between her fingers and all the way up to the wrist. Adam interpreted this meticulousness as some sort of apology. Soffía was not one to admit mistakes or to ask for forgiveness directly.

"Can't you call Bergsveinn and ask about this conversation with Arngunnur that she couldn't remember?" he asked. "I would really appreciate it if you tried that first. Let's not waste any time with a trip to Mosó. I'm expecting two clients, I can't have Gunninga reschedule their appointments yet again."

Soffía took a deep breath and seemed to pull herself together. She took out her phone and had her index finger poised over the screen when it rang in her hand.

"Hello," she said as she slammed the phone to her ear.

Since Soffía did not introduce herself, Adam assumed that she knew the caller. He guessed it had to be a work call. Margrét had recently told him that her mother did nothing but work, exercise and watch Netflix. She rarely met her friends and had never been persuaded to try Tinder, not even before the pandemic.

"You're the only one she wants," Margrét had said, almost accusingly. "Why else do you think she suggested you work with her in this needle case?"

"Maybe because the police are under loads of pressure and I'm a smart psychologist?" Adam asked in return, a little hurt... perhaps more than just a little. He thought that with this supposition, Margrét was undervaluing his professional skills. This was also complete nonsense on her part. Soffía certainly had no interest in renewing their relationship, they had been in complete agreement that their marriage had run its course.

"Why can't you just get back together?" Margrét didn't give up after just one attempt. "You're not dating anyone else either and nobody understands why you split up. You're the typical couple who complement each other."

This would have been the ideal juncture to tell Margrét about Jenný. But she had come out with all this so unexpectedly that Adam had not been prepared for the Conversation with the big C. But the question was whether he would ever be able to discuss this with his daughter.

Soffía was finishing the work call and Adam was trying to dispel thoughts of the difficult conversation with Margrét.

"OK, I'll see to this. I'll call the doctor. Bye."

Soffía ended the call and looked thoughtfully into space for a moment. Adam desperately wanted to know what was going on but pretended to be completely indifferent. If she sensed his interest, she would just wait longer to explain the matter to him.

"Emil has been moved from A&E," she finally said. "There was space on the oncology ward. Or they made space. They put a bed in a waiting room. And some doctor contacted the station."

"The police station? Why?"

"Emil's mother called from Tenerife. She wants to come."

"What's that got to do with the police? "Adam didn't grasp the connection. "Is the woman on some wanted list? And why is a doctor at the National Hospital getting involved in this?"

Soffía sighed.

"She was asking the doctor to explain the situation to Víðir."

"Which Víðir?"

"The one and only. So she doesn't have to quarantine."

Adam barked with laughter, even though the matter was deeply serious.

"She wants to come here from a country that is one of the worst affected in all of Europe, skip quarantine and go directly to the National Hospital?" He looked at Soffía in amazement. "Why didn't someone just say no right away?"

"The situation is better in Tenerife than in mainland Spain."

"It's still bad. There are restrictions and people who come from there must quarantine, no question. Here, relatives of dementia patients aren't even allowed to see them in nursing homes, even if they swear to stay in isolation at home between visits. You shouldn't trouble Víðir with this. The whole country is in an unprecedented situation, she'll just have to accept it."

"But Emil is dying." Soffía's mouth was tightly pursed, her eyes unusually bright. "Imagine ... if this was Magga."

"Of course I understand his mother's situation, Soffía. Very well, in fact. But rules are rules."

They were silent for a moment.

"Will he die in the next few days? Could he have weeks, or even months? Then the situation could improve, both here and in Spain. Until then they can talk to each other online."

"She's called him." Soffía sighed. "A video call. But he was on strong painkillers. Drowsy and confused. That's why she's so desperate to come home."

"And are you really going to go to Víðir with a request for an exemption?"

"I promised to ask."

Soffía turned her attention to the phone, scrolled down the list of names and tapped the screen with her finger when she found the number she was looking for. She took a deep breath as she waited for an answer. Moments later, she spoke.

"Hello, Víðir, this is Soffía. Could you call me? This is about a sick man who's connected to an investigation. His mother is the next of kin. But she's in Tenerife. Is there a way to exempt her from quarantine?" She paused to catch her breath. "I know you're swamped. Sorry. Talk soon."

Adam shook his head. There was nothing to be envied about the work being done by the trio who were the public face of the Covid prevention measures.

"Make a choice." Soffía turned to him, as if challenging him to a duel. "Come with me to see Bergsveinn, now or in the morning?"

"In the morning," he replied instantly. "But I still think you could do this over the phone."

"I'll be outside at eight-thirty."

"OK. But you're definitely going to call ahead so you know he'll be home?"

"Take it easy. I'll let him meet us at the guesthouse."

"But you're dropping me off at Sáló now, aren't you?" Adam had heard a note of finality in her voice. "I have all sorts of things to sort out before my clients arrive."

Soffía snorted as she put the car in gear and drove off.

"Did you think I'd just drop you in a ditch?"

Adam left that question unanswered.

DECEIT

TUESDAY 07.04.2020

Approximately eighty individuals were diagnosed with Covid-19 yesterday.

More than six hundred people are in home isolation.

The health administration team urges Icelanders to stay home for Easter.

The British Prime Minister has been transferred to an intensive care unit.

38

It was only a quarter past eight when a text message told Adam that Soffía had arrived. He had actually been ready for a while and was wondering if he should call Björn before another session with the police. Adam had been too tired to talk to him after coming home from the clinic the night before. Without a clear head, he didn't feel comfortable contacting Björn.

It was probably too early to call now and besides, it wouldn't do to spend only fifteen minutes talking to him. He would have to try to reach Björn later in the day. So Adam put on his winter shoes and coat and hurried out to meet Soffía, who put on a mask when she saw him approaching the car.

"Didn't you say half past eight?" he muttered.

Soffía said nothing but put her foot down so vigorously that the car spun ninety degrees on the slippery road. She cursed into the collar of her coat, straightened the car and drove off at a more sedate pace.

"Dóri's given up on the idea of stirring up trouble." She was gloating. "He'd have come out worse. The chicken!"

Her caution while driving did not last long. As she turned onto Hringbraut, the car slid across the road. Adam managed not to complain about this carelessness, seeing as Soffía had brought him news of interesting developments.

"We need to talk about more than just the phone call with Arngunnur. With Bergsveinn, I mean. The investigation team got in touch. There's a suspicion of insurance fraud."

"*Insurance fraud*?" he repeated slowly, as if practising the pronunciation of a foreign word. "In connection with the arson?"

"Yeah."

Adam digested this for a moment.

"Do you mean that Bergsveinn may have...?"

"It looks that way."

"But... Soffía, this changes so many things. Then the arson isn't part of the attacks on the siblings' businesses."

"Agreed." Soffía nodded her head vigorously. "Perhaps he just took the opportunity. Maybe hoped that we'd pin it on the needle maniac. Which we naturally did."

Adam's mind was in overdrive.

"But then how was this discovered... Fraud? I don't know anything about fire investigation."

"He had just upped the insurance. By a hell of a lot." Soffía gestured with one hand.

"Upped it?"

"Y'know. Increased the insured value of the property. The payout if something happens. That always rings alarm bells."

"That's hardly enough, in itself?"

"No, but then the scene was examined extremely carefully."

"And did they find something?" Adam could hardly imagine a more tedious job than a fire scene investigation, it must be like looking for a needle in a haystack.

"Traces of glue." She sounded proud of her colleagues' success. "The letterbox on the front door was glued down."

"Down?" Adam asked, confused.

"Closed. Glued shut. Well, or it could be. Seems to be."

"It's not certain?"

Soffía did not answer the question directly, but explained that if the team's theory was correct, the fire could not have had its origins outside the building.

"Maybe someone broke in first and then started it," Adam suggested.

"No signs of a break-in."

He suddenly realised what this meant.

"Yes. But if Bergsveinn started the fire, Soffía ... deliberately and inside the building ... it's not just insurance fraud. His brother could have lost his life in the fire. This is much worse than if it had been someone else, like the needle guy, someone who didn't know about Emil sleeping in the cellar." He broke into a fit of coughing. "Bergsveinn endangered a human life. That makes this an attempted murder."

Soffía was nodding like a wind-up toy while Adam was talking.

"He gets to walk around a free man and we're going to meet him, as if nothing has happened." Until now Adam had had a fair amount of faith in the Icelandic police but he found this overwhelming. "Why hasn't he been arrested?"

"Preliminary results from the investigation just came in." Soffía seemed to enjoy seeing Adam so agitated. "And now we're on our way to see him."

"Are you going to arrest him? Just you alone and without any protective gear? What if he punches you and tries to run away?"

"Well, then you can chase him."

"I have no authority to do so!" He suspected Soffía was joking, but was not sure. In Britain, lawbreakers could be subject to a citizen's arrest if no law enforcement officer was present. Maybe this also existed in Iceland. "I'm not getting closer than two metres to him."

"Relax." Soffía rocked with laughter. "There are more than us on the way."

Adam was very relieved. But when they drove into the street where the small hotel was, there were no signs of police backup.

"The patrol cars won't come right away." Soffía seemed to have read his thoughts. "I want to talk to Bergsveinn first. Before he figures out what we know."

"Should we go in without backup?" Adam did not like this idea. "This is an alleged murderer, Soffía!"

She slid the car into a tight parking space in front of the guesthouse, switched off the engine, and peered out the window.

"We'll be completely safe," she said calmly. "The place looks to be packed with builders."

Adam's Covid anxiety soared to new heights. He had thought it bad enough to meet Bergsveinn alone. Should he now wade through a crowd of strangers to talk to an alleged criminal?

Lights were on inside the hotel and a man in white overalls could be seen filling window frames while another wearing a baseball cap was scraping a wall. Although both had masks and all the windows were open, Adam was still uneasy in this unexpected situation. But he could hardly consider leaving Soffía alone for this, seeing as he was already there. He would just have to be very cautious.

He felt calmer when Soffía put on gloves without a word and winked at him as she did so. This showed him that she understood his concern. Together they then ventured into the lion's den, her in front and him, a little unsure, a few steps behind.

I'm turning into Prince Philip, he thought. *Follow your wife like a puppet while she's at work, without having a clear role to play.* Actually an ex-wife in this case, which made it even more awkward.

They came to a brand-new door, as the old one had been destroyed in the fire and its remains were probably in the fire investigator's lab. The door was open so they did not have to knock or ring the bell, and Soffía took the opportunity to stick gloved fingers through the letterbox as she stepped into the hall. This letterbox was not glued down.

"Good morning, folks!" Soffía called but got no answer. "Bergsveinn? This is Soffía. Are you here?"

"Jesus," yelped the white-clad figure at the window in a shrill voice, and dropped his scraper on the floor. "You gave me a shock!" The woman pulled off large black headphones with paint splashes with one hand. She put her other hand over her heart. "I'm sorry, I didn't hear you! Then all of a sudden I saw a black shadow."

Soffía did not respond to this.

"Bergsveinn is supposed to meet us. Is he here?"

"Is that the owner? I think he's in the basement."

Now the other painter had also noticed them, a man with cheerful eyes. He pointed with his index finger down at the floor, a sign that they should head downstairs, but by then Soffía had already headed into the living room and was on her way to the basement steps. Adam hurried after her.

Bergsveinn heard footsteps on the stairs and came to meet them. He was stony-faced and did not bother to return Soffía's polite greeting, instead turning on his heel to go into a windowless room that seemed to double as a storage room and an office.

"I moved the office temporarily into the store room while Emil was staying here," he explained, offering them a seat on garden chairs. He himself sat down in front of a laptop on a small wooden table from the same set of garden furniture.

"How are you coping with getting the place back together?" Soffía sounded as if she was really interested in the answer and squeezed out a smile. She reminded Adam of a cat creeping up to its prey with its belly on the ground.

"It's going well, thanks. I've got good builders. But there's something wrong with the online bank, it's driving me nuts."

Bergsveinn stared grumpily at the computer screen with no apparent interest in what the police wanted. Soffía straightened up on the hard wooden chair and coughed to get his attention.

"We saw Arngunnur yesterday," she said. "She is, naturally, in shock. The fact that you had called her recently came across as odd."

"Oh?" Bergsveinn tapping absently at the computer. "Arngunnur and I rarely talk to each other."

"Exactly. That's why you should remember why it was that

you called her." Soffía's words were almost drowned out by noise from the floors above where someone was using a grinder. Bergsveinn groaned theatrically and pointed at the ceiling.

"I'm also under pressure now."

"You talked about Emil. In this call. And maybe letters and a computer. Emails, maybe?"

"Computer? It's possible that I mentioned this problem with the online bank." Bergsveinn pointed to the laptop on the desk. "I just don't remember. But not email. Or ... I don't think so."

"Bergsveinn!" Soffía's patience was running out.

"OK, OK." He tore his gaze away from the computer and looked straight into Soffía's eyes. "It was just this thing with Emil, where he would go when he's released from hospital. Arngunnur has always got on better with him than the rest of us have. So I was asking her to help me sort him out." The hotel owner looked around and then back at Soffía. "I can't have him here any longer. The place is packed with builders during the day and deserted at night. It's no place for a sick man."

"What could your sister have done?"

"I was hoping she would invite him to stay with them. At least then he would be around people. Of course I didn't know about Katrín and the accident when I called, and Arngunnur hadn't told anyone."

"By sorting out Emil, you meant take him in, then?"

"Well, yes. Or, at least help me make him understand that he could not come back here. That's just what we were talking about. I told her about the fire, she told me about Katrín and then she pretty much hung up on me. So nothing came out of the call, which is why I hardly remember it."

Footfalls from upstairs and an echo of conversation indicated that the reinforcements Soffía had requested had arrived. It seemed to Adam, however, that Bergsveinn didn't notice.

"*Bergsveinn.*" Soffía crossed her arms and addressed him portentously. "This isn't looking good."

39

Bergsveinn's face flushed red, as quickly as if someone had turned a switch. Adam had no doubt that the man had something to hide. But had he really started a fire that could have killed his brother? He was not as convinced of that as Soffía was.

"Tell me the truth now," Soffía continued in a dramatic tone. "Did you just increase the insurance here?"

"It wasn't me." His voice quivered like a violin string.

This response seemed feeble for a grown man, and Soffía laughed.

"Just like that! You mean someone else increased the insurance? Because it was raised, you know that. By quite a lot."

Now not only was Bergsveinn red-faced, but beads of sweat appeared on his forehead.

"I have this in hand with the insurance company. This is between me and them."

Soffía waited for further explanation, watching him intently. It worked. Bergsveinn wiped his forehead with the back of his hand before continuing.

"I don't understand what happened. The insurance value was set too low, I know that, and that was a mistake. But now the amount is unbelievable. And it wasn't me who asked for this increase. Why would I want to be paying higher premiums while the hotel's empty? Do you think that I have nothing better to do with my money than hand it to some insurance company?" He was angry and it made him bolder. "And what are you asking about insurance for? It's not a police matter."

"Yes, Bergsveinn. It's a police matter if the letterbox on the front door was glued shut. That means the fire couldn't have been started by someone outside. The source of the fire must have started inside the building. There was no indication of a break-in. And there was a sick man in the basement, your own brother. That adds up to attempted murder."

Bergsveinn was on his feet as soon as Soffía dropped that final word. Adam also got up quickly, ready to step out into the hallway if the man were to start throwing furniture around. All the same, he was more concerned about him spraying saliva at them. After recent civil defence briefings, Adam knew all about droplet and airborne transmission.

"Hell!" Bergsveinn lifted his arms in exasperation but did not touch any furniture or anything else in the store room. "What's going on? Don't the police have enough to do with the pandemic and everything that comes with it? Do you also need to persecute innocent citizens?"

Soffía turned to Adam.

"Can you call the guys upstairs?" she said. "They're taking this gentleman down to the station."

But Adam did not have to call anyone. Two bulky police officers, masked and gloved, stood in the hallway and now approached the store room. They had crept very quietly down the stairs.

"To the police station? Are you out of your mind?" Bergsveinn dropped back into the chair. "Are you arresting me?"

"Do you keep your passport here?" Soffía showed no signs of sympathy for Bergsveinn, who leaned forward on the table, his face in his hands.

"No," he sighed in resignation, without looking up. "Why would I? It's at home in Mosó."

"Start by taking him home," Soffía said to the uniformed officers who now stood in the doorway. "He needs to get his passport. You go inside with him. Then bring him to the station."

Soffía's only concession to Bergsveinn was to ask the officers to use the basement door, so he would not have to be escorted past the builders.

"You don't understand, I haven't done anything! Am I to be taken in a police car like a criminal? What do you think the neighbours will say? Can innocent people be treated like this?" Bergsveinn complained as he was led out.

"What's the deal with the passport?" Adam asked as the door closed behind the three of them.

"I don't want to let him have an opportunity to leave the country. He'll most likely be released after questioning."

He decided not to ask how Bergsveinn would be able to flee the country, now that there were virtually no passenger flights.

"Have you heard from Víðir?"

They got to the car and Adam was pleased to see Soffía pick up the sanitiser without him having to nag.

"Yeah, he called last night. Emil's mother gets an exemption. With extremely strict conditions."

"Understandably."

"But it's difficult to find flights. So she isn't coming right away."

As soon as Soffía had finished with the sanitiser, she pulled out an open bag of liquorice sweets from her coat pocket.

"Want one?" She offered the bag of sweets to Adam, who shook his head.

"Don't you upset your stomach by eating liquorice so early in the morning?" he asked.

"I'm not a delicate flower like you." Soffía popped two into her mouth and chewed energetically. "That's just what I needed."

"Look, didn't you find Bergsveinn's explanations strange?"

"What explanations?" Soffía snorted. "He just denied everything."

"But saying that somebody else must have changed the insurance so his guesthouse gets a higher payout. Don't you think that's odd?"

"It's all very odd with this needle business and *everything connected to it*. And before I forget, more needles were found. Late yesterday, in two shops. But all whole needles so I'm leaving someone else to worry about them. Is that all right with the shrink?"

Adam nodded and watched thoughtfully as Soffía stuffed more liquorice into her mouth, then crammed the bag into her pocket and started the car.

"No, wait," he said as she was about to pull away.

She looked at him in surprise.

"The needle thing and everything connected to it," he muttered to himself. "That's what you said yourself. Did you mean that you thought the fire here was related to the needles and all that?"

"No, I just meant..." Soffía stared back in surprise. "Yes, Bergsveinn is naturally connected to the other issue. Therefore... What are you thinking?"

"I'm thinking you were a little too quick to arrest Bergsveinn."

"He hasn't been arrested."

"You know what I mean. As far as he's concerned, it's as good as being arrested, being publicly led out to a police car."

"So what?" Soffía said and her black tongue showed.

"This could be part of the needle case," Adam said hesitantly. "As you yourself inadvertently said."

She waited for a further explanation, looking doubtful.

"What he said about someone else increasing the insurance amount. I know it sounded childish. But Bergsveinn doesn't come across as stupid. Would a man with his business experience really try such an obvious fraud?"

"Adam, we know nothing about this man's business career, only what he's told us himself. He may be an addict. Or connected to the drug trade. Cornered people make mistakes.

They do stupid things. The kind of stuff anyone else would know can't add up."

Adam knew that Soffía spoke from her long experience in the police. She had become acquainted with an underworld where completely different rules applied to those in the society where normal people lived. Most of what he knew about crime came mainly from thrillers on television. But he had gained extensive experience as a psychologist over decades and could be perceptive about people.

"I agree that Bergsveinn didn't tell us the whole truth," he admitted. "But I still found him credible in connection with what you accused him of. He almost started crying when you didn't swallow what he told you. I think someone sent the insurance company a request to raise the insurance value as a prank."

"This was some damn prank! He would quickly have realised that the premiums were higher. Then he could have got it changed. Or not, since he had too low a valuation before. Problem solved."

Soffía felt this was clearly settled because she drove off.

"I need to get home now, I'm expecting a call," Adam lied.

"It'll have to be a short call then. You'll be following the Bergsveinn interrogation. OK?"

Adam's answer was drowned out by a phone call that Soffía was quick to answer, and a male voice echoed through the car.

"Hi, this is Gummi, from forensics. I just wanted to let you know that it's confirmed about the glue, in connection with the fire at the guesthouse. The letterbox had been glued shut."

Adam looked at Soffía in surprise, but of course did not interrupt the conversation between the two colleagues, waiting instead in shock with a questioning look on his face.

"Great. Thanks for this."

"Then what you asked about this morning. I checked and there were three fire extinguishers in the building, all recently serviced. Two were still in their brackets, but one was lying on the floor where the man was found. He seems have grabbed it and tried to put out the fire but gave up, either because he was overwhelmed by the smoke or because he couldn't get it to work. These things aren't light and I understand from the paramedics that he's no strongman."

"No, exactly. Listen, it was great to get this. Bye."

Adam almost forgot what he had been waiting to say to Soffía when he heard her say goodbye to this Gummi before ending the call. Did the woman show everyone more courtesy than to him? He decided, however, to not mention this for now.

"You're just now getting confirmation of that thing with the glue? You claimed this was fact and accused Bergsveinn of attempting to murder his brother."

He made it clear that she had also told him about the glue on the letterbox as if it was a fact.

"You heard what the man said." Soffía shrugged. "There was glue. No harm done."

40

Adam wanted to call Björn as soon as he got home to Kaplaskjólsvegur, although not without first allowing himself time to make tea. Everything was better with tea at hand and for this call there was more need than ever. He was going to break a rule he had always respected. It could have serious consequences, but he was nevertheless convinced that he was doing the right thing. Today, Adam was going to break confidentiality.

Björn answered, short of breath and his voice thin, a split second after Adam had pressed the call button. He had to be consumed with worry, obviously tired from lack of sleep and no less in need of help than Rebekka.

"Hello, Björn. This is Adam, the psychologist. I really don't mean to intrude, but ... sorry, am I bothering you?" Adam had only just stopped himself from asking the man if everything was all right. That would have been a very unfortunate choice of words, seeing as it was unlikely that anything was going well for Björn at the moment.

"You and your daughter have been on my mind," he added hastily, not wanting to give him false hope that he might have any useful information or advice to offer. "Is there any news of your daughter?"

Björn sighed heavily into the phone and Adam moved it a little away from his ear.

"Nothing good, I'm afraid, nothing good, no. She refuses to move in with me even though I've been trying to persuade her.

I think it would be better for both of us."

Adam agreed. Rebekka needed to be in a place of safety. But her mental state was probably too splintered for her to see that for herself.

"I have told her many times that of course she will have complete freedom, even if she is living here with me," Björn continued. "She could bring these men she's sleeping with home, if that's what she wants. I wouldn't be annoyed by it, or with the cannabis. If I just knew where she was and could only take care of her in between her binges, or whatever you want to call them. Make sure she's eating. Then I'd feel better and so would she, I'm convinced of that. But she won't even consider it, unfortunately."

Adam checked the time. Soffía should have arrived at the police station by now and would soon start Bergsveinn's interrogation, which he had to watch. He had to get to the point.

"Do you know if Rebekka has found someone to analyse the genetic material from the sportswear she put in the vacuum pack?" he asked cautiously.

Another long sigh echoed over the phone.

"I know little more than what her friend tells me and she says she doesn't know how it's going. They rarely meet, the girls, even though they're flatmates. My Rebekka seems to have turned day and night around. But this man, her biological father, it's a real obsession." Björn inhaled sharply. "I don't know how this will end, Adam, I'm telling you the truth. I thought nothing could be worse than losing Fanney but, you know, this is so much more painful. Because Rebekka should have her whole life ahead of her, her whole life, and because she doesn't want any help..."

"This must be an incredibly difficult time." Adam knew that only those who had been in Björn's situation could fully understand his pain.

"I'm trying to get her to meet Jenný again," Björn continued, "but there's little I can do when she doesn't answer the phone and I have no idea if she's getting my messages, she answers them so rarely."

Adam cleared his throat and tried to calm his nerves.

"Look, Björn. I need to tell you something in complete confidence. Something that I absolutely shouldn't talk about at all, because it's connected to some consulting work I undertook for the police. So I'm not exaggerating when I say that you mustn't tell another living person about this. But maybe you can still do something – something to stop your daughter – when you know what's at stake."

"I don't understand what you mean. Is Rebekka involved in some police case? Is it the theft, this sportswear, or some illegal substance?"

Björn sounded even more worried and tense than at the beginning of the call, but Adam had gone too far to be able to turn around.

"No, nothing like that, Björn. Not directly. But the man she has her eye on, the one whose clothes she snatched, he has become very worried about his own welfare. Very. And now he's hired a bodyguard. You know, a weightlifter type, you understand?"

Björn was silent for so long that Adam was worried that he had walked away from the phone.

"Are you still there?" he asked carefully.

"I'm just taking this in. Look, do you think he could harm her? The bodyguard?"

"Not if she stops tracking her supposed biological father."

"And you think I can get her to stop?" Björn's voice demonstrated how helpless he felt.

"Even if you mention neither me nor the police, you could tell her, and her friend, that you know for sure about this weightlifter. It's no longer a game. This is cold, hard reality. These men will not hesitate to use violence. Would that make her think twice?"

"I'll try, I'm ready to do anything." Björn still sounded like he could hardly swat a fly, let alone anything that required more energy.

Before saying goodbye, Adam reiterated that Björn was welcome to contact him at any time, as was Rebekka. He then apologised repeatedly and said he had to end the conversation, he was needed at an important meeting.

He hadn't realised until he had hung up that when he mentioned Rebekka, he had not mentioned that it was Jenný she could call, not Adam. But the anxiety in his stomach eased almost immediately. Even if Björn had noticed this or he suspected something, the desperate father no doubt hardly cared, and had other things on his mind.

Adam was surprised that Soffía had not yet tried to open a connection over Facebook. Had Bergsveinn demanded a lawyer, as was common in police interrogations in films? That might explain the delay.

After making sure twice that both the computer and the internet connection worked, he used the time to put a frozen blueberry waffle in the toaster and ate it greedily with a scoop of ice cream. It was not a meal time, let alone a coffee break, but he needed something sweet right now. And it turned out, he need not have hurried, as there was still nothing from Soffía.

When the phone finally did ring, he was immersed in a BBC News report on the pandemic. Hardly anything else was on the news these days.

"Did you forget me?" he asked in an attempt to strike a light chord, even though he was half annoyed.

"Don't be childish." She had never been one for humour, unless cruel teasing could be classified as a joke. "I'm letting Bergsveinn cool his heels at the station. He's not very happy with that."

"Aren't you at the station?"

"No, just coming out to the car. From the hospital. Emil's doctor called me."

"Is he dead?"

"No. But he doesn't feel well. Mentally, I mean. He's naturally on some high-strength painkillers."

"Wouldn't it have been better to call his siblings? Or let him talk to his mother on Skype or something?"

"He had just talked to her. It did him no good. And the siblings are not a good idea. There's a ban on visiting. I had to follow the regulations and wear a space suit. I needed two nurses to help me put it on."

"Are you going to tell me what's going on, Soffía, or should I keep guessing?"

"I could have done with you there. But I didn't get the green light for that."

Adam expected this was meant to be a compliment, even a kind of white flag, as he waited further explanation.

"He's suffering terrible paranoia. Maybe it's the drugs. What do I know? He's furious with everyone. Even his mother. You should have heard the language he used."

"Didn't you ask the doctor if this could be due to his medication?"

"It affects people in different ways. He said something about old wounds. Emotions that come to the surface. Emil thinks everyone hates him."

"Isn't there some truth in that? You're now going to interrogate the man who could have put his life in danger, just a few days ago. His dog's dead, although no doubt by accident, and no one wants to let him live with them."

"He didn't mean that," Soffía objected. "Or I don't think so. When he was little, he said. Pretty devastating bullying, going by the descriptions."

"Bullying? Tell me more."

Countless alarm bells began to ring in Adam's head, telling him to pay more attention to this. This was the mental anguish of a very sick person, but nevertheless fascinating from a psychologist's point of view. To him this problem seemed to be taking a sudden new turn with this fresh information.

"The big kids, he said. They locked him away. Beat him up. Pissed in his schoolbag. Never left him alone. For years, you understand. They told him to go and drown himself in the river. He thought about it, really thought about it," Soffía sighed. "Hell, kids can be really revolting."

"Did this happen at school?" Adam waited for the answer with bated breath.

"He didn't say. And yet. The thing with the school bag must have happened there."

"Soffía, I think I've solved this thing."

"What thing?"

"Well, the thing that you wanted me to help you with."

"The needles?"

"Not only that, pretty much everything, in fact."

"Really? Are you going to explain this then?"

Adam took a deep breath.

"Not right now. Drive down to the station and get coffee and whatever. Give me some time to think. And then call before you start questioning Bergsveinn. That's absolutely crucial. Not when you're already in the room with him, but before you go in."

"Yes, boss."

This could almost be classified as a goodbye and even something close to a joke.

41

Adam sat down at what served as both kitchen and dining room table in his small living space. There he spread out handwritten notes and printouts from the internet and immersed himself in the details. Among the aspects he concentrated on was the chronology of certain events and the whereabouts of certain individuals, as far as it could be determined. Most of the time, though, he wondered about the people involved.

He was certain that his guess was right. This was not tangible, scientific evidence that could be examined and analysed under a microscope. But he was certain he was on the right track, or as sure as he could be of a theory formulated more or less independently at home. Decades of experience in helping people to work their way through psychological turmoil and to process volatile emotions had brought him the intuition and sensitivity that now came in useful. After all, he believed that it was exactly this ability that Soffía had in mind when she brought him in.

The only problem was that if his hypothesis turned out to be correct, it would be better for the police to address all the siblings together, not just Bergsveinn. But doubtless the pandemic rules made that impossible and in addition, Arngunnur had just lost her partner. Adam left Hafdís out of his reckoning, and as she was in a nursing home, there was no point in involving her in this.

It could be possible to talk to the siblings remotely, but

Adam had doubts that this would work. The matter was also far too sensitive for him to ask Soffía to meet him and the siblings in the open air, such as in Laugardalur or Nauthólsvík. He scratched his head with a pen, and started when he realised there was no cap on it.

He was writing down key words when Soffía called.

"Well? Now I can't keep Bergsveinn waiting any longer."

"He didn't set fire to the guesthouse."

"Are you sure? What about him increasing the insurance valuation?"

"That wasn't him either. But I'm not yet quite done figuring out this thing with the glue on the letterbox."

Soffía let out a long growl, as if someone had stepped on her toe.

"How can you be *sure* of anything at all? You're a psychologist. Not a detective."

"I'm naturally not a hundred per cent sure, Soffía. But I have a theory that I feel is going to turn out to be correct. Is there any chance that you can gather the siblings together, that's to say the four who are not in institutions?"

"Do you think that Dóri and Sessí set fire to Bergsveinn's place? And maybe Arngunnur too? Katrín was injured on the night of the arson, remember. They were at home in Grjótathorp."

Adam slid his finger down the list he had just finished writing.

"Yes I know."

"This consultant position has gone to your head, Adam." Soffía seemed to have swung from intense interest to despondency during the course of the call. "You're a good psychologist, I will admit that. But you're not Poirot. And I can't bring all these people together. We're not in an Agatha Christie story."

"But this affects all of them and it's much better to talk to them all at the same time."

"Have you forgotten about Covid-19?"

"Isn't there a meeting room at the police station, or a space, where everyone can keep two metres apart? There aren't that many of us."

"Maaaaybe," Soffía drawled. "But I can't plan anything without knowing more. Put your cards on the table. Right now. You're not directing a one-man show here. Not with me standing on the sidelines wondering what's happening next."

Adam took a deep breath and so told Soffía his theory, as quickly as he could, and she listened silently until the end.

"Christ, Adam," she groaned when he had finished. "If this is true... This is going to be ridiculously complicated."

He agreed with her.

"I'm not sure this sort of situation has occurred before. Here in Iceland, I mean."

"I know," he agreed. "This is something special."

"But we have to talk to them all together. I agree. That's simplest."

Adam was relieved not to have to expend more effort convincing Soffía. He himself had no desire to go to a police station through which countless people passed every day. But it would be ridiculous if everyone but him were there. Soffía also assured him that the police had a strict separation between departments, so there were only a few people walking around each part of the building.

Soffía finally made her decision.

"OK, no problem. You come here. Now I have to calm Bergsveinn down. He's going crazy in the next room. Then I'll call the other three. Do you want me to send you a car? You can also take a taxi and claim it back."

Adam did not want to walk up to Hlemmur in this cold weather, but he was also reluctant to get into a car with strangers.

"You'll have to pick me up," he said stubbornly.

"You've become the devil's very own prima donna! Adam Poirot." Soffía hesitated for a moment. "All right, then. But I don't know when. I'll call when I'm leaving."

An hour passed before the call finally came. He went outside straight away and she was there within a minute.

"You can do the talking," she said on the way to the station. "This is your idea. But what do we do if it doesn't add up?"

"I've no idea," he admitted.

"Very reassuring."

"Have you told your superiors about this?" Adam had a horrible thought that the senior officers at the station might line up at the back of the room, perhaps in full dress uniform. That would make him extremely nervous.

"Listen, calm down. This is just a theory. Let's see what they say. We can't be certain of getting a confession."

Adam was relieved to hear that the senior police officers would not be present like a panel of examiners. When they walked into the half-empty room that felt like a classroom, he immediately felt overcome with nerves. The body language of the four siblings, who were each in a corner of the room, did nothing to put him at his ease.

Arngunnur was staring into space and looked as if she were on another planet. Her colourful dress, carefully gathered hair, bracelets and necklaces were in stark contrast to the puffy, unfocused eyes above her mask. Bergsveinn paced in one corner with a face like thunder that could hardly be missed, despite the black mask. Dóri and Sessí were both preoccupied with their phones, sitting with their backs to a small table, not even looking up when Adam and Soffía walked into the room.

"I've told the others how you treated me this morning," Bergsveinn called, unnecessarily loudly. "And how I've been made to wait here for hours. Like some kind of criminal."

"I did offer my apologies," Soffía said, failing to sound particularly apologetic. "Some urgent stuff came up."

"That's not my problem," Bergsveinn sneered, folding his arms.

"Yes, it is. To a certain extent. I was called to the National Hospital. To your brother."

Now all the siblings looked up as one.

"Is he ...?" Arngunnur asked, trembling.

"He isn't dead," Soffía clarified quickly and the four of them immediately relaxed.

"Did he say anything?" Bergsveinn now stood still with bated breath. "Why did he want to talk to you, to the police?"

Adam tried to interpret these few words of Bergsveinn's. He could make out tension, that was understandable. But also confusion, perhaps a hint of relief. It was a strange mixture but matched Adam's previous deduction, and he now took over from Soffía.

"Did you suspect there was something Emil hadn't told the police?" he asked, trying not to sound like a bit-part actor in a cop show. He was not sure that he had managed it.

"No, not at all. I just asked." Bergsveinn waved his arms. The movement undoubtedly meant to demonstrate his lack of concern, but it made him resemble a badly-controlled puppet.

"Why have you been covering for your brother?"

"Covering ...?"

For a moment Adam thought Bergsveinn had failed to understand. He glanced at Soffía, but her face was impassive.

"Yes, what's more you allowed yourself to be brought here in a police car," Adam continued. "You could've avoided that humiliation if you had told Soffía what you knew to be the truth."

"But I don't know... Didn't know... Didn't want to... I only suspected ..."

All of Bergsveinn's arrogance had evaporated in a flash. He collapsed into a chair in his corner and stared at the floor.

"That Emil set fire to your hotel?"

"Yes."

42

Adam and Soffía did not have to guess whether Bergsveinn had told the siblings about his suspicions. Steindór and Sesselja gasped and erupted into a babble of questions. Even Arngunnur stared in astonishment at her brother and seemed to understand what was going on.

"You tried to tell one person about this idea, didn't you?" Adam asked, and Bergsveinn nodded his head silently. "You called Arngunnur. But then her partner was lying seriously injured in hospital and the message didn't properly come across." Adam cleared his throat. "Maybe you didn't speak clearly enough, Bergsveinn. Arngunnur only vaguely remembered that you had mentioned a door, a letter and a computer, so at first I – Soffía and I, that is – thought that the matter might have been about an email."

"Rubbish."

"I know. The part about the email was wrong. You told your sister about the front door. That's to say, you'd glued the letterbox shut, probably to prevent junk mail..."

"They ignore the stickers asking for no junk mail," Bergsveinn interjected. "It was the only way to prevent my guests from having to wade through advertising flyers on the way in and out. Superglue."

"So what?" Sesselja looked questioningly at Bergsveinn. "What does that have to do with what you said about Emil?"

"Emil didn't know that," Adam replied. "He tried to make it look like the fire he lit at the front door had been started by someone outside using the letterbox."

"Are we supposed to believe this?"

"Why would Emil have started the fire?"

"Didn't he suffer smoke inhalation?"

"But he tried to put out the fire."

"Was he really so jealous?"

"What for?"

"This can't be right."

Steindór and Sesselja were talking over each other and all eyes were on Bergsveinn.

"You must have realised this right away." Adam made this a statement, not a question.

"Not really." Bergsveinn sounded dazed. "It was such a shock. The damage, everything I had created, the furniture ... all wrecked! And worrying about Emil. I mean, he was found on the floor, injured, and him a cancer patient. I felt so terrible about it, I wasn't thinking clearly. It wasn't until the next day, when someone mentioned the fire starting inside the front door. Then... then..."

"Why did you just call Arngunnur?" Dóri sounded more angry than surprised. "Why didn't you talk to me? Or Sessí? Why didn't you warn us? He could also have started a fire at our place."

"I thought maybe Arngunnur could talk to him. She's always reached out to him. In any case, he was in hospital. Laid up there, it wasn't as if he could do you any harm."

"You should have let the police know," Sesselja said accusingly. "Why cover up for an arsonist?"

Adam noticed that Soffía was becoming agitated. She no doubt felt uncomfortable with him, this outsider, in charge, even though she had suggested herself that he take the lead. Even more so now that the siblings were starting to talk among themselves. He would have to rein them in.

"You may have been suffering from feelings of guilt," he suggested.

Bergsveinn started.

"Guilt? I felt sorry for the man! He has a tumour the size of a lemon in his head, he had just lost Mango. Was I supposed to drop the police on him? And what? Lock him up for arson, while he's seriously ill?"

"Guilt," Arngunnur echoed in a flat voice. "Going back to the old days, he means."

Adam latched on to this thought.

"You're not exactly of an age to talk about the old days," he said. "But if you mean when you were kids, I think you've hit the nail on the head, Arngunnur. I suspect that what you siblings have been dealing with these last few days is due to things that happened when you were little. Young, that is. Younger."

"What are you really talking about?" Dóri stared at Adam and Arngunnur. "Something more than the fire at Svenni's place? And what guilt? I have no guilt."

Soffía stepped up and took control, quietly and decisively, without a word. Adam instinctively took two steps back.

"There's more to this than arson." She glared so pointedly at Dóri that his shoulders sagged. "The needles, for example. Negative reviews. And the cyberattacks. More than likely."

"No, wait, wait, wait." Sesselja raised her hand as a signal that she wanted to speak, but held her other hand to her throat, as if she had difficulty breathing.

Soffía gestured for her to speak.

"Am I supposed to understand that you are blaming Emil for sticking needles into fruit in Arngunnur's shop and in our toilet rolls? Our brother?" Sesselja was hoarse with emotion. "And... and in the cocktail sausages he himself was going to give to people? And the needles in all these supermarkets, all over the country. It's absolute rubbish! I mean, his dog died because of this! He loved Mango."

"A guest at the gallery gave the dog a sausage," Soffía said. "Emil didn't intend to harm the animal. But he himself had to be hurt by a needle. That's to say, his business. To divert our attention from him. And it worked."

The atmosphere in the room had become electric and all the siblings were in shock. Arngunnur was no longer in a daze, instead turning her bracelets in endless circles and her face twitching as if she had a nervous illness.

"But strangers? Arngunnur's customers and me and Sessí? Was he going to hurt them?" Steindór demanded. "And the customers at Nettó and those stores too? What had they ever done to him?"

"Emil is nothing to do with what happened at the supermarkets," Soffía stated loudly and clearly. "We withheld important information from the media. In connection with the needles. So that we would know if others were also at work."

"What information, how?"

Soffía pretended not to hear the question but suddenly pointed triumphantly to Adam, who was completely taken aback by this.

"That was on Adam's advice. He has been an enormous help."

She wasn't going to tell the siblings what Adam's advice had been. That made sense. Needles were still being found in supermarkets and it was important that as few people as possible knew that all the original needles had been broken in two.

"What did you say about computer problems?" Bergsveinn stared open-mouthed at Soffía while he waited for an answer.

"Weren't you having problems with your online banking?" Could Emil have 'helped' you with your computer recently? Just like he helped Steindór and Sesselja? Or even just used the computer? We could get the technical department to take a look at what he did exactly. But then that might be no use. Just take the computers to be fixed."

Bergsveinn could not answer because Dóri, sitting rigidly, broke into a fit of profanity.

"Damn that wretched fucking boy! Did he wreck our computer system? Why the hell? Is it the tumour in his head that's making him do this? Is he the one who has been stalking me and broke into the car?"

"No, Steindór, I don't think Emil had anything to do with that."

Soffía looked at Adam with surprise at having let this slip out.

"We can't say anything about that now, Adam. Is that right?"

"No, maybe not," he said apologetically. "That's still unresolved."

Without warning, Arngunnur stood up slowly. She leaned heavily on the chair and looked beseechingly at Soffía.

"What about Katrín? What about my steps? Was it... Emil?"

"Well, what do you think, Adam?" Soffía passed the question to the psychological consultant.

"I strongly suspect so, yes." He found this the most difficult of all the facts discussed at this strange meeting, as the ice on the steps had taken a life. "I'm so sorry, Arngunnur, I'm truly so sorry."

Adam saw in the look that Soffía sent him that she thought it was foolish of him to talk as if he or the police had something to apologise for. But to him the form of words was familiar from his mother tongue.

"I don't know if it was premeditated or coincidence that Emil passed through Grjótathorp that night and had a bottle of water on him," he said. "But both the vet and you, Bergsveinn, have stated that Emil was in a state of despair after his dog had to be put down. So it's likely he wasn't in his right mind. No doubt his illness and the drugs have also played a part. It was later that evening that he set fire to the guesthouse."

A deathly silence fell over the small meeting room of the police station and there was almost palpable grief in the air. The siblings would need some time to process this information.

But instead of giving them a chance to recover, Soffía took

the opportunity to continue. She proudly revealed, without prompting, that after a great deal of work a young police officer on her team had found important footage from a security camera. The recording showed Emil walking fast along Austurstræti ... with a two-litre soft drink bottle in one hand.

Adam was so taken aback by this tactless move that he had to lean against the wall for support.

43

"Aren't we going to talk about the reason for this misery... this horror?"

It was Arngunnur who lanced the boil. The numbness had gradually faded from her face, and it had been replaced by a harsh impatience that Adam had not seen in her before. Behind the counter of the small health food store, she had always been relaxed and smiling, kindness personified.

Soffía and Adam glanced at each other. Until Emil had been formally questioned, they had neither a confession nor a valid explanation for all the events. It was possible that they would never be able to question him properly, as this would depend on his health.

Soffía had surreptitiously recorded her conversation with him in the hospital earlier. But that recording had no value as evidence, as Emil had rambled while under the effects of strong painkillers and had repeated himself again and again. She would certainly be reprimanded for recording him, if it were to come up, and it would be even more serious if she were to allow the siblings to listen to the recording. So that was out of the question.

"I spoke briefly with Emil earlier," Soffía began to speak and Adam felt she looked uncertain of herself, and it was important for her to be careful with such limited evidence to hand.

"Did he confess?" Arngunnur asked before Soffía got any further.

"This wasn't an interrogation. He's under heavy medication right now. We can't formally interview people under such conditions. No evidence of that nature would be accepted by a court of law."

"Does anyone imagine he's going to court?" Now it was Sesselja who interrupted Soffía's story. "He won't live that long. We all know that. The man's nothing but skin and bone. It takes strength to fight cancer, physically and mentally. Since Mango was put down, Emil has nothing to live for."

"And he's taken revenge on all of us," Steindór added, bitterly. "Revenge has definitely kept the bastard going. Excuse my language. You might find it harsh, but I don't see him through rose-tinted spectacles, even though he's a sick man. A crime is a crime, regardless of the perpetrator's health."

Now Adam could not stay silent, as Dóri was touching on something in this matter which was his field as a psychologist. He took two steps forward.

"You mention revenge, Steindór. Guilt was mentioned earlier. Would you explain the use of these terms in more detail, perhaps in connection with the strong suspicions of what Emil has done ... and in connection with the past?"

"There's not much to say." Steindór glanced at his siblings, one by one. "Is there?"

Nobody answered, but every eye was on him.

"Emil was the youngest of us," he continued, "and we felt he was Dad's favourite. He was like a little prince, with a bedroom that was bigger than the living room where we lived in Borgarnes." Dóri coughed. "I guess that... Yes, it could be said that we... Well, speaking just for myself, I couldn't stand him."

Sesselja picked up the thread when Steindór seemed disinclined to continue.

"There was nothing wrong with him, as such," she explained. "He was a very ordinary kid, just something of a softie. But his mother had taken our mother's place. A week after Dad got rid of our Mum, Halldóra was sleeping in what had been her bed. Only a week! Then she changed everything she possibly could in the house, re-arranged the furniture that my mother had chosen, the pictures that my mother had hung, the curtains and the floors and everything."

"Do you remember how quickly she killed all the herbs that Mum was growing, the ones that my father got from that gardener?" Bergsveinn added. "I'm sure Halldóra just simply stopped watering them."

"But the hardest thing, for me at least, was how my father behaved, how he changed." Sesselja spoke up again. "It was as if he'd never had a child before. He would give Emil a bottle at night so Halldóra could sleep and even changed shitty nappies. Our father!"

"So you were jealous of Emil?" Adam addressed the question to all the siblings.

"Not that I remember." Arngunnur was the first to answer. "But I was thirteen years older than he was, a generation apart really, and grew up in Reykjavík. He never bothered me at all. It was rather Hafst... Hafdís that I was jealous of. And maybe a little of you, Svenni. But my life in the city was my world so it didn't matter to me. I was just a visitor to the farm in the summer and could never get back to Reykjavík soon enough."

Bergsveinn frowned.

"You still took part in teasing him. Wasn't it you who locked him in the potato store?"

"No, I was the one who let him out. The poor little thing had wet himself and I thought he'd never stop crying." Arngunnur suddenly put a tissue up to her eyes. "But I'll admit that I didn't say anything about it to the rest of you, which I should have done. You were all so horrible to him and the boy hadn't done anything to you. I should have grassed on you to Dad or Halldóra. I don't understand why I didn't. I'll never be able to forgive myself."

Arngunnur sighed. Adam felt she was showing incredible

composure in light of the fact that the bullying seemed to have led to the death of her partner. But at this moment, the dominant emotion was self-blame. Later on anger would take over, and this was a part of the grieving process, even in normal circumstances, let alone in a situation like this.

"Did Hafdís also take part in this?"

"At first. But then she went to stay with her grandparents in Sweden."

"So it was Emil alone against all of you?" Adam sadly shook his head. The bullying seemed to have lasted for years.

Now Soffía could no longer be a spectator. She took a step forward a little too far, he thought. The two-metre rule had clearly been forgotten.

"Emil described to me the bullying you inflicted on him." Soffía looked from one sibling to another. "His description was horrifying."

"It's the morphine," Dóri muttered obstinately.

"That doesn't make any difference. It was disgusting. Even if you could attribute half of it to the morphine... Well, it's still disgusting. For year after year."

"Halldóra knew about it." Bergsveinn looked defiantly at Soffía. "Sometimes she tried to tell us off, but we told her what would happen if she told Dad."

"And what would've happened?"

"We would have told Dad she was mean to us."

"Was she?"

"We would have refused to come to the farm. It would have worked. Mum tried to stop him from seeing us right after the divorce, and Dad went nuts. Halldóra knew he couldn't bear it if we stopped coming. So she told Emil to toughen up and fight back. Which, of course, he never did."

"Until now," muttered Sesselja behind her mask.

"His mother? Really?" Soffía's eyes were on stalks. "But wouldn't your father have stood up for Emil? He changed his nappies and gave him a bottle feed at night?"

Bergsveinn snorted.

"He didn't do it for Emil, he did it for her, for Halldóra. So she could sleep, so she could relax. He adored her! But my father thought Emil wasn't tough enough, always making things and drawing. He called him the glitter boy."

"Were any of you your father's favourite?" Adam asked, even though he could hardly speak for contempt for these people. He suspected he knew what the answer would be, yet it also came as a complete surprise to him.

The siblings all spoke at once, each in their own corner. Adam heard one of them say Hafdís and another Hafsteinn.

"Was it Hafdís?" he asked.

"Yes," they replied as one.

"Or Hafsteinn, as I said. As she was called then," Arngunnur added.

"What do you mean?" Soffía was back in the driving seat.

"Hafdís is trans." The name flashed like a neon sign in front of Adam's eyes. *Hafsteinn? Steini?* Trans? Could there be a third sibling who could be a candidate for Rebekka's biological parent?

44

Adam was forced to hold off speculating about Rebekka's paternity, even though he found it difficult to control himself. Soffía showed the siblings out and attended to the formalities. Bergsveinn's questioning had been suspended and she no longer required him to surrender his passport.

No matter how unpleasant the man was, he had neither raised the insurance for the guesthouse nor set it on fire, that was clear. And while the siblings were certainly all guilty of atrocious bullying, decades later this was not something the police could do anything about.

"What if Emil recovers and makes a formal complaint?" asked Adam, who felt they were getting off too easily.

"If he recovers? Then he'll find himself facing charges. The bullying stuff is beyond the statute of limitations. He wouldn't be able to report that as a crime."

"But they destroyed his life, Soffía. They have caused irreparable, lifelong harm to his psyche. And his mother, too, she may be just as bad. An adult, a parent, who was supposed to protect him." Adam could hardly speak about it without tears appearing in his eyes, so he tried another tack. "Do you know that there has been research into the relationship between trauma, such as physical assault, and cancer?"

"What do you mean? That people get cancer from mental trauma? Rubbish!"

"I'm not asserting anything, I'm just telling you that there have been theories about it and scientific research has been going on for many, many years. The incidence of cancer has been shown to be higher in individuals who have been assaulted and suffered other severe traumas. But how people deal with it does make a difference. That's where psychologists come into it."

"What about people who survive wars?"

"The consequences of a trauma don't necessarily appear like a bruise right away, Soffía. This can linger in people for decades. And then the causal relationship isn't always obvious, maybe trauma weakens the immune system or increases the likelihood of cell mutation or something like that. Research into this still has a long way to go."

Soffía rolled her eyes and sighed.

"I'll send you links to some articles about it," he added hastily. "You might have time to read about it once this case is closed. You must be tired after all this."

He could not be bothered to argue with his ex-wife. It was, after all, one of the benefits of divorce – no more marital strife. Not unless you ended up in the unfortunate situation of working with your former spouse, as he had. But now, as always, he wanted to get home more than anything else. He had been experiencing an overwhelming homesickness over these past few days.

"OK, OK." Soffía raised her arms, as if a gun had been aimed at her. "But what am I supposed to do with Emil? If he could stand on his own two feet, then I'd have arrested him. But this is a crazy situation. A dying man is guilty of..."

"Sabotaging consumer goods," he said.

"Exactly. And then the ice on the steps. That's more complicated. How am I going to unravel that?"

On the way out to the car, Adam advised her not to rush. She was not under any time constraint.

"I would be inclined to wait and see if Emil recovers. And talk to his mother when she arrives. Apart from that, this is no longer my area of expertise. I'm just a psychological consultant, remember."

"Of course I'll discuss this with my superiors. But first I just want to try and understand..." She paused in the middle of the sentence to answer the phone. "Hello, love."

The caller must be Margrét. Soffía spoke in the affectionate, gentler tone that she used with their daughter. Which was why Adam was taken aback when he realised something was wrong. He indicated to Soffía that he also wanted to talk to Margrét, but she ended the call anyway.

"You can call her later," she said. They were sitting in the car and Soffía started the engine. "She'll be staying at my apartment for the next few days. A boy she was at a party with this weekend has been diagnosed with Covid."

Adam felt a chill.

"Who? When? And... where were they, inside or outside? Did she sleep with him? Then she's definitely been infected."

"Calm down, man! She has no symptoms. And she's on the way to get a Covid test. Right this minute. That's why I need to get home quickly. She'll be coming straight from the health centre."

For the first time, Adam noticed that Soffía was heading east, not west. He was about to protest, but then realised in time. Soffía was in a hurry to get home to fetch clothes and toiletries.

"Are you going to move out in the meantime?" he asked.

"What else? You know what isolation means."

"Of course but... Can't she stay at her own place?" Adam could not think clearly, even with all the Covid-19 information he had absorbed lately, his thoughts had come to a standstill inside his head.

"The kids she rents with, Adam." Soffía sounded like a mother trying to explain something to a small child. "She could have already infected them. But these are the rules."

"Sorry." Adam's initial chill had receded and now he was hot and flustered. "It's great that you can lend her the apartment. But where are you going to be staying?"

His voice quivered.

"Do some breathing exercises," ordered Soffía, who seemed calm. "You've held relaxation courses! You must know some tricks. Magga isn't sick. And she's young. Young people quickly shake it off."

"There's nothing universal about that, Soffía," he objected, curt and trembling. "And you remember how sick she got from just ordinary flu when we were in Wivenhoe? Her temperature hit forty degrees and we drove at a hundred miles an hour to the hospital. Remember?"

Soffía sighed.

"She was two years old! And you had her wrapped up in a wool blanket. Calm down, will you?"

Despite the stress, it had not escaped his notice that she hadn't answered the question of where she intended to stay while Margrét was in isolation. What would he say if she asked to stay with him?

By his own standards Adam had become remarkably calm, given the circumstances, by the time Soffía brought the car to a halt outside a three-storey apartment block in Grafarholt. He had never been to this part of the city before. If he owned a car, he would no doubt have had a chance to explore the neighbourhood and check out the building his ex-wife had moved into, but he had made do with Street View.

"Nice place," he muttered, as the house was much smarter than his old apartment building on Kaplaskjólsvegur. There were also no basement apartments here, so Soffía's home was not only bigger than his, but also had to be brighter. Yet he would not have wanted to swap.

"Come in with me," she commanded. "I can't leave you behind. Not in a police vehicle. Not with the engine running. And you'll die of cold if I switch it off."

"Do you think I'm going to steal the car?"

"That's the rules."

Adam pretended to be indifferent as he got out of the car, despite being quite offended. Soffía usually had little regard for rules; she was no doubt trying intentionally to annoy him.

She definitely found this amusing. But because he was curious to see her home, he chose to follow her instead of sitting in a cold car feeling hurt.

He did not want to have to take off his winter boots only to have to lace them back up again after a couple of minutes. So he just stood on the large rug by the door, where he had an unobstructed view of the living room and kitchen, and looked around with interest. Meanwhile, Soffía hurried from bedroom to bathroom and back with a bag to which she constantly added things.

The television was new and huge, but Adam didn't see anything else he had not seen before. There was their long grey sofa, which would have filled the living room in his basement apartment, their shabby dining table and chairs, and a coffee table that had also been too big for him to take when they divided their belongings. Up against one wall was a half-empty Billy bookshelf with some familiar books – everything Arnaldur Indriðason had ever written, practically every one of Kristín Marja Baldursdóttir's books and half a shelf of biographies of famous people, Nelson Mandela, Malala, Whitney Houston and Michelle Obama.

At the time of the divorce, Adam had got the double bed, the Jamie Oliver pans, and the English tableware set that his parents had given them as a wedding gift. In any case, Soffía had never liked the tableware. He had been happy to buy a new and smaller sofa and a new table. It had been a major turning point in his life and he felt it was appropriate to embrace change.

But here at Soffía's place, time seemed to have stood strangely still. Their old home had simply been moved up to Grafarholt. All that was missing was Adam sitting absorbed in a book or computer on the sofa, it was like jumping back a few years in time.

Admittedly, the photographs of Margrét, the mirror and the painting by Pétur Gautur, which had been a wedding gift from Soffía's parents, would also have to be lowered. These had all been hung so high on the walls that anyone would imagine that giants or people walking on stilts lived here.

"Right, let's go then." Soffía was ready, with a crammed bag on her shoulder and a laptop under her arm. She threw both into Adam's arms before he could turn and open the door. The phone that controlled Soffía's life had rung and she was immediately immersed in a work conservation.

"All right. I'm coming." The person who had called her was clearly very excited. "I'm actually up in Grafarholt. But I was on my way west anyway."

When Soffía had hung up on the excitable person on the phone, she took her stuff from his arms and sighed loudly.

"That was Dóri," she said. "I thought I was free of this bunch. His hired beefcake has caught the stalker. It's a young girl. Doped up, he said. She broke into the house on Seltjarnarnes. And now he wants me to turn up and handcuff her."

"Then I probably need to tell you a few things," Adam said, shocked.

Soffía pushed him ahead of her.

"In the car. You can confess your sins on the way."

45

The unbelievable happened. Soffía didn't jump down Adam's throat when he admitted that he knew quite a bit about Steindór's stalker and had kept it to himself. Anticipating a furious diatribe, he had half-expected her to stop the car and throw him out. But that did not happen.

It could have been that she was more worried about Margrét than she wanted to show, or maybe other things paled into insignificance in comparison to their daughter possibly being infected. Adam did not try to identify the cause of this unexpected placidity, but was just suitably grateful.

She did not even get annoyed with him giving her no more than the basic facts about Rebekka, only what she needed to know so that she could take a sympathetic stance in dealing with this young woman. Adam was still bound by confidentiality rules concerning his client. He did not tell Soffía which illness the girl was struggling with, only that this was one of the worst any person could find themselves facing, and that the police would have to treat her gently.

"Two perpetrators. Two, Adam. And both are too sick to be prosecuted. Unbelievable." Soffía grabbed a handful of liquorice-filled chocolate balls and chewed with great concentration.

"There's no comparison there," Adam objected. "Emil endangered people's health, and both Katrín and his dog lost their lives. Rebekka hasn't hurt anyone, just frightened a man who was convinced that someone was harassing him, and these are completely unrelated."

"I'm a cop, not a judge." Soffía's breath carried the smell of chocolate as she spoke. "I can't overlook someone committing a crime. Not even if one's suffering and another's a jerk."

"But the girl hasn't done the man any harm, just watched him and aimed a laser pen at his curtains." Adam had not told Soffía that Rebekka had broken into Steindór's car, stolen his sweaty clothes and sent them for a DNA analysis.

"And the reason she's stalking him is an illness? I'm supposed to believe that? Is this some mental condition?"

"I've told you everything I can."

"You'll have to come with me. If you're going to have any say in this. Otherwise I'll just arrest her."

Adam was fully aware of this, which was why he now had a gnawing pain in the pit of his stomach. He had no idea how Rebekka would respond to meeting him, but she might also see the person she knew as Jenný. It was simple-minded to assume that she would not realise. Although he did not want her to be suffering in any way, he hoped that she would be too confused to make this a matter of discussion, at least while Soffía was within earshot.

He desperately wanted to call Björn and ask him to head for Seltjarnarnes, but said nothing. Soffía would never agree to the father of a burglar being brought to the scene when the perpetrator was not a minor. But when they entered Steindór's home, Adam was relieved that Björn was not there. It would have been unbearably painful for the man to see his daughter curled up in the foetal position on the floor, with a distant expression that indicated that she hardly knew where she was.

"Jesus," Adam groaned, kneeling beside the girl. "Rebekka, my name is Adam. I'm a psychologist. Rebekka?"

No response.

"She's completely drugged up and hasn't said a single word since we found her. The woman who cleans for me let her in.

She doesn't speak Icelandic or English and didn't know what the girl wanted, so she just kept an eye on her until I came home."

Dóri sat in a low armchair with his legs stretched out and held a sheaf of papers. The bodyguard stood with his arms folded, leaning against the wall, looming over Rebekka. His doorman pose next to the helpless girl was ludicrous, and greatly disturbed Adam.

"Isn't this unnecessary?" He directed the question at Soffía and gestured to the bodyguard. "Rebekka can't do anyone any harm in this situation."

Adam had expected Steindór to protest. It would fit his character to pretend that he was being threatened by the unfortunate girl on the floor, and Adam was ready to speak his mind. But there was no such exchange. Dóri's attention was entirely on the papers he was now waving in the air.

"We found this on her, these ancient letters. And I know who wrote them. I know the writing, it tilts to the left and has little circles over letters that should have dots. What's this junkie doing with letters from my sister?"

Adam got to his feet and strode towards Steindór.

"I know this girl and she is seriously ill!" Adam's voice trembled. "If you speak disrespectfully one more time, I will not be responsible for my actions!"

"Have you looked at her pupils?" Dóri was not about to be intimidated by a long-haired psychologist.

Soffía stepped forward and took Adam's arm.

"Just calm down," she whispered. "Let me deal with this."

Soffía turned to Steindór but did not have a chance to address him before Adam continued.

"She has an illness that I suspect your sister has."

Steindór stared at Adam open-mouthed.

"Doesn't Hafdís have Alzheimer's?" Soffía demanded. "It's on the list."

"The person who compiled this list for you didn't take enough care with his work." Adam was so sad that he could hardly speak. "He listed the symptoms, not the name of the illness."

"Hafdís has Huntington's." Dóri was back on track. "It's like a mixture of Alzheimer's and Parkinson's, only worse. But what about it? I don't understand what this illness has to do with it."

Adam hurried to answer before Soffía could say anything.

"These letters you're holding were written to a young woman named Fanney."

"That fits." Steindór waved one of the envelopes.

"Fanney worked one summer in Borgarnes. And had an affair with... well, Hafsteinn. Wasn't he called Steini?"

Steindór nodded his head in confirmation.

"But then Hafsteinn went to Sweden and left Fanney with a broken heart. We can say that he ran away. Either Fanney didn't try to contact him or Hafsteinn forbade your family from revealing his whereabouts."

"We didn't know where he was." Dóri sounded like a spoilt child. "Neither did his relatives back in Sweden, not for months. When he finally showed himself, he wanted to be called Hafdís."

"The child had probably been born by then."

"The child?" shouted Soffía and Steindór at the same time. Adam pointed to the girl on the floor.

"Rebekka Rósa, yes. And she has unfortunately inherited the condition that caused Hafdís to be admitted to a nursing home in the prime of life."

Dóri stared at Rebekka, and the look on his face was such that Adam would have attacked him if Soffía had not held him back.

"Put something under her head," Soffía ordered the bodyguard.

"Adam, you call her father. And then an ambulance. I need to talk to Steindór for a bit."

It came as a surprise to Adam when Rebekka asked him to come with her to meet Hafdís.

They had met regularly at Sáló after she was discharged from the hospital and had moved home to her father. That said, Rebekka came to see Adam, and not Jenný. Rebekka had never mentioned the name. Maybe she had simply forgotten Jenný, as she had hardly been herself when they met. Maybe she just saw nothing remarkable in the psychologist's behaviour.

Since they had made progress with conversational therapy, and Rebekka had taken medication to help, Adam knew that she was ready to take the step of visiting Hafdís. But he was surprised that the girl chose to have him by her side instead of Björn. The father and daughter had recently re-established strong ties. Rebekka's explanation demonstrated this – that she wanted to protect Björn from seeing how ill she would eventually become.

When they arrived, however, Adam was not allowed to go with her into the nursing home. Visits were still subject to severe restrictions, and despite Adam doing his level best and asking Soffía to seek help from the authorities, the director of the nursing home would not be moved. Rebekka had no choice but to meet Hafdís alone.

Björn and Adam waited outside to be the girl's help and support after what would be an emotional reunion. Adam was glad that Rebekka's father was there too and was able to take her into his arms when she came out in tears. Although the pandemic appeared to be receding, Adam had not begun to hug people.

In Adam's opinion, Björn had performed admirably under the terrible circumstances that fate had allotted to them. Among other things, he was taking an active part in a project that Rebekka had unexpectedly become involved with after getting in touch with Tove, her newfound aunt in Sweden. As Hafdís's power of attorney, Tove had established a relief fund for Icelandic trans people a while ago, and Rebekka and Björn threw themselves into it together. Adam hoped that the fund's work would continue to be rewarding for Björn when Rebekka would no longer be able to take part.

DECEIT

It warmed Adam's heart to see Rebekka hugging her father in the parking lot of the nursing home. When might he and Margrét next have such an intimate moment together?

Adam had not yet talked to his daughter about Jený. He blamed it on the pandemic, but he knew this was just a pretext.

To Soffía's great relief, Margrét had not fallen ill with Covid-19 and she continued living with her mother after her isolation period ended. Soffía was clearly pleased with this, and she and Adam helped the girl buy an old car, which meant that she no longer had to take long bus rides.

But Adam had not accepted repeated invitations to Grafarholt. He used the virus as an excuse, as mother and daughter both interacted with numerous people every day. The truth was, however, that he suspected that Soffía would pin him down regarding a conversation she wanted him to have with their daughter. His concern was that she could simply announce to Margrét that her father had something important to share with her. From that moment on, there would be no escape.

In fact, there was more to it. Adam had found it odd, even a little discomfiting, to go to Soffía's home. It had been like unexpectedly stepping into a previous life, with all the old furniture and the memories that came with it. However, he could not properly define why his ex-wife's home had affected him so much. Perhaps there was a loneliness in him that he did not acknowledge, a longing for companionship? Or was he afraid of being sucked back into the past and having to leave Jený behind? He did not know... or did not want to know.

He declined Björn's offer to drop him off at home. They would probably prefer to talk in private after Rebekka's visit to the nursing home. Adam also enjoyed the walk. He was going to stop off and buy a pink sparkling wine for Jený and maybe he would get a ginger shot in Arngunnur's shop.

Adam now shopped even more often at Arngunnur's than before and recommended the small shop to anyone who would listen. In doing so, he tried his best to support this woman for whom he had a growing respect. Arngunnur had shown incredible empathy when she had invited Emil's mother to bury him next to Katrín. And Adam suspected that she looked after her half-brother's plot with the same care as she did her partner's.

One day, he would ask Magga to drive him up to the cemetery so he could lay flowers on both graves.